By R. COOPER

NOVELS
Play It Again, Charlie
A Boy and His Dragon

NOVELLAS
Let There Be Light
Some Kind of Magic
Winner Takes It All
A Wealth of Unsaid Words

Published by DREAMSPINNER PRESS
http://www.dreamspinnerpress.com

A Boy and His
DRAGON

R. Cooper

Dreamspinner Press

Published by
Dreamspinner Press
5032 Capital Circle SW
Ste 2, PMB# 279
Tallahassee, FL 32305-7886
USA
http://www.dreamspinnerpress.com/

A Boy and His Dragon

Cover Art by Paul Richmond
http://www.paulrichmondstudio.com

ISBN: 978-1-62380-269-1
Digital ISBN: 978-1-62380-270-7

Printed in the United States of America
First Edition
January 2013

This would not have been possible without help from the ladies of Ladywood, the discussion group/book club/bowling team that never bowls. But it would never have existed at all if not for those who came before.

To the original Bertie, and his Godric.

FACTS ABOUT DRAGONS:

1. They have existed since before the first written human records in almost every human culture.

2. They "came out" around the turn of the last century when the other magical Beings started to emerge from hiding both during and after the First World War, though many did not come into public view until the mass exodus of Beings from the countries torn by war and strife during the Second World War. This includes Russia, China, Northern Africa, the islands of the Pacific, and most of Europe.

3. Like fairies, they are said to possess powerful magic.

4. ?

CHAPTER 1

THE dragon was staring at him.

Arthur couldn't move. He actually, literally couldn't move. His legs wouldn't carry him. He was certain that if he even tried to back up, head out the door, run toward his bike, he'd collapse to the floor and then… and then he wasn't sure what would happen, but it probably wouldn't be good. Best-case scenario, he wouldn't get the job, and he *needed* this job; worst case, the dragon might eat him.

It didn't matter what he'd read. It didn't matter that there hadn't been a reported case of a dragon eating a human for decades. None of that mattered because Arthur got one look at that dragon's size, at his strong jaw and his white, wicked teeth and knew that the dragon could swallow him whole if it wanted to.

If *he* wanted to, Arthur corrected himself, only a little hysterically. The dragon was a he, was a *Jones* of all things, and no one with the last name Jones should be threatening. When Arthur left Professor Gibson's office with the contact information, he had even thought it was funny that the dragon in need of an assistant was a Dr. Jones. Dr. Jones was even a historian—maybe not an archeologist, but close enough. Arthur actually had a tiny feeling of hope, as he prepared for this interview, that this job might not be too terrible, that he'd get it even without the best qualifications, that maybe it would give him a chance to get ahead of everything for once, give him room to breathe.

He swallowed air then choked and wondered if his face was now red. It was embarrassing, but it could have been the heat in here and that was what he would say if asked. He was so hot. The fall air outside had left him chilled even after pedaling halfway across town, but the startling heat inside the house was starting to make him feel dizzy.

If he fainted, either from fear or from the heat, it wasn't going to get him the job. He needed this job, he reminded himself. He made himself think of the phone calls, the letters, and his sister counting on him. He looked back at the creature studying him from the upstairs landing.

The creature, the dragon, stared back for another moment, and then opened its mouth so a long forked tongue could loll out. Arthur quickly looked elsewhere, anywhere but at that open mouth and those teeth. They made him think of saber-toothed tigers or daggers carved of ivory.

The banister was of dark wood, with sloping balusters that unfortunately did not block his view of the dragon lying— standing—on four legs as it peered at him. It seemed frozen, as if Arthur had startled it, which made no sense because Arthur would swear that he'd heard a rough voice bark "Come in" when he knocked on the front door.

Not that he knew if the dragon could talk like that, and not that he was quite ready to look at its mouth again. He focused on the claws instead: sharp, sharp, black-tinted talons, five on each hand, or paw. Seeing five claws depicted in dragon art was important to many dragon societies—he remembered that from the reading he managed to get in on the subject before today's interview, the reading he had done late at night while jotting down a quick list of irrefutable facts about dragons. Arthur knew it was nerdy, but he'd always liked lists and facts, and he'd enjoyed doing the research for today so he wouldn't make a fool of himself. Clearly, he'd been unsuccessful.

He inhaled a deep, heady breath of warm air and heard the sound of the dragon doing the same. Arthur tried to think about his list of facts again.

The number of claws a dragon had in any depiction of him was a sign of nobility: the more claws, the higher the rank. Or it had supposedly been, back before dragons walked as freely among humans as they did since the other Beings came out of hiding. Arthur remembered that fact and focused on it. Facts were steady, even if they could change. It was why he liked learning and why he picked a major that left him surrounded by books. Facts were calming.

He lifted his head to look at the dragon again. The dragon's body was a little bigger than a large man's, with the tail making it even longer. There were wings at its back—small, leathery wings like those of a European dragon that couldn't fly—but unlike a European dragon, this dragon had a mane, ebony black and somehow lighter than air as it shifted in an imperceptible breeze. The mane looked soft, like the tiny beard under the dragon's chin. That beard was something usually only found in Asian varieties of dragon, Arthur remembered distractedly. This dragon was built more like an Asian dragon too. No towering height as it stood on its hind legs, no fat belly, no plates down its back like the old pictures of what dinosaurs looked like; it was sleeker, exactly like a big lizard, with the famed gleaming, shining scales down its back that rippled like water when it moved.

Legend held that dragons had eighty-one scales on their back, and each one held more magic than most humans could ever hope to touch. The legends also said dragons liked to feast on those who would attempt to take one but would give them freely to those they deemed worthy.

Arthur swallowed. The dragon hissed, making Arthur jump. He tried to push away the thought of stolen scales and the exorbitant prices people paid for black-market dragon parts. He imagined this dragon in pieces for sale and felt ill. Money wasn't something that should matter that much, but he knew it was and always would be to some people, to desperate people.

He thought of his sister again, and the messages on his phone. Then he frowned and looked right at the dragon, since it was still looking right at him.

The dragon—Dr. Jones, Arthur forcefully reminded himself; this was *Dr. Jones*—pulled its tongue back into its mouth and flared its nostrils. Arthur had two distinct impressions; one, that the dragon was smelling him, the way reptiles scented the air, and two, that the dragon found him amusing.

Maybe it was those eyes. He couldn't look away from them once he met them. They were almost all pupil. Big black spaces that shone and had impossible layers. Like agate, like molten gold or lava rock, they gleamed as blackly as the silvery onyx of those scales, with only a thin circle of pale brown to show the dragon's eye color. The dragon had long eyelashes, flirtatiously long, Arthur decided, and then he felt the heat in the house all over again with a sudden awareness of his body, of how he was standing.

He moved. He didn't think he was imagining the glittering of those dilated pupils; he just didn't know if it meant he was supposed to be lunch.

They said dragons no longer ate people, but Arthur's gut knew that was only *mostly* the truth. The fluttering in his stomach said the truth was that dragons didn't eat people anymore unless the dragon was provoked or someone tried to steal its treasure, and—as many states operated under the Castle Doctrine, which said a man's home was his castle and he had the right to defend his property—such behavior would be totally acceptable in most courts of law.

The problem was the matter of how much the dragons might enjoy it. All of mankind's uneasy relationship with magical Beings could be summed up in dragons: worshipped and feared across the globe since the dawn of time.

Arthur's legs were still weak, which made him think about falling to his knees. This in turn reminded him of the last few lines of one of the articles on dragons he'd glanced through, where the author wondered if dragons had truly been praised for their wisdom and benevolence, or merely to appease their terrifying hunger.

Hunger. Arthur was hot, dizzy, and breathing too fast. This dragon wanted to consume him whole, he was suddenly certain of it. His chest tightened, his heart thundering even as his mouth went dry, and he reached out, vaguely recalling childhood stories about knights battling dragons; wishing for any kind of defense. A shield maybe, since he wouldn't use a sword.

The moment he moved, the dragon's mouth fell open wider in what Arthur could only describe as a grin, and then those long eyelashes swept down over one eye in a definite wink.

"My apologies," the dragon rumbled slowly as a hint of smoke scent carried down to Arthur, who was gaping. "But I thought it best that any applicants confront the beast, as it were, head on."

Maybe it was the quiet British accent or the soft apology or maybe just that bold wink, but Arthur put his hand down and cleared his throat so he at least wouldn't seem as stupid as he probably looked a second ago.

"Dr. Jones?" He let out a long breath and watched the dragon angle his head at him for another moment in a move not unlike a cat—perhaps a Cheshire cat with that grin—before Dr. Jones moved back in a sinuous motion. Only when he turned did Arthur register the statue on a table behind him on the landing. It was a stone gargoyle. It had to be there as a joke.

Arthur opened his mouth to ask, but the dragon was moving away, heading down the stairs, and unless Arthur came forward he couldn't keep it in sight. He flicked his gaze back to the gargoyle, which looked dusty even at a distance and had the same relaxed grin. Strange for a creation intended to guard and warn and frighten.

The dust all over the stone wasn't that unusual, as Arthur learned when he carefully took a few steps into the room and looked around. He wasn't sure whether to call it a study, a living room, or a library. It could have been any of those. If the room had a defining feature, aside from the great fireplace against one wall or the short swords covered in cobwebs on display by the door, it was the shelves and shelves of books. They all looked old, but that could have been due to the dust covering every surface. Even the table against the back of the velvet couch by the fire looked like a relic.

There was no sign of treasure, but Arthur hadn't really been expecting to find any in the living room. The books were far more interesting in any case. He had a suspicion that Dr. Jones, in addition to being a very poor housekeeper, had no system of organization. There were what looked like pamphlets and hardcovers next to encyclopedias and paperbacks of various sizes. There were comic books on one shelf by the fireplace, which was no place to keep any sort of paper good, much less any kind of book. Arthur itched to rescue them.

If the rest of the house was like this, there was no way he could work here, not without taking care of this… this *problem*, this… *disaster*. Yes, Arthur decided, it *was* a disaster. He might not have his master's yet, might not ever have it, but this was unacceptable.

He heard footsteps and turned just as the dragon came back into view, or rather, as Dr. Jones came back into view. Dr. Jones had changed into the form dragons usually took when dealing with humans: a human-looking body, albeit one that would never be mistaken for a true man.

His skin shimmered. That was the only word for it. It shimmered as though the sleek black of his scales was just beneath the surface. His nails—both finger and toe, as he was barefoot— were shorter now and blunt, but still darkly tinged as if he had nail polish on. In place of his feathery mane was black hair, which he was smoothing away from his face as he walked.

His face. Arthur's thoughts stopped for a moment, frozen. He should never have agreed to this interview. Whatever he'd been expecting, this handsome figure with bedroom eyes wasn't it. He wasn't overly tall or muscular, but there was strength there, a presence that took up space in the room, and in Arthur's mind. *Power*, Arthur thought so fiercely that he almost said it out loud. Even while disguised as a man, the dragon gave the impression of power. His muscles rippled as he stretched and seemed to adjust to his new body. There was stubble along his jaw; he looked like the kind of dangerous, sexy man who always had a five o'clock shadow, the kind that would rasp and burn against skin and leave it red and used, or so Arthur had seen in movies anyway.

Arthur could stop shaving for days and have nothing to show for it. He had the faintest possible trail of blond hair on his lower stomach, it was true, but that was as dangerous and sexy as he got.

He dropped his gaze, he had to, because the man must have been naked as a dragon and had obviously just stepped into some sweatpants on the way downstairs. The idea of him naked knocked the breath out of Arthur. He blinked in surprise at the lack of chest hair until he remembered what he was dealing with, only to immediately wonder how all that skin would feel against his and if the man's hair would be as feathery and soft-looking as his dragon mane.

He shivered, then banished the thoughts with a shake of his head.

Despite how rude he'd been and stupid to stare so much, when he looked up he found the dragon giving him the same up and down. The dragon's tongue came out, darting into sight just for a moment, wet and pink and not forked, and then he inhaled. Arthur could only guess at what he smelled like. Sweat, he would guess, from the bike ride over here and from nerves. Hopefully not so aroused it was noticeable. He resisted the urge to check his armpits, but only because he doubted it would matter.

Dr. Jones's eyes were all pupil again, just for a moment. He offered Arthur a slow smile. "You didn't run. I do like that."

"You… you do?" Arthur's mouth was inexplicably dry. A few minutes ago he'd been petrified, and now all he could think was that he refused, absolutely refused, to embarrass himself any more. The man was a historian. Once Arthur got over his appearance, he was going to remember that most historians were full of themselves and often boring, and he was going to feel very foolish.

Anyway, there were more important things here than a sexy scruff and a cultured, if rumbling, voice that hit Arthur like hot coffee on a cold morning. Like a job with a tremendous opportunity that he couldn't ignore or risk losing.

But that smile, no, that *grin*, that Cheshire cat grin, made him frown.

"Then you shouldn't scare people."

It was a mistake. Arthur tensed, waiting for some furious reaction to his scolding even as he was forced to admit that he had, in fact, just scolded a dragon as though it was his baby sister, but after a second of silence, Dr. Jones's gaze seemed to turn to liquid.

"Did I truly frighten you, pet?" Dr. Jones continued into the room, stopping by the table to reach into a small, tarnished silver chest. He seemed very sorry, but only briefly. "I thought you were about to pull out a sword and brandish it at me for a moment there." He pulled out one cigarette, then two, but he put the second one back after a sideways look at Arthur.

Arthur glanced down, not sure where anyone could get the impression that he was any kind of threat. But it was close enough to what he had been thinking at that moment to make him wipe at his warm cheeks.

"Sorry. I was startled." Or terrified, but Arthur really needed this job. The dragon hardly seemed to notice the lie.

"Mind if I smoke?" he asked, apparently to make Arthur shiver, but the cigarette at his mouth was already lit when Arthur raised his head. The smoke curled around him like a halo, lit by overheard lights and the crackling fire. It didn't smell like tobacco. It was sharper, herbal. The smell grew stronger when the dragon came closer to him.

His hand rolled with the cigarette in it. It was an elegant gesture Arthur couldn't have emulated if he tried. It made him think of aristocracy again. So did the slight fold at the corner of each of Dr. Jones's eyes and the arch in his eyebrows. Arthur felt like he was talking to the descendant of an ancient line, and he wasn't measuring up.

"I'm supposed to find a *very qualified* assistant." Arthur got the impression Dr. Jones was quoting someone. "Yet Gibson recommended you." There was enough of a beat to make Arthur's pulse speed up. He hadn't known that the professor had recommended him. Professor Gibson had only said it was a shame to see Arthur's potential go to waste and then told him about the job opening.

He couldn't ask what the professor had said. But he opened his mouth, having at least expected to have his credentials and experience called into question.

"I am working towards my degree." Or he would be, if he ever found the money again. It wasn't likely, but he couldn't quite make himself admit that yet. There was always a chance. If he could do what he had to, maybe everything would be all right. As it was, his time away from school, his "sabbatical," kept getting longer and longer. He closed his eyes just for a moment. A sword wouldn't have been all that bad. It might have made him feel stronger and not scared and dead tired.

He opened his eyes. "And as for the others, who? Reilly? Birch? Not one of them has half my drive." Archival studies was a field with limited opportunities, especially at a smaller university, but Arthur was damn good. He would have been working on his doctorate by now if things had gone his way. But they hadn't. The others weren't as good, and they didn't need this job nearly as much as he did. It was *his*.

His voice trembled with everything he wasn't saying, but if anything, Dr. Jones seemed to like it. When Arthur tried to speak again and explain the arrogance in that statement, he got waved down.

"There's no shame in having pride in one's work, if that pride is justified." Dr. Jones put the cigarette to his mouth, then licked his lip and Arthur wasn't sure if he was still smelling the air or tasting a fleck left behind from that cigarette, which looked hand rolled. "As for whether or not it is, that's a wait-and-see matter, isn't it?"

He exhaled. Arthur watched the streams of smoke rise upward with a fascination he hoped wasn't too obvious.

"What is that? It's not tobacco." He remembered himself. "If you don't mind me asking."

He had a feeling that the timidity in the question surprised Dr. Jones, but after a moment, he nodded. "Herbs. I suppose they're terrible for me, but I feel like they clear my head." He took another long pull from his cigarette. Arthur did his best not to watch the man's mouth as he did, but there was a small part of him that wondered if that was the dragon's intention in smoking like that so close to him. If he'd been the Cheshire cat from *Alice in Wonderland* before, he was more of the Caterpillar now. A possibly stoned caterpillar, Arthur decided to himself, only to give a small jerk when Dr. Jones started waving his hand, and his cigarette, around him as he stepped back. The smoke followed him. So did Arthur, though at a distance. He wasn't sure what else to do; this was the strangest interview he'd ever been on.

"Your GPA is, or was, quite high. Your employers at your various internships had nothing but fantastic things to say about your work, and your areas of study are varied enough to keep you interesting. Then there's Gibson's opinion of you, which you seemed surprised to learn about."

"I...." Arthur couldn't think of what to say to that. Dr. Jones didn't give him the chance to try.

"He says you're smart, focused, and determined." He turned back. Arthur froze, but he knew the surprise was all over his face again. The professor had never given any sign that he valued Arthur's work so much. Arthur thought of him saying that, committing that to paper, and bit his lip. Dr. Jones made a low noise, a *tut*. "You look exhausted to me."

Arthur reached up but didn't touch the circles under his eyes. He wanted to squirm when the dragon's voice softened. "Now that I've got a good look at you, I find myself wanting to ask who's been taking care of you, because they've been doing a very poor job."

It wasn't that Arthur wanted his potential employer to find him attractive. He was nothing special—young face, blond hair, "cute in a wholesome way," someone had once said—but it was something else to be dismissed completely. He scowled and stepped up. He didn't *think* he was going to get eaten, at least, not today.

"I take care of myself." He had, for years now. But he wanted to bite back the words the second they were out. The dragon's voice only rumbled lower, grew even softer.

"Is your name *really* Arthur MacArthur?" His tone was courteous and careful, but only for a moment. "Did your parents hate you?"

Arthur shook his head and answered anyway, with only the tiniest frown. Maybe it was the heat, or the smoke, or being so close to someone so hot, or that pride that Dr. Jones had talked about, but he was having a hard time remembering to stay quiet.

"No. Arthur was my mother's father's name."

"Don't worry." Dr. Jones let out a sigh. "No insult intended. My parents hated me, you see. I don't know if you're aware, but most dragon families give their offspring names to reflect the family's sense of pride and power. Sadly, my parents chose to honor an old family branch and thus: Philbert."

Arthur was inhaling, the stinging, oddly refreshing herb smoke on his tongue as the name sank in. He coughed, then tried to cover it. His eyes were wide and watery. *This* creature's name was *Philbert?*

"That's ridiculous." It just slipped out. Worse, when Arthur tried to think of something to mitigate that horrible faux pas, more came out. "Do people call you Phil?" He couldn't help it. This man, this dragon, was named *Phil*. Phil the Dragon. Not even around those teeth was "Phil the Dragon" a terrifying possibility.

Dr. Jones sniffed.

"Do people call you Mac?"

People barely called Arthur at all. "No."

Dr. Jones pursed his lips and angled his head for a moment. "Really?" Intrigue, or the cigarettes, made his voice seem smoky. "May I?"

Arthur suppressed a shiver. That was all he needed, to imagine this man breathing out a special nickname, something just for him. He'd always thought that might be nice, but with that voice, it also might kill him.

But it wasn't going to happen, so he shook his head. Dr. Jones gave another sigh but then looked thoughtful.

"You're right. Arthur is so much better. Arthur MacArthur…. It sounds like something from an epic saga." When his eyes came back to Arthur, they were heavy. Arthur glimpsed his tongue again, wet against his lip, against the paper of the cigarette. This time

Arthur couldn't hide his shiver at all, but he could look away, focus on what he had to gain from this job and not on whether he smelled tasty or not.

"Is this part of the interview?" Arthur regularly confronted collection agencies. He could do this, even if it meant facing a thousand hot stares and feline smiles.

With a dramatic gesture, Dr. Jones shifted away to find an ashtray, or whatever he was using for an ashtray. His back was as breathtaking as his chest, if not more so. There was something obviously different about the skin there, shining with almost-scales and playing over muscle, looking sleek to the touch, smooth, all the way up to the back of his neck. There was no sign he had recently, or ever, lost a scale. But then, Arthur didn't even know if that part of the story was true; he only knew people thought it was.

It turned Arthur's stomach and made him shake, but it let him take his eyes off the man in front of him and focus on the questions he was asking.

"You have transportation? Do you mind smoke? Can you type quickly, use a computer?" Dr. Jones turned back in time for Arthur's answer.

Arthur nodded to all of them, though he thought of his bicycle apprehensively and decided not to mention that he didn't own a car until he was asked directly. He was getting good at indirect lies... too good, really.

He stayed where he was and let the doctor circle slowly and turn back around to fully face him.

"What's your favorite period in history?"

That was a new one. Arthur let himself frown as he repeated the question to buy time. But he honestly couldn't say. His interests truly *were* varied, and the courtly romances and adventures of the Middle Ages written to describe earlier periods were too embarrassing to admit to. He hesitated and Dr. Jones added to his question.

"Well, when you minored in history, what was your thesis on?"

Arthur jumped. "The Wars of the Roses." He glanced up and then stared down at his feet, trying to figure out the point of the question. Dr. Jones pressed him for more.

"Really? Bloody Old England? Do go on, Arthur."

"With… uh… with what?" It wasn't that he couldn't keep up; he just couldn't see how this was relevant.

"Lancaster or York?"

The question was so distant it echoed, and Arthur turned, not certain when Dr. Jones had left the room. Arthur had thought he was coming closer, but he must have gone into another room, maybe the kitchen that Arthur could see part of through one open door.

"Lancaster." He shouldn't have hesitated at the answer. He turned again at the flash of motion to one side and noticed the second door coming out of the kitchen as Dr. Jones emerged from it. His cigarette was gone.

"Why? Because they win?"

Dr. Jones was not an old dragon. Some of them lived to be a hundred. He appeared to be in his thirties, but his use of the present tense to describe a historical event was disconcerting, as if he was older than he looked and had lived it. That wasn't possible; even for a fairy, that would be ancient.

"No, I…." Arthur squeezed his eyes shut at the embarrassing truth and then opened them wide when he realized he had to keep an eye on the dragon. It was too late. Dr. Jones was close to him again and watching him with an intent expression. It only got more so when Arthur tried to wet his lips. "When I was kid… I liked stories about King Arthur."

Dr. Jones beamed at him, hopping on the balls of his feet in clear delight.

"Of *course* you did. And?"

Arthur knew he ought to shut up before he revealed all of his nerdiness and what a lonely kid he'd obviously been. He really should. But Dr. Jones settled into his space, hot and bare chested and interested, and his heart started pounding.

"The House of Lancaster had a red rose but also a red dragon as their emblem." There was nothing more arrogant than explaining something to someone who probably already knew all about it, but Dr. Jones's gaze didn't waver, not even when Arthur realized he was talking about dragons to a Being and dragon historian. "Because they were Welsh, who are the People of the Red Dragon. And in some stories, the red dragon myth was a foretelling of the existence of Arthur. *King* Arthur I mean, not me. Obviously." He could not have sounded like a bigger dork.

Dr. Jones closed his eyes and sighed so deeply that his shoulders moved with it. When he reopened his eyes, Arthur blinked. A reptile, or something like a reptile, shouldn't have a gaze so hot. There was warmth coming from Dr. Jones too, radiating across the small space between them as if he wasn't cold-blooded at all.

"You truly are a pearl," Dr. Jones declared at last, quiet and purposeful.

"What?" Arthur took a step back only to stare with stinging eyes.

"You," the voice rumbled slowly for his benefit, "are a *pearl*, Arthur."

Arthur's mouth opened, but no sound came out. No one said things like that, and if they did, they didn't say things like that to him, not since his parents had been alive. His social life was nonexistent. With two jobs and school and his sister, it had had to be, but back when he had a social life, he'd never heard anything like that either. There was nothing pearl-like about him.

He suddenly remembered why he was there and dropped his head.

"Does that mean I'm hired?" he asked at last.

"Oh yes." Dr. Jones nodded. After a pause, Arthur dared a look up. Dr. Jones seemed pleased with himself, but his watchful stare was not as reassuring as it should have been. Arthur started to speak, then couldn't think of what to say. He had the job, which meant regular hours in a safe, warm place—*if* a dragon's lair could be said to be safe; it was definitely warm—with more than decent pay. And he would be close to the university again, and even closer to a chance to finally get ahead of the financial mess he was in.

He had the job, Arthur thought again, and then went weak. He put a hand on the table to stay on his feet and ignored the concerned way the doctor leaned in his direction. Arthur almost smiled at him, then tossed his head, because he shouldn't smile, not with his reasons for being here.

He straightened.

"Thank you. I will do my very best work for you." He felt even hotter at how serious, how formal, he was, but held still as he watched the arrested expression come and go in shining dragon's eyes.

Dr. Jones's mouth turned up, leaving Arthur to internally wriggle in humiliation at how obviously the myths of dragons were going to his head if he was pledging himself like a knight at a tournament.

"I'll need you several days a week," Dr. Jones said.

Arthur hadn't thought he could make a bigger fool of himself. No amount of frowning could hide the way his eyes went wide to hear those words or disguise what he'd obviously been thinking about.

"And some of your nights too, I'm afraid." Dr. Jones said it on purpose. He had to have. Arthur kept his face as blank as he could. Dr. Jones exhaled in obvious disappointment and went on. "I'm afraid I can't tell when something will strike me, and in the meantime, there's always something to be done."

"You're writing a book." It was like Arthur had forgotten everything he knew once he'd walked in here. Everything but bits of feudal lore and fairy tales.

"Yes, Arthur, very good. I'm writing a book." In his place, Arthur might have been far more condescending. "It's why I need an assistant. So you will be here tomorrow?"

He didn't say a thing about a background check. Arthur didn't glance around for the treasure, but this was a dragon: naturally there had to be treasure here somewhere. Of course, dragons were supposed to be hard to fool. Perhaps background checks didn't matter when dragons could peer into souls.

Arthur bit his lip and raised his head and only then realized that Dr. Jones was still talking to him, stepping close with burning heat and a cleansing brace of herbal scent to exhale a question with breath so warm that Arthur shivered when it hit his skin.

"Unless I can persuade you to stay a little longer?" He was too much, too close, and dangerous and strange, and Arthur needed this too much to risk it even for someone so... incredibly fucking sexy. He did his best to try to convince his legs to carry him away and failed when Dr. Jones continued. "I could offer you my take on what lengths those Woodvilles might get to if given the chance."

At least it let him speak.

"What?" It took Arthur way too long to remember the Woodvilles' role in the Wars of the Roses. At this rate, Dr. Jones was going to regret hiring him any second now. *Breathe*, Arthur told himself. He needed to breathe, and to do that he needed cool, fresh air free of sexy, smoky dragons and their sexy, smoky scent. "I... have to go. I have work."

He always had work. It wasn't a total lie.

Dr. Jones pulled back with a pout. A *pout*. "Whatever else you're doing, I'm afraid you aren't going to be able to keep it for long if you're mine."

Arthur swung a look over to him. Dr. Jones licked the corner of his mouth in a way that did not disguise his smile. "I mean, if you work for me." He shrugged in a half apology for his innuendo or joke or whatever it had been, and Arthur realized that he was glaring. At his dragon employer. But he couldn't seem to stop. In fact, his glare only grew fiercer at the man's next words, which revealed how not sorry he actually was. "I'm the demanding, possessive type."

Arthur had been planning on quitting his day job anyway, but he was going to keep his weekend job of delivering Chinese on his bike. He didn't say any of that though, because he wasn't risking anything at this point. When Dr. Jones stared at him for another moment and then took a step back to wave him toward the door, a wave Arthur could only describe as regretful, he almost reconsidered his decision.

Then his instincts kicked in and he moved toward the door, keeping his back to the wall and his eyes on the smiling predator in front of him.

"I'll see you tomorrow, Dr. Jones."

"Philbert, Arthur. Philbert. Or Bertie or Jones, to my friends."

Jones. It was perfect. Arthur stumbled but righted himself and concentrated on work, the job. The job that could answer his prayers. *Jones*, his mind repeated anyway, but then slid on to *Bertie.* It was adorable. There was no other word.

Adorable. Arthur had the faintest thought that maybe the threat from dragons wasn't at all about being eaten, not with his mind holding onto the soft little nickname like it was made of gold. *Bertie.* He could almost hear himself saying it between kisses.

"I'll be here early," he promised too loudly, trying not to think of kissing his new boss, not now, not ever while he was in this house, and saw Dr. Jones open his mouth, as though the very air or Arthur himself was delicious to him, delicious and edible.

"I look forward to it," he called back as Arthur hurriedly ducked away. His voice was so light that Arthur could have imagined it, but somehow he didn't think so. Especially when the words seemed to follow him home.

HE WAS worried about rain but, though the skies had threatened it, he made it back across town to his apartment just as the first sprinkles were starting to fall. The approaching wet winter was going to be a problem now that he was working farther away, but it was something for him to worry about later.

For now he had a job, a good job. He almost couldn't believe it. Since dropping out of school, taking his sabbatical, he'd worked two, sometimes three part-time jobs, anything he could to keep the apartment and put food on the table, but fighting for jobs with younger kids in a college town, kids who had cars and no competing work schedules, had been starting to take its toll. His paychecks had been getting smaller, his hours reduced. Sleep was something he fantasized about.

Finally, that might change. Arthur carried his bike up the stairs with him, taking the back way by the dumpsters because Mr. Cruz, nice though he was, almost never went there and rent was due in a few days, and that was a conversation Arthur didn't want to have today. Not with his blood pumping and his cheeks hot despite the chill in the air and the growl in his stomach that he was almost used to.

It was amazing he hadn't gotten hit by a car; the way his thoughts were spinning, he hadn't been paying much attention to traffic. The moment he could think calmly, he was going to remember all his near misses, but for now he smiled as he unlocked the door and made sure to make plenty of noise to let his sister know he was home.

Kate was in the small kitchen, and Arthur only smiled wider to see her dressed and attempting to make dinner. The pot of boiling water meant noodles and not their other staples, peanut butter and jelly sandwiches or mac and cheese, and though Arthur would have been happy to never ever smell another MSG-laden bowl of instant noodles again, his stomach rumbled at the thought of a hot meal.

Skimping on food was one of the few ways they could save money, and it wasn't too bad if he let himself get hungry enough that it all seemed delicious.

There was a smile on Kate's face, or a hint of one. She never smiled with her mouth as much as her eyes. They were the same blue as Arthur's, but Kate plucked her eyebrows to make them even thinner, though they were usually slanted downward in an uncertain frown. The steam made her pink. Arthur took off his helmet and left it hanging from the handlebar of his bike while he took in her outfit.

There were very few clothes Kate owned that could be considered respectable. Her wilder, younger days weren't that far behind her, and she hadn't had the energy or the money to buy new clothes since she'd come to live with him. What she had on might be her best: clean jeans, low heels, a smart blazer.

"You went out?" He couldn't keep the excitement from his voice. The apartment was clean, dinner was on the stove, and Kate had gone out. Even if he hadn't found a job, this would have been a good day.

"There was an ad for a weekend shift at that sex shop downtown." Kate rolled a shoulder nervously. "I don't think they're going to want anyone who has to check 'yes' when asked if they've ever been arrested for something. But I thought I should try." She was dismissive, trying to play it off, but Arthur came forward to wrap her up in a hug. He couldn't help it. Kate was about average height for a girl, and Arthur topped her by an inch or two, but the way she reacted to the embrace made her seem tiny and fragile. She stiffened, the way she still did sometimes around displays of emotion, but then relaxed. She didn't hug him back, but Arthur heard her swallow.

"How did you get there?" He pulled back after a second to give her space and let her regain control of the situation, and she shrugged again, though she was too tense to be nonchalant.

"I took the bus." She was too pale, paler than Arthur, because she was inside most of the time. Arthur watched her closely as she put the dried nest of noodles into the water.

"They'll call." He had no idea if that was true, but she needed to hear it. Kate was young and pretty and smart, even if she didn't believe that. "If those people don't want you, then fuck them."

She snorted but didn't acknowledge his faith in her. "How about you? How did your interview go?"

"It wasn't even an interview," he blurted out, then shut up and slid past her to remove his jacket and wash his hands in the sink. His face and neck felt hot. It wasn't a good sign that just thinking about his new boss made him flush all over.

"So you didn't get it?" Kate pressed when he didn't go on.

"No, I got it." His smile came back, bigger than before. He didn't think even splashing cold water on his face would have any effect on his red cheeks, but whatever. At least for now he had a job, a *real* job. He turned around and put his back to the sink. Kate was studying him. The steam was making strands of her hair fly around her face. Arthur had the same fine blond hair, and he had the sudden horrifying thought that it must have been just as frizzy in the heat of Dr. Jones's house, making the faint waves that never went away even more pronounced. He usually just combed it and left it alone during the day, growing it to cover up his ears, which he thought stuck out a little, but he had at least tried to keep it neat under his bike helmet for the interview today.

Kate opened her mouth but seemed to change her mind and shook her head. "If it wasn't an interview, then what was it? This was the dragon, right? The professor?"

"He's a doctor." Arthur had no idea what expression was on his face to make his sister blink rapidly at him the way she was doing before the noodles called her back. "He has a PhD and a house like you wouldn't believe. Books everywhere." And a face and body out of Arthur's fantasies, but she didn't need to know that any more than she needed to know that the man had been flirting with him.

"You *would* focus on the books and not the treasure." She didn't bother with a strainer; she used a spoon and tilted the pot over the sink, leaving some of the water in with the noodles so they could pretend it was soup.

Arthur's smile faltered at the mention of treasure.

"There wasn't any treasure." Arthur scowled at her. "Unless you count those books, which I know *you* don't. I…." It wasn't that he hadn't thought of treasure—of course he had. He was desperate, and people had stolen more for worse reasons than needing money. He didn't want her thinking of it though. He didn't want any part of his desperation to reach her.

He shrugged when she made a face back at him for pointing out how little she liked to read.

"I don't need it anyway," he lied. "The hours will be better, I never have to work a graveyard shift behind that supposedly bulletproof glass at the gas station again." He would quit without

notice and not feel even a little bad about it. "And I will be around—
" He stopped, not sure whether he wanted to say *around the
university again* or *around Bertie*. There was no way he could say
the name Bertie around his sister. She would ask questions. He
should say *Dr. Jones*, or *a well-known historian*. He should tell her
that he hadn't seen the dragon breathe fire and that Bertie was an
appalling housekeeper for someone with magic and money at his
disposal, or maybe ask if she ever had a thing for men who smoked.

No, that he'd keep to himself. It might alarm her to think of
him ogling his boss, or make her think Arthur was going to let
himself get harassed by some creeper for the sake of a paycheck. It
was hard to tell how Kate would take news these days. As she had
told him, repeating what her sponsor had told her, without the
alcohol and weed clouding her mind and messing up her brain
chemistry, her mind had to relearn how to react to things, and it
didn't help that her thoughts were clear for the first time in years.
Some things seemed to hit her harder than others, so Arthur had to
choose his words more carefully.

After everything that being wasted had led her to, all the
trouble of the past few years, Kate was a lot more scared and
protective than she used to be. Arthur was just grateful to have his
sister back. He could deal with her worrying as long as it meant she
wasn't depressed again. She left the house today, had thought
enough of herself to apply for a job. He wasn't going to distract her
now.

"I'll be around someone that I have a feeling is brilliant," he
settled on, though he knew it was true as he said it, from the little
thrill it gave him. He'd never met anyone who talked about history
like it was alive and present. He wanted to know what Bertie might
have had to say on the Woodvilles. Maybe someday he could ask.

"Well I'm happy that you'll be doing something you like
again." Kate made a face. "And that you won't be in that gas station
all night anymore." She got down two bowls. "Though it's a shame
you'll never see the treasure. Imagine having money like that." She
shivered. "Maybe it's good that you won't see it. I'd be too tempted
to steal it."

Arthur put his head down and shut his eyes at the thought. He hadn't thought about treasure. But he had thought, in something a little more than passing, about scales. Dragons were said to lose their scales from time to time. He read that and although he had already wanted the job, he couldn't help but think that picking up a discarded scale so he could sell it hardly counted as stealing. Maybe it didn't. But even before he walked into that house and saw that beautiful, terrifying, extraordinary creature, it had felt like something secretive and wrong.

Now he saw the dragon, Dr. Jones, shirtless—the muscles of his back, the hint of shining scales along his spine—and flushed with color that he was going to blame on the weather if Kate asked.

She didn't. She only handed him his bowl of noodles and a fork, and then went into the small space they called a living room because of the old couch against one wall. It was Kate's bed at night.

He wasn't doing anything wrong, Arthur reminded himself firmly. He wouldn't be stealing, exactly. He'd do what he had to do, if it was even possible. No one would be hurt, despite what his suddenly tight stomach was trying to tell him.

He ignored it and followed Kate to the couch.

"I'll still be working weekend nights delivering food." Hopefully it would be a mild winter. He couldn't afford to get sick.

That only made Kate sigh. He recognized the guilt in it and hurried on in an attempt to keep her from fretting even more about Arthur working so hard to support them.

"You should have seen him," he offered, only to stare at his noodles when she looked up. His tone had been warm. Even knowing teasing him about a new crush might lift her mood, he hurried on. "He's different, even for a Being, and you know how they can be." Talking to Beings was often confusing; they could speak the same language as the humans they interacted with, but it was as if the words meant something else to them.

Like with fairies. Fairies weren't flirtatious, they were shockingly direct. Elves were usually impatient with humanity's slowness. But they both looked more or less human. Even as a man, Dr. Jones—Bertie—had seemed something other. Even with arms and legs and opposable thumbs, he seemed like something special.

"I might stop by the library tomorrow on my way, to get his books. Professor Gibson recommended me to him, and he doesn't do that lightly, so I should be prepared. I wouldn't want him to get disappointed in me."

He wondered if Kate would have found Bertie as fascinating as he had because Bertie's magic made him fascinating, or if Arthur had found him fascinating for completely personal reasons. Not that he was going to ask her, or ever have a chance to introduce them.

She was watching him, her eyes round, and Arthur tried to remember the last time, if ever, he'd gone on like this around her. She hadn't been interested in his studies back when she was high all the time and running around with her asshole boyfriend, and though she guessed he liked boys back when he was in high school, he'd never shared details of his love life with her.

Not that this was about his love life. This was about work and a chance to get ahead of his money troubles, to maybe even someday go back to school. It *couldn't* be about his love life.

"Disappointed?" Kate echoed him. "Who would ever be disappointed in you, Arthur?" She must have meant it, because the twist of her lips was shy before it turned rueful.

For the second time that day, Arthur's mouth fell open.

He thought of a similar approving look from a man who had called him a pearl, and quickly ducked his head to stuff noodles into his mouth and avoid any more talk about his new job.

His sister cleared her throat and set about eating too, as if she was suddenly just as starving as Arthur was.

CHAPTER 2

IN THE morning, with the clouds momentarily parted to allow some sunshine and with Arthur no longer worried about being late to an interview, he could take a moment to study the outside of Dr. Jones's house, which was as old and impressive as the inside had led him to believe.

There were nicer areas just outside of town, higher in elevation the way they were higher in status. Sprawling estates hidden on the edge of the woods, though even the rich wouldn't venture too far into the forest since a pack of weres had taken up residence there a few months ago as part of Thomas Kirkpatrick's Reclaim the Woods movement.

When they were little and their parents were alive, Arthur and Kate used to go hiking in those woods with their family, though Kate had enjoyed it far more than he ever did. Arthur missed his family more than he missed the thought of walking for hours through the dense trees, but he did wonder for a moment about the werewolves, and if they were anything like dragons, as some said they were.

Dr. Jones most likely could have afforded to live somewhere else, in one of those bigger, pricier estates, but this was still a wealthy neighborhood: clean streets lined with orange and brown oak trees that were losing their leaves, a place where doctors and lawyers and intellectuals with family money lived.

He would never have thought it was a house full of treasure from the outside. Perhaps that was why Dr. Jones didn't ever seem to lock his door. After knocking for a few minutes, Arthur tried the doorknob and frowned when it turned. It was even stranger to get inside and notice the alarm system keyboard next to set of wrought iron hooks for keys and to read the note: *Here is your key, Arthur, and the code to the alarm, in case I ever turn it on.* It was as if Bertie was daring people to rob his house.

Arthur shoved the note and key into the pocket of his jeans before edging in past the entrance hall. The probably antique, probably very valuable Art Deco brass lamp above him was on, as was every light inside, though there was no fire in the fireplace. It didn't affect the heat any; it was just as warm inside the house as it had been yesterday. Arthur unzipped his jacket and then paused to listen for Dr. Jones, but there was no dragon on the upstairs landing and no man by the wide table. There were no sounds at all to indicate he wasn't alone.

There was, however, another note on the table, and next to it, held down by the silver chest filled with those hand-rolled herbal cigarettes, a stack of money.

Arthur, the note read—and the cursive had enough turns in it to look like calligraphy—*please be a dear and buy me more printer paper and a few packets of things from my herbalist.* There was a card for the herbalist on top of the note and a scribbled blur that looked like a printer's serial number.

Arthur stared at the money, certain it was too much as much as it was a test. It had to be a test. He wished he had the kind of money to throw away on tests of his employee's virtue. But after a second, he sighed and zipped up his jacket again before grabbing the cash and the card with the herbalist's address on it.

He stopped to take a long look around, but there was no one, no Bertie. It wasn't exactly how Arthur had thought his first day would go. He glanced upstairs with a frown, just in case, and then sighed before turning and heading back out.

He locked the door behind him, for the sake of those books if nothing else.

ARTHUR'S small backpack normally held a cup of instant noodles and books from the library, but now it was packed tight with printer paper and a large, wrapped bundle of herbs. The herbal place had turned out to be an occult store, the kind of place with premade-purpose candles in the front for magic hobbyists, and serious items for witches and wizards in the back, behind a curtain. The employees obviously knew who the herbs were for when he asked for that combination, because Arthur was suddenly treated to wide smiles and even given his choice of a free candle. When he chose a protection one for his sister despite the array of wealth and fortune candles right in front of him, the old man who must run the place patted his hand.

He was certain the scent of the herbs clung to him as he unlocked the door and slipped back inside the house. He only realized that the scent wasn't coming from him after all when he heard that voice and swung his gaze around until he found Dr. Jones, lying on his sofa in front of a blazing fire and spinning a small yellow globe in his hands.

He looked the same as he had yesterday. Arthur hadn't been imagining how attractive he was or letting the adrenaline go to his head. The only change was that today the man was dressed in jeans and wore a white shirt unbuttoned at the throat. His feet were still bare.

Arthur quickly looked at the globe, which had the faded colors and faint scrawl of an old map, the kind of map that might have had a terrible sea creature or dragon drawn on it as a decorative warning. He had the feeling that Dr. Jones would find that very entertaining. "Here be dragons," indeed.

He knew he was right when Dr. Jones saw him studying his toy and winked at him. Arthur didn't jump, but he could have.

"Hullo, Arthur," he was greeted playfully.

"Hello, Dr. Jones." Arthur stopped with his hand on the zipper of his jacket, without thinking why except that slowly easing down any zippers didn't seem like a good idea given how hot those few words had him feeling. He was flushing again, sticky beneath his clothes, and he blamed the fire. "I have your things." He paused. "And your change." He didn't fail tests.

But if it was a test, it wasn't a harsh one. Dr. Jones nodded, waved it off, and didn't seem even a little interested when Arthur came in and set his backpack down on the table.

"I have to say, Arthur, you are looking scrumptious today. Perhaps it's the color that being outside gives you. And please, call me Bertie. Or Jones. Anything but Doctor."

"I'm…." It wasn't the fire. Arthur's face was stinging now. He was burning up but still wasn't sure he could take unzipping his jacket with *Bertie* teasing him like this. He raised his head to meet the man's gaze. There were things he could have said to that. Comments about it being hot in here, maybe, but Arthur had never had any practice at flirting, and anyway, Bertie's grin clearly meant it had been a joke. Arthur was cute, but he wasn't *scrumptious*.

He cleared his throat. "I'm pretty sure that's not appropriate coming from an employer." For a moment when the doctor didn't respond, Arthur thought he'd sounded too stern or rude, which made no sense until he remembered what he'd said to Kate about Beings and humans speaking different, if similar, languages. He offered a small smile just in case, though he couldn't quite bring himself to look over and see if Bertie was watching him shrug off his jacket.

There was only the sound of fire consuming wood for a few seconds while Arthur reminded himself that for all he knew, dragons were just this flirty with everyone, and it had been too long since he had anyone but Kate to tease him. He took a breath and turned back.

The doctor's eyes looked almost black, shining and wet. Arthur's mouth was suddenly dry.

"Unless you're planning on eating me," he pushed out, since, judging from yesterday, Dr. Jones liked things out in the open.

Arthur barely kept his voice from trembling and licked his lips when his remark made those eyes grow hooded.

"I make no promises." Bertie took his time responding, as if he was thinking about it after all, and then made a low noise, as if he was pleased by something. He set down the globe, stood up, and either didn't see Arthur's eyes go wide or was pretending not to. He rolled one hand and sighed. "Have you read my books, Arthur? I gather from that comment that you have not."

Arthur hadn't realized his shoulders were tense until he let out a breath at the subject change. He shook his head.

"Not yet. I got copies from the library this morning."

There was something different in Bertie's smile at that. It made him look less dangerous and more like a kid at Christmas. Arthur had to stop himself from scuffing his shoe on the floor or smiling back at him.

"How sweet of you." Bertie nodded to himself. "And thorough. As I was saying, as you may have noticed, I'm something of a historian." Arthur nodded too in order to keep the man talking. "Sadly, I am not a very organized historian." He didn't seem to appreciate the small sound of agreement that Arthur couldn't hold back. Bertie pursed his lips and spent a moment considering Arthur, and Arthur had the strange feeling that now Bertie wouldn't eat him because Arthur was beneath him. He surprised himself by feeling insulted and lifting his chin.

He supposed criticizing a dragon to his face wasn't the wisest idea. Most people probably wouldn't dare.

Arthur wanted to apologize yet couldn't do it. There were inches of dust and no order to those books at all. "I thought I was here to organize things for you." It was as diplomatic as he could get.

"So you are, Arthur. So you are." Bertie, a name Arthur couldn't seem to stop thinking though it was somehow too cute for a man like this, let out a small huff and then nodded. "You're correct of course, but you might have thought of my feelings."

Arthur's jaw went slack. Thankfully he kept himself under control when he saw the sparkling glint enter Bertie's eyes. A second later Bertie grinned. It was a joke. Bertie hadn't been angry at all.

That's what Arthur got for being so obviously wary of him. Bertie was making fun of him. He crossed his arms. Bertie instantly lost his grin.

"Once again, Arthur, you're right. Back to business. I have a bad habit—" When he paused to inhale, Arthur realized his eyebrow was arched. Bertie only sailed on with another low, pleased sound at Arthur's effrontery. "—or *two*, and one of them is that I write notes about things I want to put into my books as I am researching them, and I tend to leave those notes everywhere. I tuck them into things. I've found them on the floor, under rugs, even in the refrigerator. But mainly I leave them in books as I'm reading them."

Arthur instantly got what the man was saying. He looked wildly around the room, for a second anyway, before focusing back on the supposedly brilliant dragon in front of him.

"Part of your job will be finding them. Now, granted, I don't always use every idea in them—they're usually things I want to add to keep the text from becoming too much boring prose—but I do like having them, and trying to find them once I'm ready to write can slow me down considerably."

Arthur waited until he was sure Bertie was done talking and glanced around the room, the mess, again. That his heart was racing at the idea of straightening all those books, looking at them, reading them, and classifying them, didn't matter. It was hardly the work of a research assistant. Or even a personal assistant.

"You're serious?" Arthur didn't move as Bertie came around to get himself a cigarette. He didn't light it, just let it touch his lips.

"You don't want to do it?" The unbearable sadness in his voice reminded Arthur that he promised to do his very best work. Stupid though it was, he'd offered up his services to Dr. Bertie Jones—crazy, flirty dragon—just yesterday.

He inhaled and considered it. It wasn't exactly like having his own library, but it was as close as he might ever get. He swallowed.

"Can I dust while I look? Or open a window? It's stuffy in here, and it's not good for the books."

Bertie's head went back and he looked affronted at the word "stuffy." This time Arthur didn't go nearly as tense as he had before. Bertie looked too pouty again for him to feel too worried.

"But I can get so *cold* at times, Arthur." It was the last thing Arthur expected to hear. He looked down at his sweatshirt—it was fall outside after all—and then over at Bertie's thin white shirt and bare feet. He possibly spent more time studying them than he should.

Bertie's lips were closing around the white paper of his cigarette when Arthur finally looked up. The tang of herbs and smoke filled the air, and Arthur felt about as hot as the burning red cherry.

"So wear socks." He knew why his voice was rasping. The man had a tendency to make his throat go dry. He sucked in a long breath and thought about work, his job, looking through every page of every book in this house. "I can buy them for you if you like."

"Socks? You unromantic soul." There was amusement in Bertie's rough, rumbling voice, and then Bertie took a drag from his cigarette with a flare of light and fire that was reflected in his eyes. Arthur waited, absolutely certain he was being teased, for Bertie to exhale and then lick his bottom lip. He was not disappointed.

He got his eyes up in time to await more instructions.

"Very well. Clean if you must." The topic was dismissed as if it were nothing, and Arthur scowled because it ought to matter if the room, if these *books*, were taken care of or not.

"I must," Arthur insisted, and Bertie's eyebrows rose in surprise. He took another drag.

"But don't disturb anything," he warned a second later. Arthur angled his head at him.

"Could you even tell?" His disbelief was too real for him to worry about being rude. He got a grin for a reply.

"I will give you that hit, Arthur. It was a bull's-eye." He inclined his head graciously and spoke as formally as Arthur had the day before. "You may straighten to your heart's content… straighten everywhere if it please you, Arthur MacArthur."

"Everywhere?" Arthur immediately glanced up the stairs. He hadn't seen any other rooms downstairs yet, but the rooms upstairs were going to be the ones considered more personal and private. Even if there wasn't a treasure up there, it was where Bertie's bedroom would be.

Arthur raised his hands before he looked back. "I just don't want to end up an entrée."

The lack of humor in Bertie's expression made him freeze. He could see the brown of his eyes now, so much of it, with his pupils narrowed to slits like an angry cat's.

Arthur's stomach tightened. Treasure really was, in his sister's words, *srs bsns*, to dragons.

"Sensible humans respect a locked door," Bertie hissed quietly, but a moment later he dropped his head and heaved a sigh. Arthur bit back a comment about how he hadn't known Bertie knew how to lock a door.

"Sorry, I…," he started instead, and Bertie jerked his head up and waved at him to shut him up.

"I'm hardly Bluebeard, Arthur. Nothing behind any of my doors will be as interesting to you as what is out here. I'm becoming very convinced of that." There was a half smile on his face and he seemed to have forgotten that he was smoking. Arthur put out a hand as a trail of ash fell to the carpet. Bertie's smile only grew.

Swallowing while considering the lack of teeth in that smile, Arthur tried a subject change.

"So you're working on a new book then? What's it about?" That smile said Bertie thought the world, or maybe just Arthur, was delightful. Scrumptious. A pearl. Arthur was so hot he wanted to strip his sweater off—not that he would dare, not with those eyes watching him.

"The Welsh red dragon," Bertie announced slowly, with a flourish of the hand not holding the cigarette.

Arthur snapped his gaze up to see if Bertie was joking.

"No, I'm not teasing you." He was immediately reassured. Though now Arthur had to wonder if dragons could read minds. He hoped not, because then it was only going to take one stray thought whenever Bertie put anything near his mouth and Arthur was doomed.

"Arthur." Just hearing his name on the heels of that thought made Arthur give a whole-body shiver. "I am a Being, and most importantly, a dracologist, and I've been researching the long lost red dragon of Wales for some time now."

"Long lost?" Arthur could do this, he could focus even while in mild shock and with a dozen explicit fantasies about his new boss pressing on the edge of his thoughts.

"They haven't been seen in centuries. Even by the standards of an often-reclusive people, that's going a bit far." The soft, serious tone brought Arthur back to his senses. Bertie turned away to stare at the fire. Even knowing it could be more teasing, Arthur didn't think so. He stepped closer then stopped and studied the edge of black hair against Bertie's neck, the faint gleam of hidden scales.

"Perhaps they are extinct," Bertie spoke to the fire, then twisted to look over his shoulder, staring right into Arthur's eyes. "Or perhaps they are hiding while they wait for Arthur's return."

"I… um." Arthur licked the corner of his mouth and rubbed at his cheek because he knew it was flaming red now.

"I do shock you sometimes, don't I? Sorry, Arthur." Bertie's laugh was quiet. He faced the fire again. Perhaps he really was that cold. Arthur would have to think of something else to keep him warm while protecting the books. Socks definitely. Maybe those warmed ones; he didn't care how unromantic it was.

"If you can make sense of my notes once you have them, it would be very helpful, but I am sure it's impossible. Simply finding them will take up your time. Other than that, you will be doing odd errands and research. Keeping track of mail… and taking messages, should you find my phone. It's around here somewhere. I don't know what else to have you do," he admitted, tossing his cigarette into the fire. "My publisher recommended an assistant. I'm afraid I've never trusted one before." Bertie paused, going still, and Arthur didn't think he'd reacted, didn't believe he'd even *thought* anything out of the ordinary or suspicious, but when Bertie turned his lips were parted and Arthur caught a glimpse of his tongue.

"So," Bertie mused a moment later, his eyes narrowing, "so I don't know quite what to do with you."

"We can work that out as we go," Arthur murmured, though cleaning would take up any free time he had. Free time. He felt weak again. It had been a while since he had much free time, and to be spending it even in a small way, doing something he loved, felt like a vacation. "You're already being more than generous, so really anything you want is fine." He shut his mouth with a click and looked over. But Bertie apparently felt it was too obvious for his form of flirtation, or at least he left it alone and continued to speak with his usual smoky intimacy.

"You are going to be a steadying influence, Arthur. I can tell. You're just what I've been waiting for."

"Okay." Arthur got the word out, that's what mattered to his dignity. He shifted to one side. "Do you… want coffee or something?" Maybe he just was supposed to start going through books now, but Bertie continued to stare at him, even wrinkling his brow in a frown.

"Why?" He seemed confused. "Do you? Well, help yourself if I have any. You do seem tired, pet. And hungry. Did you even get time to eat breakfast before I sent you running around? If there's no food, we'll have to see about getting some before setting to work. I had a housekeeper once who bought my food for me, but she got tired of walking in and finding me naked after I shifted. You'll notice I have donned clothes just for your human sensibilities."

He cracked his neck and lifted his arms for a stretch, or to display the clothes he'd put on for Arthur.

"If it's as bad as you say, I should get started," Arthur said quickly while watching that body move and *not* thinking about it without any clothes. That was for later, when he was far away and less likely to embarrass himself. "Earn my keep."

He almost bit his tongue at his phrasing. This house, this man, seemed to bring it out in him. He'd never been so tempted to put inappropriate slants on all his words before. It was probably because Bertie seemed to find them so amusing. Of course he planned on earning his keep. He wasn't being kept, that was ridiculous. It was just that the pay was already generous. He didn't need to be fed too.

"Work?" The very word seemed to make Bertie tired. Arthur abruptly realized why Bertie's publisher wanted him to have an assistant. They'd probably even tried to hire one for him, some drill sergeant to keep on him task. The thought made him straighten and put his shoulders back, because he had his work cut out for him.

Bertie took one look at Arthur's posture and sighed again. "If you must, Arthur. If you must." He tasted the air once more before sliding closer, his footsteps silent on the thick rug. "Unless...." The same part of Arthur that knew approaching unknown snakes was a bad idea knew that hanging onto Bertie's every word was only going to get him in trouble. It didn't keep him from listening, even if he frowned. "You want to talk some more, or have a bite? Just a nibble?"

Arthur's hunger must have been in the air. Bertie's stare said he could tell that Arthur's stomach was growling and that Arthur hadn't had any breakfast at all. It also hinted he knew what talk of bites and nibbles was doing to Arthur's brain.

Arthur hadn't done anything like that with his one real boyfr— with Clematis. There was a lot he hadn't done with Clematis that he'd wanted to do, but during all those light kisses and sweet blowjobs, when he wanted more, he hadn't realized "more" might include love bites. He pictured teeth against his skin and couldn't stop his breath from coming faster.

Arthur closed his eyes briefly but kept his frown in place.

"I'm fine, thank you," he got out before opening his eyes again and watching Bertie tap one dark fingernail against his mouth. It was just as distracting, if not more so, than watching him smoke. Arthur might have a thing he hadn't previously been aware of for painted nails on men, in addition to his new interest in cigarettes and biting.

"If you *insist*." A tiny puff of smoke escaped Bertie's lips, like an exclamation of annoyance. "Then find a place to work. I will be in my study if you need me for anything."

His raised eyebrow wasn't very subtle. If Arthur hadn't still been red, it might have made him blush. He didn't want to imagine what the air might smell like, but luckily Bertie's tongue did not make an appearance, just another grin. "And I do mean anything."

To save himself, Arthur turned on his heel to look at one wall of books and didn't look back until the heat had minutely lessened, the scent of herbs was gone, and he felt that he was alone.

He pulled in several lungfuls of air and tugged at his sweatshirt. Anything to feel cooler. He looked around before yanking it up over his head and felt marginally better in just his T-shirt.

For a second or two, he stared at himself: at his arms with their faded freckles and light hair, at his legs in jeans that were looser than they'd been when he bought them. Then he frowned harder.

Fairies, or at least *one* fairy he knew from personal experience, weren't really interested in a human's physical appearance as much as people thought. Despite being gorgeous and spending a lot of time kissing him, Clematis had seemed more interested in Arthur's reactions to his attentions than in Arthur himself; in what he could get out of Arthur instead of what Arthur wanted.

Dragons were Beings too, just like fairies. All this attention had to be simply how dragons were. It was at odds with the myths of them kidnapping people and keeping them in their lairs or eating them, but Arthur was suddenly sure the people writing those stories hadn't wanted to admit to getting tongue-tied and flustered when a giant lizard winked at them.

At least he was reasonably sure he wasn't going to be roasted alive now, and he had a job with a boss who wasn't going to push him hard or treat him unfairly. In fact, Arthur had a feeling that being frequently red-faced and suffering through various stages of arousal was going to be the most difficult thing about this job... that and resisting the urge to respond.

He wondered if Bertie was that languid about everything, if his soft pet names meant he wouldn't take charge in bed, if Bertie saw Arthur as someone to top him the way other people seemed to, or if Bertie would fuck Arthur the way Arthur had wanted Clematis to. He was a strong and powerful dragon, but did that mean he would hold Arthur down and push him open the way Arthur had only ever done with his fingers? Would he, if Arthur asked him to and promised to be his?

His breath hitched at that last errant thought. It was too strange to be his. It had to be the house or something he'd read about dragons giving him that idea—maybe one of those old stories about dragons keeping maidens in their lairs.

Just in case dragons *could* read minds, he shoved the thought away and locked it up tight. The books were in front of him. Mountains of them. Hordes waiting to be cleaned and alphabetized and put in their proper place, which did *not* mean near a fireplace. With a grim smile of determination, Arthur pushed his shoulders back and set forth to bring order to chaos.

CHAPTER 3

IF THE dust didn't kill him, the lack of organization would, Arthur thought fiercely and not for the first time. Just piling the books into some kind of order without stopping to read or glance through them had taken up most of his first two workdays.

While many of the books were obviously loved and well-read, they were also so thick with dust that whenever he moved one he had to pull his head back to avoid the shower of dust motes that followed. To make it worse, Bertie must have been eating or drinking while reading a few of them, somehow getting a few thick leather covers wet; and combined with the heat of the room, there were now spots of mildew on them.

It was completely unacceptable. How Bertie had ever found what he was looking for was a mystery to Arthur, because although there was evidence that Bertie's books had once held some sort of order, or attempt at order, it was clear that Bertie put books wherever there was space for them regardless of title, subject, or author.

Arthur fully intended to correct that problem, as soon as he'd been through every book in the house. So far, he hadn't even made a dent in the main room. It didn't help that in addition to trying to create stacks to help separate the books and wiping them down and setting aside the ones in need of repair or replacement, he had to flip through them all page by page to find any scraps of paper with notes on them.

There was a pretty sizable pile of notes so far, actually. Arthur was kind of proud of it, though not nearly as happy as he was to see his hard work starting to pay off. The room might someday look almost like a real library.

He glanced at the evidence of his hard work again. Not all of the notes seemed to be about dragons. An edition of *Psychopathia Sexualis* had had two notes in it, one reading simply "move 7 to 2" and the other quoting an entire passage from Ovid. Arthur found the Ovid later and checked it; Bertie must have been quoting it from memory because he only got one word wrong. They were probably lost notes from a previous book, and so far there was no obvious rhyme or reason to which books they might be in, or why.

"Poetry quotations in a copy of *Grimm's Fairy Tales* printed around 1930 lying on its side underneath three volumes of a travel series," Arthur muttered to himself because the house was quiet. Bertie didn't keep the fire going when he was out or not spending his time in the living room. Right now he was in his study writing, or pretending to, or just staying out of Arthur's way.

Bertie had tried, halfway through the first day and early on the second, to distract Arthur, probably so he wouldn't feel bad about not working while Arthur was working. Arthur's face and hands were streaked with dust, his arms were full of heavy tomes, and he'd once again skipped breakfast. He usually did, but it still didn't put him in a good mood, and dragon or not, Bertie took one look at him on both occasions and disappeared into his study with a chastened look on his face.

"He *should* feel bad," Arthur huffed as he straightened and stretched. He'd found a sliding ladder for the bookshelves that had been being used as a kind of coat rack, and going up and down on it all day was making his tired muscles shaky. "Nobody should treat books this way, I don't care how brilliant they are."

"You're quite right, Arthur." The cheery note in Bertie's voice and the fact that he'd heard Arthur complaining made Arthur stop where he was and wet his lips before turning around. It got him a mouthful of dust that made him gag.

It was hot in the room even without a fire. Arthur was very conscious that he was red-faced, sweaty, and dirty. His fingers looked like he'd been fingerprinted with black ink. He knew without looking in the mirror in the downstairs bathroom that his hair was sticking to his forehead in a vague wave. He'd stopped being too concerned with wearing just a T-shirt and jeans the moment Bertie had made it clear he planned on leaving Arthur alone while he worked.

It was a completely appropriate thing for an employer to do, and Arthur liked working alone; he got more done. He didn't know why it had made him frown to see Bertie disappear into his study without commenting on Arthur's bare arms or remarking on how his body looked with fewer clothes on or giving him any kind of flirty wink, but it had.

Okay, Arthur *did* know why it bothered him. Even not wanting to risk anything, even knowing that it was just flirting and didn't mean anything, he wanted Bertie to say something nice about him again in his heated, seductive voice with that cultured accent. He wanted Bertie to stare at him and call him a pearl.

Arthur really, really needed to get out more, because his crush could no longer be denied, and he was only going to embarrass himself if he kept on like this. He scowled at the thought, and because he was itchy, tired, and hungry, and he'd made a lot of progress and Bertie hadn't said anything. Arthur realized he was starting to whine internally just as Bertie darted out his tongue to wet the corner of his mouth.

Bertie had on jeans and a large, floppy sweatshirt with the university's logo on it. It looked comfortable and soft and like it had cost more than Arthur's jeans. Knowing that the sweatshirt, that *all* of Bertie's clothing, was for his benefit only made Arthur scowl harder.

"It's a mess now, but when I'm through with it you should be able to find things without too much trouble," he insisted as the silence went on. Bertie blinked but followed the direction of Arthur's hand as he pointed at the stacks. Arthur's heart was beating hard. "Some of these are expensive. All of them are valuable. You shouldn't let them get dirty," he explained slowly, hearing the irritation creeping into his voice but unable to completely suppress it.

"Of course, I—" Bertie began. Arthur thinned his lips and Bertie shut up.

"*This* stack has mold. I might not be able to save them." Maybe it was because he'd never seen books in this condition, but Arthur flung one hand out accusingly at the books under discussion. "The other stacks are either volumes that belong together in a collection or pieces I have yet to classify." He wasn't even going to go into the dried leather bindings on the older books.

He would swear his snappish words echoed through the room. He wiped at his face, probably smearing sweat and dust all over it. Bertie watched him with wide, shining eyes. He wet the corner of his mouth again, but this time it looked more like a gesture of uncertainty. It didn't seem very dragonlike, but it reminded Arthur of who, of what, he was dealing with all the same, and he abruptly shut his mouth and shook his head.

"I mean, I can arrange them however you like, if you give me time to devise a workable cataloguing system that suits your needs…." His voice lowered as he gestured at the books again. He couldn't make himself apologize, not with the state of this room when he started. But Bertie wasn't speaking, so he had to. "And you should have space on your shelves when I'm done, for more books, or… whatever." He gave another small wave, this time at the pile of dusty knickknacks he hadn't looked at or tried to clean yet.

"It's a good room," he added, not sure why, though it *was* a nice room. Someone, probably Dr. Jones, had the bookshelves built in so it looked like the library of an old mansion. He looked back over to see if Bertie was angry and caught the lift of his eyebrows. The eyes below them were getting warmer by the second. Arthur tugged at the collar of his T-shirt and wondered why he'd ever missed those stares when they only made him feel like he was on fire with blushes.

"You're awfully flushed," Bertie announced after a moment. "Perhaps you *should* open a window."

Arthur would *love* an open window.

"Really?" His surprise was genuine and probably all over his face with the dust, and it left Bertie upset with him, judging from the chiding noise he made.

"I'm not a monster, Arthur." As though to prove it, he smiled. Not a grin but a real, wide smile. Arthur could feel his lips curve up to match it, because it was a nice smile even if the man couldn't take care of his books. Arthur's smile was probably a little dopey, but Bertie was pleased with him after all and Arthur... didn't know how to react except to smile goofily in return, but then he hadn't eaten much today. He felt the smile disappear from his face when Bertie peered at him for a moment longer and then scowled. Arthur had no idea why his smile would make the other man frown, but one second he'd been delighted with Arthur and now he just looked disappointed.

"Arthur." He hadn't thought Bertie could sound stern. Fierce and scary, outrageous, and sexy he could do, but stern was new. It was also, like many things about his new employer, interesting. And by interesting, Arthur meant hot. He waited and Bertie threw up his hands. "You didn't eat, did you?" He wasn't really asking, Arthur could tell from how Bertie didn't pause for an answer after the question. "I was willing to let this go the other day, but this is quite enough. You've been taking the phrase 'starving student' a little far, I think."

"I have not." The denial was instant. Arthur wasn't even sure where it came from because he was busy watching a dragon put his hands on his hips to scold him. "I'm not starving myself on purpose here."

The protest was overridden with a wave of one hand.

"I have something I'm sure. Cheese, if not bread. Fruit. You might need something more substantial."

Fruit. Arthur almost drooled.

He was so hungry his stomach had given up on growling to get his attention and turned itself into a solid, aching knot, and he forgot to bring his cup of soup today. He'd wanted to forget it. The taste, the smell, all of it. He never wanted to eat instant noodle soup again. It was bad enough filling the Styrofoam cup with hot water in the kitchen and slurping it down quickly so Bertie wouldn't see him eating it. Arthur had had a feeling that the dragon would have something to say about his diet, and now he was right.

"I can eat at home, it's okay," he tried, not sure what the protocol was when your employer wanted to feed you. It had never happened to him before, though he did sometimes get the cancelled orders and mistakes on the nights he delivered food. "I just forgot to bring my lunch." And eat breakfast, but who was counting?

Bertie must have been, even while hiding out in his study. Or he *could* read minds, but it wasn't something Arthur could contemplate at the moment.

"Really," he tried again, putting some force into the words and raising his chin, "you are already being more than fair."

"Are you frightened that it's a trick? I thought you better than that, Arthur."

It stopped him.

"Trick?" Arthur smoothed his hands down his pant legs.

Bertie's eyes narrowed. "A serpent offering you food doesn't always have to be anything malevolent." With his arms crossed, he looked indignant and Arthur suddenly understood what he was referring to. He hadn't thought about it like that at all and hurried forward to make up for his cultural insensitivity.

"I'd love some fruit," he started, and then caught the look on Bertie's face, a bright, mischievous one that he didn't do a very good job of hiding. It *had* been a trick, only he'd been tricking Arthur into feeling guilty so he would eat. Arthur stopped short and pursed his lips.

It was embarrassing to be caught like that, but he couldn't seem to feel any spark of anger. "I don't suppose you have any apples." He changed his tone as smoothly as he could, and Bertie confirmed that he *had* been playing with Arthur when he snorted a little at Arthur's reply. "Or figs," Arthur went on, "or pomegranates for that matter, since there are several theories about what that forbidden fruit in the Garden of Eden was, as I'm sure you know. It's never identified as an apple in the story."

"Excellent." Bertie drew out the word of approval with a sibilant hiss and briefly closed his eyes. He turned the moment they were open again and led the way to the kitchen. "Come with me, precious, and we'll find you a treat."

ARTHUR had been sent to the bathroom—a small half-bath just down from the kitchen by the laundry room and a side door that probably led outside to the detached garage—to wash up. The bathroom had a dwindling supply of toilet paper but plenty of issues of National Geographic with address labels still stuck to them. The room was also as dusty as the rest of the house, although it consistently smelled of the lemon verbena in the hand soap.

He made a note to use the change Bertie had never asked for to buy more toilet paper since that seemed safer than poking around the rest of the house looking for a supply closet. He had to admit that he didn't know enough about dragons to know how complete their physical changes were when they shifted to human. It was possible Bertie didn't use his own bathrooms and so wouldn't know he was low on toilet paper. It wasn't something Arthur wanted to ask about, exactly, but he did want to know. Maybe not about that so much as how human Bertie's body was—not that he had a way to ask that wouldn't give away the reason for his interest.

He ought to stop thinking that way in any case. It wasn't going to happen. Arthur had admittedly attracted a fairy once, but it wasn't like anyone had been beating down his door since then. The few looks of interest thrown his way hadn't lasted once people realized he'd have no time for them.

He had time now, he realized suddenly while looking at his reflection in the bathroom mirror and drying his face. But he instantly pushed the thought aside because it wasn't going to happen. He sighed as he headed back out to the kitchen.

The kitchen was empty. Arthur took a moment making sure he looked composed before he went searching for his employer. Bertie was in the main room, leaning against the couch with a large bowl of fruit resting on the table behind it. He had a bunch of red grapes in his hand. Of course he did. And of course he was eating them one at a time and licking his lips after each one.

Arthur approached carefully, stifling his second sigh because he should have been comforted to see a dragon eating fruit and not people. *Comforted*, not turned on.

There was a pomegranate in the bowl, surprising him, but he left it where it was, not wanting to make a mess over a rug he couldn't afford to replace. He avoided the bananas too—no way could he take Bertie's response to those right now. He chose more grapes and tried not to push too many in his mouth at once when he realized they were seedless.

"God." It slipped out with the first bite, breathless and edgy. It had been a long time since he had fresh fruit. He really shouldn't be making noises over some grapes, but they were so good. He popped a few more into his mouth before he forced himself to slow down and eat properly, then he looked over at his employer.

"Poor, hungry Arthur." Bertie breathed the words without looking at him. He was glaring at the fireplace as though annoyed to find no fire burning inside. "If you won't feed yourself, you'll force me to do it." When Arthur stopped chewing, Bertie glanced over at him. His eyes, though still full and black, lacked their usual glitter. "Humans are so—" He gestured as if starting to understand something that he didn't feel like explaining. "—fragile."

Arthur's eyebrows drew together. He wasn't fragile. He knew how the world worked better than Bertie did—he was willing to bet on it. The world with money and magic was a lot different than the world without it.

"While we're on the subject," Bertie said as though he'd read Arthur's protest before he could voice it, "there are guest rooms here, Arthur, as well as this couch, which is very comfortable. You are welcome to stay if you find yourself here late. I've seen what you call transportation." He turned up his nose at the very thought of Arthur's bicycle. "Riding a bicycle isn't very safe at night even with those reflective lights."

Arthur bit his tongue before he could point out that he delivered food all over town on that bike: at night, in the rain, on busy streets. He had a feeling that the less Bertie knew about his other remaining job, the better.

"My bike keeps me in shape." It was an invitation for Bertie to look him up and down, and Bertie did not waste the opportunity. Arthur fought not to shiver as those eyes took their time traveling from his shoes to his face as if Bertie was imagining what was hidden by Arthur's clothing. Arthur didn't think of himself as a strong man—he was too little for that—but he could ride up hills other delivery boys couldn't manage and could carry most heavy loads without losing his breath.

He closed his hands under Bertie's stare and saw Bertie's eyes go back to his forearms. Bertie exhaled and then his lips curved up. Arthur went on quickly before Bertie could say anything about what he thought of Arthur's shape.

"I'll be fine, really. There's no need to…." The word *worry* stuck in Arthur's throat. His eyes burned for a moment. "You barely know me," he whispered, then tossed his head and looked at his feet when Bertie looked like he wanted to say something. This wasn't a normal job, but Arthur didn't deserve that, not with part of his intent in coming here so… dishonest. It didn't matter that he would never take anything from Bertie. The fact that he ever considered it, as if any part of Bertie was for sale, made him feel terrible. "I've looked after myself for a long time."

"Not bloody well enough." It was the most British Bertie had ever seemed. He sounded like an old colonel. "Now *eat*."

Arthur ate another grape before putting the remains of the bunch down. There were tiny oranges too. He laid two aside to take home later and then discovered almonds under the fruit. He should have asked whether Bertie was a vegetarian dragon or why he got so much fruit, but he didn't. He crunched almonds and then ate a few more grapes. He wouldn't say he felt better when he was done, but his stomach didn't feel nearly as tight, and the heat of the room didn't seem so overwhelming.

Bertie watched him, though whenever Arthur glanced back at him, the dragon would slide his attention back to his cold fireplace. After a couple of missed glances, he coughed and put his arm up along the back of the couch.

"It pains me to say it, but maybe you ought to go home for the day, Arthur."

Bits of almond stuck in Arthur's throat. He swallowed them all, not without pain.

"You're sending me away? I can work harder." He came around the table to stand in front of the couch only to freeze when he received Bertie's full attention. He immediately turned to all the books, all his piles, his plans. He hadn't done nearly enough.

"Arthur." Bertie's lips were parted, just a little. "You can always stay."

"Then why…?" Arthur changed his mind after he asked. First he was told to stay and eat, now Bertie wanted to send him home. He didn't want to go. Bertie hadn't even seen a fraction of what he was capable of yet.

His own desperation to impress wasn't nearly as confusing as his sudden need to stay. His paycheck hadn't even been his first thought.

"Do you want me to go?" He didn't like how quiet his voice got or the puzzled look Bertie shot him, as if he honestly didn't know how to answer Arthur's question.

"Of course not," he rumbled, sounding more like himself as a lizard than as a man. "I simply thought… perhaps… you were overwrought."

"Overwrought?" Arthur repeated the Victorian-sounding word in disbelief.

"Exhausted?" Bertie changed it quickly. "Weak with hunger?"

"Oh." Arthur's breath rushed out of him. Bertie had been worried. His earlier thought returned and hit him hard. "You were worried about me?" He stopped himself from asking more. "Oh," he said instead. "I just... I just need a break. I don't need to go home."

"That's a relief." Bertie drummed his fingers along the back of the couch and Arthur caught a whiff of acrid smoke. "You have no idea how irritating it is going against your instincts, even for a little while."

"I have an idea," Arthur defended himself without thinking, remembering the fantasies he'd had about Bertie talking to him in that fire-and-smoke voice while he pressed Arthur facedown to the couch cushions and fucked him the way Arthur would beg him to. Then he blinked, because that last comment hadn't made any sense. "Wait, what?"

Bertie turned away, his nose up in the air as if Arthur wasn't worth an explanation or he thought Arthur wouldn't understand one. The warmth in Arthur's stomach vanished.

"We really *are* speaking a different language. *Beings*," he muttered under his breath. He wanted to flop down onto the couch, but he couldn't with Bertie there and wouldn't have anyway because that couch was made from a velvet so fine that just touching it once had made him sigh.

Bertie turned back to stare at him and raised one eyebrow, which meant he'd heard that remark. Arthur hurried forward only to stop once he was a foot from the couch. Bertie's gaze stayed on him, and though his pose was relaxed, like some kind of emperor, a few grapes still in his lap as he lounged, the very air around him seemed hot and still.

Whenever the air had been that hot and still, Arthur's mother had used to call it earthquake weather, which Arthur had never understood. Not as a child anyway, though he was getting it now. At this exact moment, he suddenly understood how the potential for a disaster could be felt in the air. It was almost as if the house itself was watching him.

"I'm sorry. I don't... I haven't read your books yet." Actually, the two he got from the library didn't seem to be about dragons at all, and what he looked at on the library computers hadn't said much. The information on trolls and werewolves and demons was far more complete. He supposed they were a bigger threat and had needed to be studied more. Dragons... no one knew for sure how to classify them: lucky protectors or fearsome beasts. Maybe both. "I don't know about dragons. Are you... typical?"

"Are you typical for a human?" Bertie idly picked up the grapes and dropped them onto the table behind him without looking to see where they fell. Arthur couldn't read his expression and tell if he was angry or disappointed or teasing him again.

"That.... I know there's no such thing as typical." He'd never tripped over his words so much but he never meant to hurt anyone. "I'm sorry. I didn't mean to sound like a jerk, it's just that I've never met anyone like you."

There was no change in Bertie's face, but something in his posture seemed to ease. He melted back into the velvety cushions. The air around them no longer seemed to portend disaster, but Arthur wasn't breathing any easier yet.

"Do you mean someone who doesn't like watching a person suffer needlessly?" Bertie sat up just for a moment to twist around and flick open the silver chest so he could take out a cigarette. "That *is* sad, Arthur."

Arthur's mouth opened and closed for a moment.

"That isn't what I meant," he protested, but of course Bertie had known that. He'd said it too pointedly for it to be a mistake.

"Ah, so you mean someone who flirts outrageously with you?" Bertie stuck the cigarette in his mouth and winked at Arthur's slight squirm and subsequent frown. "Or do you mean a Being? Surely you must have met a few."

"There was a fairy in one of my classes." It just came out. Arthur wasn't sure why, because Bertie and Clematis weren't alike at all, and Bertie was hardly going to be interested in a fairy Arthur had known once.

"A fairy?" Bertie instantly proved him wrong, settling in on the couch again to study Arthur. He seemed to know the whole story already, and it made him frown. "And did he or she like you?" His voice deepened.

"Yes." Arthur wasn't sure where this was going and answered as carefully as he could. "Yes, he did." Clematis had eyes like a cappuccino, swirling shades of warm brown, and long wings like green Depression glass, and the broad shoulders of a swimmer. Despite his muscle, he weighed almost nothing at all when he pounced on Arthur for that first kiss. His glitter rained gently down on Arthur, his come tasted sugar sweet, and his body felt almost fragile under Arthur's clumsy human fingers.

Then he was gone. Arthur frowned and focused back on Bertie.

It wasn't that he wanted to make his orientation clear, to let Bertie know he was available and possibly interested. Even if both of these things were true. He hadn't been planning to talk about himself at all, but after being so insensitive, it only seemed fair to offer Bertie something of himself in return.

He didn't think it was that big a deal, not with Bertie admitting that he'd been flirting, though Arthur still didn't know whether his flirting was personal to Arthur or just a habit. This was a college town after all, and Bertie was a man of learning and intelligence and unlikely to be a bigot about Arthur being gay. Anyway, dragons, like many other Beings, didn't have the same hang-ups about morality that a lot of humans did, or at least, what morality they had was different.

"Yes." Bertie stared at the unlit cigarette in his hand. "About that…." His pause was heavy and his slight frown made him seem pained again. "You should watch yourself around Beings, Arthur. Some of us have a definite type when it comes to humans. A taste, if you will."

He raised his head and met Arthur's shocked, wide-eyed stare. Arthur couldn't quite process what Bertie's look was telling him. He thought faintly that if Bertie was trying to say *Arthur* was the preferred boyfriend material for creatures of unbelievable magic, power, and beauty, then that was ridiculous because he wasn't anything special to look at. He'd never be an underwear model even if he ate normally and gained some weight back. He was a good student who loved his choice of career, if he ever got back to it, but he wasn't a genius. He was, he thought tightly, a skinny kid with little to no free time who usually had his snub nose in a book when he wasn't working.

His conversation was lacking, too, and not just because some dragon seemed to enjoy rendering him speechless. He closed his mouth, at least, so he wouldn't ask if that's what Bertie meant, and if so, why, because he'd already put his foot in his mouth once in the last few minutes, and he didn't want to do it again.

Bertie shook himself and broke the stare.

"Were you sad when the fairy left you? He did, didn't he?" He rose in one fluid, restless motion and went over to the fireplace. With his back turned, Arthur only saw the spark and then the thin trail of smoke rising from the cigarette.

Yes, Arthur thought but didn't say out loud. He was sad when Clematis left. Sad and lost because knowing a fairy would leave was something he'd chosen to ignore during their time together. Frankly, he'd been so swept away, grateful, and happy to be with someone that he hadn't wanted to think about it.

Arthur's stomach rumbled, the snack reminding him that he did need to stop, and he ought to find some real food if he wanted to make it home without passing out.

"Yes and no." He shrugged for show, though Bertie couldn't see. If Bertie *was* tasting the scents in the air, all he had to do was lick his lips to sense Arthur's distress at the memory of waiting for a call that never came and looking for those green-glass fairy wings in his classes, only to realize Clematis must have left the school completely. But Arthur had been an undergrad then—it was years ago. He hadn't had time to think about it since then, not really. It only stung now instead of making him cry. "He was never going to make it through the history program," he dismissed it as evenly as he could. "He had no focus at all."

Bertie gave a soft snort before turning around again. Arthur couldn't read his expression, but his eyes were old and sharp, more than human. Of course he wasn't surprised the fairy left. Why shouldn't a fairy have left Arthur? It was pathetic that Arthur would even try to deny how alone he'd felt afterward, how bereft. It was nice to feel loved by someone other than his sister, and he hadn't wanted it to end. That was the truth. Having a fairy to teach him things was almost a bonus, like a dream come true—for a while.

He did his best to focus on the present and to keep his face blank, but those eyes were still on him.

"Is it true that no one can fool a dragon?" Arthur was rough and loud again, and swallowing did nothing for his voice. "Because when you look at me like that, I feel like you're weighing my soul, or at least reading my mind."

Arthur couldn't believe he'd said it. Maybe it was the embarrassment of talking about his fairy ex-boyfriend or the pity he knew Bertie had to be feeling. He really was soft-hearted for a fearsome dragon. He already offered to feed Arthur. Arthur shouldn't be dumping his problems on him too. He'd humiliated himself enough as it was. If he kept this up he'd be telling Bertie about the dream he had last night in which a gleaming lizard held him down by his shoulders and then slowly, slowly lowered its head until Arthur woke up, breathing hard.

"Would you mind if I was?" The question startled him and he jumped. "Would I find something you wouldn't wish me to know, Arthur?" The question curled slowly around him, like the trails of gray, spicy smoke.

Arthur looked over—into those eyes, at the shining hint of scales at his throat, at his mouth—and then looked away, nearly gasping in relief when his gaze landed on the piles of books.

"Are your books that successful? To pay for this house I mean." Arthur stepped back and went over to the table. He wiped his hands on his jeans and took some more almonds.

"You might say I have family money with me, but yes, the books do well enough in certain circles." Amusement—it had to be amusement—made Bertie's voice even rougher, but he came away from the fireplace, slowly sauntering in Arthur's direction.

Arthur moved again, though he didn't have a destination. Bertie stopped by the arm of the couch.

"You mean with Beings. There aren't many books on them that weren't written by humans." As Arthur discovered during his trip to the library. The Internet wasn't much better. He'd mostly found a bunch of anti-Being hate sites full of ignorance and misinformation, and human/Being fetish sites with message boards advising him to get a werewolf lover if he could.

He'd really rather not. He had enough problems. But he replayed Bertie's words and forgot all about FangandFur.com because Bertie had meant the treasure. His mythical but very real dragon's treasure.

He almost choked as he swallowed a whole almond.

"Is that in the *house*?" Unlike before, when it had been a vague concept, now he could picture mountains of gold and jewels strewn about, and the image wasn't reassuring. "You keep your family's treasure in this house? And you don't even lock the door?" Arthur was wheezing as images of armed robberies sprang to mind. People had to know a dragon lived here. "You need to start setting that alarm! What if people find out? They're going to take it and probably kill you!"

He only got his mouth closed when he realized that Bertie didn't seem to be listening. He had his eyes closed and a strange, happy smile on his face. He looked like he was dreaming about something nice and wasn't at all concerned about Arthur's panic. Ash dropped to the floor, ruining a costly carpet. Not that Bertie seemed concerned about that either.

"Oh, Arthur, stay as long as you like," he purred at last, and reopened his eyes. He came forward and around the table to pick up an apple in one hand. He spun it like that globe for one moment and then slowly stretched out his arm to offer it to Arthur. "You will stay, won't you?"

Arthur's concerns caught in his throat. He didn't take the apple, and after a moment, Bertie wrinkled his nose and set it down. He stared at it so forlornly that Arthur felt like he had to say something.

"I… I still have a lot of work to do," he remarked, and the warmth of his flush spread from his cheeks to the skin hidden by his T-shirt. Bertie instantly perked up.

"Wonderful news." He released a pleased little puff of smoke. "If you're still working around dinner time, we must get something."

"Oh, I don't know." Arthur tried to wave it off, but it was too late. Now that he'd eaten, now that he was agreeing to stay, he was also apparently agreeing to eat again. Bertie stepped away, grinning in a way that made Arthur's heart beat faster. It could have been alarm, but Arthur didn't think so. He was too hot for that.

"So, I'll leave you to it, shall I?"

"You shall," Arthur agreed quietly, trying to figure out what just happened. He'd been insulting, then revealed he had his heart broken once, and now he was to go back to work and maybe have dinner later? He glanced down at the apple as Bertie left the room, going toward his study.

It was a plain red apple, not covered in wax because it was organic—the sticker said so. He had no explanation at all for why it seemed to gleam.

CHAPTER 4

IT CERTAINLY tasted like an ordinary apple. Arthur rediscovered it later that afternoon when he realized that he was still starving, and ate it quickly before getting back to work. He hopped on his bike to head home not long after that. It was getting dark, and he didn't really want to put Bertie through any trouble in finding or cooking any food for him.

Kate hadn't heard back from the sex shop about the job and had spent her day experimenting with their small supply of food, so at least Arthur came home to a warm dinner of grilled cheese with green onion, which was... different, if not good, and Kate was happy about the tiny oranges he'd brought home.

Arthur went to bed early, had weird, intense dreams that didn't leave him in the mood for conversation, and read most of one of Bertie's books before going to work at Uncle Wu's. He was glad to get a Friday shift because it was busier and the tips were better, but it was like everyone who ordered lived up a steep hill, and now he was exhausted and sore.

The wet streets didn't help, either. Kate had been worried he'd get sick and had thrown another jacket at him this morning—which was already soaked. It started pouring down rain again on his way to Bertie's house, and by the time he got in the door, his outer jacket was a soaked, heavy mess.

It was still early and the house was dark, as if either no one was up or no one was home. Arthur thought Bertie must have left, because he was surrounded by the dull silence he was starting to associate with Bertie's absence.

He put his bag down and went to the bathroom to leave his soaked outer jacket in the sink. The house was warm, Bertie was gone, and it would be okay if he left some of his clothes in there to dry for a while. He might even poke around and find a dryer. He could do some of Bertie's laundry, if it was around, to make up for using the appliances without Bertie's permission.

He was almost glad Bertie wasn't there, because he would have had something to say about Arthur wandering around shirtless in his house, using a hand towel to dry his hair.

On the other hand, Arthur was hot all over just at the idea of how Bertie would look at him if he saw him right now. It was probably better that Arthur leave at least one shirt on.

There was still no sign of any dragons, flirtatious or otherwise, so Arthur poked around for a few minutes, sticking his head into the study to take a look. It was surprisingly well organized. It also had another deep couch, lower to the floor than the other one, and a TV, which made Arthur wonder if watching television was what Bertie did when he was supposed to be working.

He didn't go upstairs. He didn't even let himself think about it. He wouldn't have had a chance anyway. The sound of whistling startled him, and when he found the source in the kitchen—a teapot—he also found a note telling him to have a cup of tea with plenty of sugar, and a scone as well.

The scones were on a silver plate with a doily, little buttery biscuits not at all like the dry, triangular wedges he usually saw in coffee shops.

He looked over his shoulder before he took the water off the stove and then opened cabinets until he found a mug. He rubbed at his neck, though he was reasonably certain you weren't supposed to be able to tell if someone was spying on you via magic. He didn't even know if Bertie could do that, but maybe anyone could use a crystal ball or a pool of water if they had enough training.

It could have been the house itself. Bertie kept treasure in here; maybe there were wards around the house itself, letting him know when someone entered it. Of course, that didn't explain how he knew to time the boiling water to Arthur's arrival, but he hadn't gotten everything right at least. Arthur would have preferred coffee over tea—not that he was going to object.

He had his choice of tea and picked the darkest one he could find before heading out to the table in the main room to set up his ancient laptop. Only then did he look over at the stacks of books and sigh.

Maybe another scone would revive him, but at the moment all he could think of—apart from the tantalizing idea that Bertie was keeping an eye on him, watching him even now, making sure he was fed and cared for—was that he wasn't ready to lug any books around today.

He spotted the stack of notes he'd discovered so far and looked around once more. There was still no hint of Bertie, and his note didn't say anything about when he'd return.

The notes were by the couch. The couch that looked incredibly warm and soft and inviting. Arthur fell into it with a long moan. He'd been working for Bertie less than a week and already he was going to miss it when he was gone and the work was over. The tea was hot enough to make him prickle with sweat and the couch *was* velvet, or something close enough to it that he almost put his cheek on it.

He was seriously tired if he was thinking about rubbing his face all over his employer's couch. His very *expensive* couch. He slurped down his tea quickly so he wouldn't spill it and so he'd wake up a little, and then he put it on the table and reached for his laptop and all those notes.

If he typed them all up, he might be able to put them in some kind of order, maybe even figure out what exactly Bertie had to say about lost red dragons and King Arthur. Of course, that was assuming there was any order to be found.

A lot of professors were touchy about their unpublished work, but he should ask if he could look over the outline or whatever was written so far. It might give him a better idea of what to look for.

In fact, as he typed up scribbled notes written on napkins and legal pads and one business card for that same herbalist, he was definitely going to need more to go on. For a history book, many of the notes seemed to be about romance. A few were from hero cycles. Arthur had never seen "Beowulf" in the light that Bertie must have. It was clear he had contempt for the way the story played out, and yet there were hints that he was using it as an example of another trend in early cultures; the word "vilifying" had been used more than once.

Arthur made a note to reread the text. Then he added a note to look into the idea that Beings and humans had once lived together in peace; the human stories about the subsequent shift in behavior in dragons that had necessitated the Beings being heroically murdered might have some dark motivation. There *were* other stories of mythical creatures being helpful, even dragons or serpents, if you went back early enough. He never noticed it before, but Bertie was right: at some point that had changed.

He thought about it as he typed and squinted at a misspelling or two and had another hot, hot cup of tea, frowning at the screen until his vision went blurry and the world was spinning.

He saw himself in a harsh realm with a sword in his hand, desperate to prove he was master of his fate, of the world, and woke up with a cry of confusion.

The room around him was dark. Really dark. Much too dark for it to still be morning or even afternoon.

For a moment he contemplated whether or not Bertie had ever come home, because the lights weren't on, and then he became aware of the velvet crushed under his cheek and the thick comforter that had been thrown over his shoulders.

His laptop had been taken out of his lap and put onto the cushion next to him. Sleepily, he wondered if his tea had been drugged, but then he felt the heaviness in his arms and legs that meant he was still exhausted from the night before. His stomach was rumbling and his skin felt like it was on fire.

Sitting up and shooting a look around didn't make him feel any more awake. If anything, it made the spinning behind his eyes worse.

He frowned, first at that, and then at the flash drive plugged into his laptop. He searched the room for any hint that he wasn't alone, but there was nothing.

He angled his head to look up the stairs. He couldn't hear anything, but somehow he didn't think he was the only one in the house anymore. Maybe it was the way the temperature had risen despite it being darker. Not that he knew what time it was, but he doubted Bertie would come home just to tuck him in and then leave again.

He yanked his laptop over and opened it, hoping Bertie hadn't gone through all the files on it. There was no sign that he had, but there were two files on the drive. The first was labeled, "Dearest Arthur." Arthur clicked it.

This was a wonderful idea, it read. *I can read my own notes now. You're a treasure, Arthur, and you were right. Here is my outline for you to read. Be aware it's preliminary, and I will change my mind about it a thousand times. I am sure you have read* Discovering Arthur *but if you haven't, I recommend it. It's a compilation of various Arthurian and what might be Arthurian-in-disguise legends. It might not be relevant, but it might interest you. You are welcome to stay. I made spaghetti for you and you slept right through it.*

Somehow the typed words held a disappointed, pouting rumble. Arthur blinked and looked up again, not certain how he'd possibly slept through Bertie cooking anything. He couldn't believe he fell asleep at all. Anyone else in his situation would most likely be trying to get the dragon to trust him enough to let down his guard, not the other way around.

He sniffed the air, not sure if he was disappointed he couldn't smell anything, not smoky herbs, nor even oregano and garlic. At least not until he was up and in the kitchen, where the swinging doors must have trapped the steamy scent of tomato sauce inside.

Inside the fridge was a sticky note that just said his name, on top of a plastic container.

Arthur thought about leaving it. Then he thought of his sister and what she'd do for even half a bowl of spaghetti. He took it and stuffed it into his backpack with his laptop and more of Bertie's notes, hurried back into his still-damp clothes, and headed outside to get home before it started to rain again.

There was dim light from somewhere upstairs, visible through the high windows at the front of the house, that made Arthur stop and wait until he realized that the design of the house meant no one was going to appear silhouetted in that window. Then the chill made him hop on his bike and race home.

THE spaghetti was delicious: fresh sauce made with a hint of red wine, tender meatballs, fat noodles cooked al dente. To be honest though, the sauce could have come from a jar and the noodles could have been mush and Arthur still would have loved it.

He and his sister wolfed down every last mouthful, and his smile at having so much flavor to go with his full stomach lasted until Kate wondered innocently if his new boss wasn't trying to woo him with food.

Arthur blushed a red so fiery that Kate's expression went from teasing to suspicious and then to knowing, and only by burying himself in a book—one of Bertie's—did Arthur finally convince her to back off.

It was only temporary, he knew that. She had questions, and she would only have more the longer he avoided the subject. She liked to think of herself as street-smart despite the fact she'd been drunk or high or both for most of her adolescence and could barely remember time spent in the bad parts of town following around her asshole boyfriend.

Arthur was okay. He was handling things well. He hadn't made too big a fool of himself, if he didn't count falling asleep instead of working and letting himself get tucked in, and he was going to return the Tupperware and thank Bertie for the food today… and then apologize for falling asleep at work like that. Bertie might tease him, but Arthur was pretty confident it would be okay as long as he brought it up first thing today.

There was a van parking outside of Bertie's house as Arthur rode up, and he kept an eye on it as he left his bike and helmet on the porch. It was too early to check for mail, something Arthur did if he thought Bertie had forgotten, and he wasn't sure if the van was for Bertie, but he lingered just in case it was.

The name and logo were for the high-end—all natural, organic, imported—grocery store in town, where Arthur couldn't afford to buy water. He hadn't even known they delivered.

He studied it as the driver got out of the van and opened up the back, but then gave up his surveillance and turned to go inside. He closed the door behind him and caught a flash of movement from upstairs.

"There's a van outside," he called up. "Did you order something?"

"You must be more specific, Arthur." Bertie's voice was muffled, as if he was getting dressed. A sudden thump made Arthur move, but he stopped at the pissy "Damn it all!" that followed.

Before he could ask if Bertie was okay, the doorbell rang.

There was still no sign of Bertie, but Arthur heard him mumble before he raised his voice. "Could you get that please, Arthur dear?"

Arthur was already turning to do that, but he put down his backpack next to the umbrella stand first. Maybe it was the slight delay, but when he opened the door, the delivery driver paused before giving him an incredulous look. The driver was tall and broad shouldered, with blond hair that reached his neck and a square jaw that looked like part of an illustration from *Ivanhoe*. He had on a short-sleeved uniform shirt that showed off his biceps and a nametag that read "Drew." He was holding a crate full of food, and he took his eyes off Arthur for a moment to consider the short swords on the wall by Arthur's head. Unlike Arthur, he looked like he might have been happy to use a sword if he were a medieval knight confronting a dragon.

Then he regarded Arthur again, and Arthur couldn't tell if the guy saw him as very different from pieces of metal on a wall. Drew's expression was curious but calculating, as if he hadn't expected to see Arthur and didn't know what to do with him. Arthur reminded himself that most medieval knights were actually ruthless mercenaries and put his shoulders back as he lifted his chin.

"Hi," he said to be polite, but didn't move. It didn't seem like a good idea to let just anyone walk into Bertie's house, and Arthur didn't feel like moving. He ignored Drew's look of surprise, though Arthur was guessing he had the man's full attention now.

"It's groceries!" he yelled up at Bertie a second later, waiting and watching the driver's eyes go past him again. There was too much interest in his expression, especially considering that when Arthur half twisted to see what he was staring at, he didn't see Bertie. He *did* see a big house in a nice neighborhood, a big house that could have been hiding all the gold in Fort Knox under a thick blanket of dust. Even without a dragon in it, the house would have been worth a look. *With* a dragon, it was a dragon's lair, and when people pictured dragons, the first thing they pictured, the first thing even Arthur had pictured, was a dragon's hoard.

Arthur's chest seemed to tighten. His stomach knotted. If Drew wasn't looking for a dragon, then he was looking for the dragon's treasure. He stiffened just as Bertie shouted his answer.

"Oh, is that Ravi? I left the money and his tip on the fridge. Tell him his mother's soup recipe was superb."

Arthur frowned as he considered reminding Bertie that if Ravi *had* been there, he would have heard that just fine. He also frowned at Drew, who was still peeking around him. It wasn't a hard thing for him to do; he was at least a head taller than Arthur.

Arthur held out his hands for the crate but otherwise didn't shift from his spot. "I'll take it."

"We're supposed to drop it off inside the house," Drew insisted without budging, and Arthur looked up into his eyes. Drew had the face of a storybook knight too. He probably knew it. People like that usually did and acted as if the world was theirs for the taking.

If Arthur hadn't been here, Bertie probably would have invited Drew in without checking to see if it was his friend Ravi or not. Arthur didn't know Ravi or how friendly he was with Bertie, but he did know Drew, or people like him, and Drew was not stepping foot inside this house. No way.

Arthur kept his hands up. He delivered too, and he couldn't imagine that everyone wanted strange drivers inside their homes.

"I've got it. It's fine." It was possible Arthur was making a big deal out of nothing, but if it *was* something, then this *had* to be part of his job description, somewhere. And if not, then he still owed Bertie for the spaghetti.

He took the crate and hid a small, surprised grunt at the weight, a weight explained by the milk and clinking bottles of wine all on one side, a weight that Drew hadn't even seemed to notice, though he was noticing Arthur's reaction to it. His mouth turned up in a smirk.

Arthur started to turn away. Bertie's voice stopped him.

"I'll be down in a moment, Arthur dear. I'm having some difficulty with my pants."

Arthur looked back at Drew, though he was very aware of the increase of heat in his cheeks that meant he was blushing. Drew was considering him with his eyebrows raised, as if that had surprised him.

"Stay there. I'll be back with your money," Arthur snapped at him, at that smirk that said Drew thought he understood everything about what Arthur was doing there and everything Arthur felt.

His answer was a low whistle and a "Take your time, Arthur dear."

As if Arthur was going to take his time after that. He used his foot to kick the door shut and then went down the little hall so he wouldn't have to push open any doors. He deposited the food unceremoniously on the island in the center of the kitchen, then snatched the crate and the envelope of money and went back to the front door.

Drew had his mouth open to say something, but he stumbled back when Arthur shoved the crate at him, and while he regained his footing, Arthur looked at the invoice and pulled out the right amount of cash.

"Where is Ravi anyway?" Considering how hot his face was, Arthur thought his question was remarkably cool, but Drew's lips went up in another smirk.

"Out sick, so I thought I'd help him out, take care of that nice, generous dragon he always talks about."

Nice, generous dragon. It didn't sound like a compliment when Drew said it; it sounded like a weakness, and it summed up Drew's intentions. Either he was here to befriend Bertie for his money or just to take it.

Arthur thought it might be better, safer for Bertie, if he would try to act as scary and mean as dragons were supposed to be. But Arthur knew it was much more likely that Bertie would have welcomed Drew into his home and tipped him too much and chatted with him and found him as ridiculously good-looking as he was.

"Ravi sounds great." Arthur's voice was clipped, and if Drew now thought that Arthur was after Bertie too, his tone wasn't helping. This guy wasn't coming anywhere near Bertie if Arthur had anything to say about it. "I look forward to meeting him," he went on and left Drew the change but kept the rest of the tip in the envelope and closed the door. He didn't realize that he was as tense as he was until he turned around and saw Bertie watching him from the foot of the stairs.

He had pants on. Arthur wasn't sure if he was relieved or not to see the sweatpants with what looked like a brand new tear on one knee.

"It wasn't Ravi," he explained shortly, struggling to calm down. He couldn't believe he'd done that. He knew personally how important tips were. He really shouldn't have refused to tip Drew. He definitely shouldn't have been rude to Bertie's delivery driver. He was supposed to be apologizing today. Not that he could ever have imagined *Drew*.

"Of course not. Ravi wouldn't ever try to come inside my home without my permission." Bertie took a few slow steps with his gaze still focused on Arthur. His voice was lower than usual.

Arthur took a deep breath because he'd just slammed a door in someone's face for acting too interested in this house and smirking at him, and as stupid as that was, he was still flushed and wound up. "Ravi's out sick."

He was almost as agitated as he'd been after punching his sister's boyfriend, his one and only adult act of violence. His hand had been sore for days afterward.

"Do you want me to put your groceries away?" Arthur skipped around the subject of Drew and moved toward the kitchen without waiting.

"Arthur." Bertie just came into the kitchen after him, using the other doors but stopping once inside. He turned on the lights while Arthur put the envelope back. Arthur opened the refrigerator, since he at least knew where the milk had to go, but Bertie kept talking. "Arthur, there are many who don't like dragons, or any Beings. There are others who think of us as creatures to be used. They are like any other ignorant people or group of bullies in the world."

Arthur put away the milk, then took a moment to line up a carton of brown eggs with a package of butter. He didn't answer.

"You don't need to do that, Arthur," Bertie spoke up behind him. Arthur chose believe Bertie was referring to the groceries and not the person who delivered them and how Arthur had kicked him out, so he shrugged. He grabbed a paper-wrapped loaf of bread that smelled like sourdough.

He moved aside some butter, found the fridge's meat compartment, and added in pound after pound of fresh meat. He noted the meat as something to think about later; he wasn't in the mood to consider the typical dragon diet right now.

"Are you going to reorganize my cabinets too?" Bertie took the bread and slid away to pop it in a breadbox. Arthur looked up from a basket of fat mushrooms. Bertie raised his hands. "Not that I'm sure they don't need it."

"I'm not." Arthur bit his lip and lowered his voice. "I'm not anal retentive or anything. I just…."

"Prefer that things be there when you need them." Bertie made a gentle *tut* sound. "It's fine, pet."

The warmth in his voice was enough to get Arthur hotter. He picked up a tiny glass jar marked "Saffron" but had to pause to look around. He had no idea where it went. He hadn't even known what it was until he read the label.

"Here." Bertie deftly slipped it from between his fingers and came around him to demonstrate where he kept his spices. He opened a cabinet, dug around for a moment, put the saffron in its place, or more likely, *any* place, and then froze before Arthur could suggest a spice rack to keep things neat. "*Arthur.*"

The strained note made Arthur carefully sniff the air for anything unusual, but he could smell nothing but a musty spice scent from the cabinet and the lingering odor of sourdough.

"Arthur," Bertie repeated with greater urgency. Arthur came forward, staring hard at Bertie and then inside the cabinet until he saw a small brown spider sitting on a cloud of webbing.

He blinked, taking in Bertie's posture and realizing that he was frozen with fear. *Fear.* He couldn't believe it.

"It's just a little spider, or are you scared of…." He couldn't finish the sentence because a fearsome dragon of ancient and noble lineage shouldn't be afraid of anything, certainly not a spider.

"Just get it out! Out!" Bertie gestured at the door so fast that Arthur couldn't duck in time and almost got smacked in the face. He backed up to save himself and to get some paper towels, but when he came back Bertie shouted again. "No, don't kill it, just take it outside!"

"I wasn't going to kill it," Arthur huffed back, not that there was any use in arguing, not with Bertie scurrying to the opposite side of the kitchen as Arthur picked up the spider with the paper towel.

He took the little guy out the back way and left him on a stack of firewood, all the while thinking that Drew would have been surprised to see a dragon panicking over a spider. Then he took a moment in the cold air to calm down and think about that.

Maybe it was better that people thought dragons were fearless. Maybe they were less likely to hurt them that way, not like they would if they learned dragons had the same quirks and phobias as humans. Unless all that had been unique to Bertie, but Arthur didn't think so.

He locked the door behind him and tossed the paper towels into the bathroom as he passed it. Bertie was still in the kitchen.

"You know, my sister is scared of spiders too," Arthur began as he came back in. "And it's funny because—"

"My hero!" Bertie swept forward so fast that Arthur couldn't have stepped aside if he wanted to. For a second a hot, hot dragon was wrapped around him and breathlessly expressing his gratitude into his ear. "Thank you, Arthur."

Arthur stuttered something in return—he had no idea what—and then Bertie straightened and pulled back to study him.

"If you hadn't been here I would have been afraid to go in that cabinet for *weeks*." He gave a pleased sigh when Arthur rubbed at his stinging face. His next words were rumbling and indecently sexy. "Arthur MacArthur, my champion."

"Assistant," Arthur corrected without thinking, too quietly to be taken seriously. Bertie didn't.

"Feel free to get rid of as many pests as you deem fit," he continued, still so pleased with Arthur, or himself, that Arthur turned to watch him deal with the mushrooms and some bell peppers.

"I don't... that isn't...." Arthur had never fumbled this much until he came to work here. "Is a fear of spiders normal? For dragons I mean." He changed the subject clumsily and didn't care. "Like elephants and mice?"

"Arthur, I doubt an elephant would even notice a mouse." Bertie was keeping his eyes on the vegetables. "As for whether it's normal... I would simply *prefer* to never have to touch one of those nasty little buggers ever again, if it's at all possible."

When Bertie shuddered, Arthur sagged against the wall and exhaled. He reflected on that statement for a moment and then nodded. He didn't think Bertie was terrified of spiders, but he didn't think Bertie liked having them around either. And as for the rest, what Bertie had been insinuating since following Arthur into the kitchen was that *Arthur* was the one who had stepped up to kick Drew out, and he had done it all on his own. Bertie just wanted to let him off the hook, so Arthur should forget all that "champion" stuff and get back to work.

But he paused because he didn't really need to help put food away, and he still hadn't apologized for falling asleep.

"Did you want me to organize your cabinets?" he offered, to make up for that and because those cabinets needed it. Bertie lifted his head.

"Did you want to? I am sure you have enough to do." He seemed to consider it, and then his smile disappeared. "Or do you? Is that why you're picking fights with hulking brutes?"

"I wasn't picking a fight," Arthur argued before he could think better of it, though he felt a small part of his tension leave him to hear Drew described as a "hulking brute." "I didn't like the way he was looking around, and then he lied. I bet there's no rule saying he has to come in."

"No, I don't believe there is," Bertie answered, inclining his head toward Arthur so carefully that Arthur abruptly realized how crazy he must sound. As if a dragon needed his protection. Bertie might seem helpless sometimes, but he wasn't. He was sharper than most people and came with his own weapons built right in.

"I'm sorry," Arthur apologized instantly. "Of course you could have handled that...," he started but trailed off at the return of a familiar grin. He gulped when Bertie added a wink.

"You didn't like the look of him. I didn't care for the smell of him. We all have our instincts, Arthur. Let's just call it even. Not that it wasn't gallant of you. I'm still picturing you with a sword, or perhaps on a white charger, bedecked in my colors."

Arthur forced his hands to relax and open up, and forcefully redirected his thoughts away from imagining what Bertie was describing.

"Just consider pest removal another service I offer," he joked quietly but waited until Bertie grinned again before he went on. "And anything else you might need me to do."

Bertie's smile disappeared so suddenly that Arthur almost looked around for another spider.

"You *are* bored, aren't you?" Arthur hadn't thought Bertie would look so upset over someone asking for more work.

"No, no, I just... after the other night, and thank you, by the way, your spaghetti was delicious. We loved it."

"We?" Bertie only looked more upset, frowning and putting his hands firmly down on the island.

"I have your Tupperware." Arthur did his best to stay on topic anyway. Bertie frowned and shook his head.

"Tupperware?" He clearly didn't care about his dishes. His frown became a full glare.

"My sister had some." Arthur didn't want to relate all of it, how the two of them had been so grateful for real food that they'd practically licked their bowls clean. It was too embarrassing.

Bertie let out a loud breath, but Arthur didn't want to be interrupted yet. He still had to get his apology out. "It was nice what you did for me, but I shouldn't have fallen asleep like that. It wasn't what a good assistant would have done." He stopped to swallow and make sure his voice was even. "I'd understand if you wanted to go with one of the other applicants. Someone with more education." Or someone who had just the one job so he wouldn't fall asleep at his other one.

"Arthur, you puzzling little human." Bertie put down the vegetables and rolled an apple toward him. Arthur stepped forward to catch it before it fell off the edge of the island, but he didn't eat it. He didn't know what it meant, or if he liked being called a little human, even if he was.

"The first applicant ran away when she saw me. The second was qualified, but he couldn't stop telling me *how* qualified, and his favorite period in history was the American War for Independence." Bertie's expression was disdainful of either the applicant or his taste in historical subjects, maybe both. "I chose you because you didn't run, and because you were also qualified, and because your interests ran alongside mine. You also wanted it the most. You were the best choice."

"Really?" The apple was smooth and perfect against his fingertips. "I thought...." Arthur remembered Bertie's sense of smell, and his tongue, and his burning stare. "You didn't do it because I... interested you?" He wasn't asking about the flirting. He wasn't. It was bad enough that he was asking why he'd been hired at all.

Bertie's head went back.

"What kind of Being would that make me if I had?" he demanded with his eyebrows raised.

"I'm sorry." Arthur stepped forward again but stopped when Bertie's gaze met his. "I didn't mean it like... like that. I just thought you saw how much I needed it and you were... curious. That's what I meant by interested. I didn't think you were... *interested*." Arthur wet his mouth. "In me."

Bertie's head went up even higher, then lowered. He took a second while he thought that out, and he must not have found

Arthur's reasoning *too* offensive, because he finally smiled and spoke.

"Did I give the impression I wasn't?"

Arthur forgot about the apple completely. He stared so hard his eyes burned, and then he remembered himself enough to blink and look away. When he looked back, Bertie's shoulders had dropped, but he was waving around at his cabinets.

"But if you'd rather organize my spices, Arthur, I would not say you nay."

"What?" Arthur's pulse was suddenly racing. He couldn't manage anything else, and he finally moved, inching forward in a kind of blind heat. Bertie took a long, sharp breath.

"I've never had an assistant, so I might get things wrong, but I am flexible. If it makes sense, I doubt I'd object to anything you might suggest."

Arthur was imagining the innuendo in everything. Even "organize my spices" sounded dirty to him at the moment.

"If you think of anything, just add it here." Bertie tapped a notepad on the fridge. Arthur recognized the paper as one that more than one note had been scribbled on before being stuffed into a book.

"I was the best?" Arthur heard himself echo the earlier words and flushed as he stood up straight. He might as well ask if he *really* interested Bertie and completely admit how high school his crush was. "But I fell asleep."

"Arthur." Bertie frowned and took another second, this time apparently to gather his thoughts. "You don't have to solely focus on work here. I thought I told you that."

Arthur started to shake his head and was cut off.

"I dislike focusing solely on work. You love to. Neither way on its own is correct. We've proven that already since I am behind with a looming deadline and you were so exhausted that you fell asleep. But it's all right. I think we'll balance each other out nicely once we figure this all out."

"But I *fell asleep*." Arthur couldn't keep the distress from his voice, and Bertie tutted again before tossing him a smile.

"Darling, you're only human," Bertie scolded him with too much amusement in his expression and then went back to putting away vegetables. "Now eat your apple so you can battle books and dust bunnies with your full strength."

It was a nicely phrased order, but Arthur didn't move until Bertie had only the wine left to deal with. Then he saluted.

"Yes, my lord," he replied with a straight face in answer to Bertie's earlier teasing tone and turned on his heel just as Bertie raised his head to look at him with a startled, soft look on his face.

He kept the apple in his hand, and the sound of Bertie's slow, approving laugh followed him out.

CHAPTER 5

IF BERTIE thought Arthur was the best, then Arthur was going to try his hardest to be the best, and for the next few days he worked harder than ever, only stopping when Bertie insisted he stop or when he had to eat.

He was exhausted, but for the first time in years he felt good about it. Not that he was going to fall asleep on the job again if he could help it, but he felt accomplished when he got home every night and excited when he came in to work in the morning.

He knew Bertie was pleased with what he was doing, and that was what mattered right now. The other things Bertie said, or hinted at, Arthur was too busy to think about anyway.

Dreaming about it didn't count, because not even dragons could tell what a person dreamed of, and in Arthur's dreams, Bertie meant exactly what he'd been saying, and Arthur wasn't too scared to take him up on his offer.

If Bertie had meant what he'd been saying outside of Arthur's dreams, then he *was* interested, but he was leaving it to Arthur to make a move if he wanted to. Which was stupid, as Arthur always told Bertie in his dreams. Of *course* he wanted to. He wasn't blind and he wasn't immune to all that attention focused on him, but when he woke up from dreams of Bertie's mouth, of that tongue at his ass, of Bertie fucking him, it never felt real, and so Arthur just worked and turned his head whenever Bertie called him a pearl so Bertie wouldn't see his blushes.

It was better that Arthur didn't do anything about his fantasies. Arthur realized that all over again as he got to Bertie's house and heard his phone beep with a new message.

Bertie trusted him, he thought again as he reached for his key to the house and then for his phone. The message was from Dante. He had asked Dante for information a few weeks ago, but seeing that name lit up, Arthur shoved his phone back in his pocket without reading the rest.

Dante was a wealthy professional student, well known around the school as the go-to guy for anyone looking for drugs, term papers, or fake IDs. Not that he dealt with any of that himself, he just always knew a guy. Dante knew everyone, including the kind of human magicians with means enough to buy their way to greater magical power. It was the only reason Arthur had contacted him or had anything to do with him.

He felt sick, the internal warmth at the thought of seeing Bertie this morning all gone. Bertie had probably made scones again. He wanted to feed Arthur, and here Arthur was, about to find out if there was anyone out there interested in buying a dragon scale.

Of course there would be. The power in those scales, even in a scale that fell off naturally as opposed to one given freely or one removed by force, was legendary. Arthur had thought... he thought when he asked Dante that it was only a possibility he might come across one. He might find a scale in the garbage or lying around or something, an unneeded, forgotten scale to take home and sell to get creditors off his back and maybe help with the rent until he could afford someplace better.

He hadn't had the job then. Hadn't known Bertie. Hadn't been fed and called a pearl. He'd assumed Dr. Jones wouldn't even miss the scale, and though it felt wrong to have even a small ulterior motive in taking the job, he told himself it wasn't a big deal. It wasn't stealing to take someone's trash.

Stealing or not, however, it *was* dishonest. It *felt* dishonest. He knew it even then. He'd be looking his employer in the face, and instead of just being grateful for an incredible job opportunity, he'd be thinking about taking something from his home.

He scowled and reached in to turn his phone off. It worked for bill collectors, it could work for Dante. Then he looked around again, at his bike resting against the wall and then at the key in his hand.

Arthur was the only one locking and unlocking the door. Bertie certainly wasn't doing it. Maybe Arthur should just accept that even almost stealing wasn't for him. To take anything of Bertie's, much less sell it for money, made him close his eyes to fight off a wave of sickness.

Of course, the creditors would keep calling, even if Dante didn't. There were medical bills and student loans and an old credit card needing to be paid off, to say nothing of the cost of living, food, rent, clothes.

Arthur inhaled and pushed the door open, hoping the air that swept in with him would disguise the guilt twisting his stomach if Bertie should scent the air, but if Bertie noticed anything other than his arrival, he gave no sign.

"Arthur!" he called out, moving across the room like he'd been pacing a moment before and still had momentum. "Where is that volume of Neruda? I am fairly certain I left it in here."

"Ah." Arthur moved, both to hide from that sharp gaze and to seek out the book in question. "I meant to ask why there were so many notes in a book of Chilean love poems."

Bertie pounced on the book when Arthur produced it, though Arthur had plucked the notes from it a few days ago. Bertie flipped through it and then gave Arthur a wounded look to find it empty. Arthur dashed to his backpack for his laptop with Bertie right on his heels.

Arthur seemed to be the only one affected by all that warm, heavy breathing right in his ear and the near contact of their bodies. He skipped back to the couch with his laptop and sat as he opened it up, saving himself from any more torture.

Bertie still didn't seem to notice Arthur's flush or shaking hands. He looked from Arthur to the pages of the book to Arthur again while the computer started up and only calmed when Arthur found the notes in question and began to read them out loud.

Maybe reading love poems wasn't the best way to cool his heated skin. The lines were intimate, sad in a soft way that Arthur hadn't found in Classical love poetry. Even the words about sex, already suggestive enough to make him afraid to look up, were filled with a longing that made his chest ache.

Arthur read until the Neruda-related notes were done and Bertie's eyes were closed on some thought, though he couldn't see what these quotes had to do with Bertie's book. His outline, which had been bare of most details, had only suggested that not all of the dragons fled to the mountains and underground the way most other dragons had when humankind, desperate to prove itself, turned on them.

It had been the lines comparing waiting for someone to a lonely house that made Bertie shut his eyes to think. Arthur waited with his fingers over the keyboard after pulling up the outline.

"That's the one, Arthur, but only toward the end. Because the betrayal wouldn't matter, not to a wise, learned race that knew what it was seeing. They would only wait, the breathlessly romantic little darlings."

"What?" Arthur asked as he typed, because notes were notes even when he didn't understand them, and keeping track of these things was his job.

Bertie opened his eyes to look at him. "I think I'll begin the chapter with it. I do like a line that makes me cry, and I don't want things to get too dry and boring."

It was good that Arthur was used to professors who talked fast, so he could keep up. He nodded as he typed.

"You want the line to head a chapter?" He considered that. "Is that what most of these notes are about?" He thought back to Bertie's other books. One he'd finished, the other he was working on. There were quotations scattered through them, but no structure that formal. They had clearly been more along the line of thoughts interspersed with the text to humanize—if Bertie wouldn't mind the expression—the subjects of his work. "If I get more of what your book is about, I can help with that… expand the outline."

He made the offer without thinking, but there was no trace of Bertie's supposed demanding, possessive nature on his face at the mention of his unfinished book. He blinked and then closed the volume of poetry to study Arthur from his toes to his head. Arthur realized he still had his jacket on, and that he must have turned his phone to silent mode, not off, because it buzzed in his pocket.

"Did I interrupt a call as you came in?" Bertie huffed, which was odd, but Arthur had never seen Bertie fired up about his work before. Maybe he was always like that when he was excited. It must be something to see him looking over relics or in old libraries, drawing every eye with that brilliant spark, calling everyone he met "darling" and "pet." He waved the Neruda in the air to get Arthur's attention. "You can take calls, Arthur, in your free moments."

"I... this wasn't a free moment." Arthur decided that answer was the safest. Bertie glared at Arthur's pocket anyway, his words coming out so slowly they might have been the last things he felt like saying.

"Work and school, being here, must cut into your social life. A morsel like you must be wanted from all corners, even if most would be too intimidated to approach you, with that warrior's determined glint in your eye." He ignored Arthur's small jump and quick swallow as he growled the words. "I wouldn't want to deny you your fun."

"All corners?" Arthur repeated faintly, though he hadn't intended to. That was getting close to what Bertie had hinted before, that Arthur was the type to attract some Beings.

"Bold of purpose, pure of heart, fair of face," Bertie elaborated, then sniffed. Arthur belatedly noticed that Bertie was barefoot again, and despite complaining about the cold had unbuttoned the top buttons of his white dress shirt to expose his throat. "Those in your past haven't been good for you if they never told you that. Though I wish you'd smile more. It makes me want to hunt for dimples when you frown so."

Arthur wasn't frowning at the moment. He knew he wasn't. He was hot and frozen at the same time, but he wasn't frowning.

"I don't," he got out, in a wheeze if he were being honest.

"What, have dimples?"

"Have people in my past. I mean," Arthur sat up and put out a hand when he realized what he just said. What he admitted to. Bertie's mouth snapped closed like it was too late, but Arthur had to try. "Clematis—"

"Clematis is a flower name." Damn, Bertie was fast. Too fast. "Was that the fairy you spoke of before?" Arthur couldn't smell herbs, but the air seemed to be getting hotter, smokier, like Bertie's voice as he put together Arthur's words in the way that Arthur had been afraid of. "Arthur when you said you don't have people in your past... do you mean that despite the fairy...." He twitched, like he had to stop himself from moving. The very air around him grew hot, and Arthur thought of earthquakes again, something earth shattering just beneath the surface that had Bertie excited. "Arthur, are you *pure of body* as well?"

It took everything Arthur had to shake his head, though sometimes he thought everything with Clematis had been a dream. When he considered it, they'd only been together, really together, for one night, and everything else had been random and hurried, kisses and messing around like he'd done in high school, nothing more.

"This isn't...." His mouth was dry. Bertie looked like he was moments from crawling onto Arthur's lap, his heavy-lidded eyes doing nothing to disguise his wide pupils. They sparkled with interest. Arthur did his best to remind himself that if there was interest there, it was probably just curiosity, and probably amusement as well since Arthur had basically admitted to being almost a virgin. Technically, he wasn't, but one night wasn't much experience, and Clematis hadn't been the kind to bend him over a table. "This isn't appropriate." It was a weak argument, but it was an argument. Arthur had a feeling he might not have done too badly with a shield if he were in one of those old stories, though he still couldn't imagine himself using a sword, not even the way he pretended to as a child.

"I could fire you and then be inappropriate," Bertie immediately suggested, and even knowing that it was a joke, or hoping it was a joke, Arthur jerked his head up and inhaled loudly. "Arthur." Alarm was rich in Bertie's voice for a moment and then he stepped closer and leaned in to put a hand on Arthur's shoulder. When Arthur looked up he could only see his eyelashes, but his tone was serious. "I'm not getting rid of you." He took another moment, his hand hot even through Arthur's jacket, and then he smiled and met Arthur's wide-eyed stare. "Humans."

He was so quiet that Arthur blinked.

"What? We do okay." He was quiet, too, but then Bertie was leaning over him, emanating heat and touching him with gentle concern. It was mesmerizing. Arthur didn't want to move.

"Yes, but think of what you *could* do."

Arthur had to fight not to close his eyes he was suddenly so warm, wisps of Bertie's breath brushing across his cheeks.

"And dragons are so much better?" He thought it would make Bertie take offense and stand up straight, but he didn't.

"Have you even read my books about Beings? Never mind, you haven't had time yet, have you? Very well, I won't pretend I'm not hurt," Bertie paused, Arthur assumed to wait for his interruption, which wasn't long in coming.

"Neither of the books the library had was about dragons," he protested. "I'm reading the others."

"Hmm, then if you like, Arthur, I can give you a brief history of dragons… share what I know with you." It was almost illicit the way Bertie made the offer: all knowing, shining eyes and heavy breathing. Arthur felt himself staring and drew his eyebrows together into a frown at how obvious he was being.

"Okay," he agreed, his face burning up in a way that only got worse at Bertie's slow, curving smile. Arthur glanced down at the hint of shining skin visible at Bertie's collar. "What… what about the Welsh dragons?"

"I have my theories. European dragons in particular have a culture rich with romantic stories… romantic to us, that is, though most consider them old-fashioned now. How humans interpreted things is another matter." Bertie clucked thoughtfully and licked his mouth before abruptly pulling back and moving around.

"Nonetheless, it is—or *was*, you would say—a culture that views things in a larger context, a view of the world as connected and as something… beautiful. The dragons of early Europe for the most part believe in eternity through the accumulation of beauty and knowledge, and this allows them to go, shall I say, over the top sometimes."

Arthur didn't think Bertie was aware that he paced slowly back and forth as he lectured. He was like a strangely intense professor. The subject must mean a lot to him. Arthur sat up to follow his every movement. Bertie was talking about history in the present tense again, as if he was reliving it in his mind, but at least he wasn't laughing at Arthur's lack of a sex life anymore.

"That demands, well"—he waved as he talked—"big gestures. Like the courtly love stories that were written later about Camelot and knights, with people being worshipped from afar and served unto death without even so much as a kiss in return, and don't dare think that concept wasn't draconian in origin and stolen by some human troubadours. That idea of romance continues to influence us, often to our detriment." He stopped and peered at Arthur for a moment before striding back over and dropping down on the couch next to him. "It's humans, you see. You also strive, but you're so… you're just… I don't wish to say shortsighted. Blind to some things perhaps, but courageous in how you press on. There's something innately fascinating about…." He trailed off. "We can't simply let you struggle."

He wasn't making sense. Not really. Though maybe when Arthur read his books on dragons it would all click.

"I thought it was about gathering and keeping treasure." Arthur turned in time to catch how lost Bertie looked, as though Arthur had cut him off midthought.

"What?" He actually scowled for a moment and then light seemed to dawn and he grinned. "Treasure? Oh, Arthur."

The glimpse of teeth made Arthur pull back, though it wasn't in fear, not with Bertie mocking him for being short-sighted, or blind, or whatever it was he'd been trying to say.

"Cheshire cat." Arthur couldn't help snapping back his reply, especially when saying it out loud made Bertie stop and stare at him as if Arthur was the one speaking another language now. It made Arthur want to keep going and he did, not entirely suppressing his smile. "From *Alice in Wonderland*. You move like a cat too sometimes."

Bertie opened and then closed his mouth. Arthur got the faintest hint of smoke before Bertie grinned again.

"Then the question, Arthur, is… do you like cats?" He didn't seem to care for Arthur's silence, though Arthur couldn't think of how to answer. He made a scolding noise. "So serious, Arthur. What shall I do with you?"

That, Arthur could answer at least. "Set me to work." Anything rather than continuing to discuss his sex life with a hot dragon breathing all over him. He got a sigh, but Bertie leaned back against the other arm of the couch and then nodded as well.

"What will you do when this room is cleared?"

"Move on to the next room. And then the next." Arthur didn't have to think about it. Bertie nodded again while regarding him intently.

"Until the house is yours. I see." He lazily reached up for a cigarette, but he didn't light it, just kept it grasped in his fingers. "Keep that up and I won't be able to live without you."

"That wasn't my intention," Arthur rushed to answer. He didn't want Bertie to think he was pushing for a permanent position. It would be amazing, but he couldn't ask for more as it was.

"There is your education to consider however," Bertie rolled on in a rumbling whisper. He stared at his cigarette and then licked the tip before letting it rest between his lips. "Do you think I might read your thesis, Arthur?"

"Yes." Arthur had no idea what he'd agreed to for a moment, until he blinked and looked away from Bertie's mouth. "If you really want to." He'd thought Bertie would have before he'd hired him actually.

"Good." The grin returned. "I already asked Gibson for it." Bertie angled his head to the side as he said it, the strong line of his throat visible, muscle and warm skin and gleaming scales.

Arthur could only guess what those scales felt like in their real form and if, when they were like that, they were warm, too, or sleek, or hard and cool to the touch. That was what Arthur found innately fascinating, and it had nothing to do with the magic supposedly in them. It made it so much worse to realize that he had ever thought of them as something to be sold. He remembered them as being beautiful, even before he thought of them as a part of Bertie, who was crazy but kind and one of the most interesting men he ever met.

Arthur swallowed and jerked his gaze away, staring at the bookshelves that he'd already been through and emptied.

"Once again you are right, Arthur." Bertie leapt to his feet, his cigarette flaring brightly as though he'd lit it when Arthur hadn't been looking. "The grindstone awaits. I'm behind schedule as it is."

He left the book behind on the couch, apparently no longer in desperate need of it. Because Arthur had done his job well, Arthur reminded himself, and pulled the book closer.

"I can look up more quotes for you," he ventured, aware that he was frowning harder as Bertie moved away and the offer didn't call him back. He could get used to Bertie sitting close to him. That probably wasn't a good idea. For a second he glared down at the book as if the poems had created this problem and not his body, his imagination, and everything that came out of Bertie's mouth.

"First get us a late lunch, would you?" Bertie stepped around one of Arthur's temporary stack of books and pulled a book from the middle of a small pile. He let out a guilty-sounding gulp when the top of the stack fell over and quickly bent down to straighten it before glancing back at Arthur as though Arthur was going read him the riot act or point out that he was putting the books back in the wrong order.

Arthur didn't get a chance to say anything. His stomach growled before he could, right on cue at the mention of lunch. Bertie was too busy with the books to grin, but Arthur imagined one anyway.

"There's some things in the kitchen, or if you prefer, money and take-out menus in the envelope on the fridge, but we need something to keep us from fainting away, don't we? While we do all this hard work."

He stood up again, not even looking close to fainting away. Arthur tried to stay serious, even if he was being teased or tricked again.

"I really don't expect you to feed me."

"Arthur." He got another sigh for his efforts, a longer, louder one. "I am certain any other assistant would not have done at all. You're… you're a very good boy." He cleared his throat and moved quickly on. "Look at what you're already doing for me, putting my house in order."

Arthur hadn't thought of it in quite those terms. It made him feel a bit like a hausfrau, but Bertie didn't give him time to reflect on it or protest.

"I'd like to keep you as long as possible, and I can't do that if you're dead or in a hospital because you won't feed yourself."

There were counterarguments, Arthur was sure, but he couldn't seem to think of any. Maybe that touch had scrambled his brain. He glared at the book of love poems again.

"Okay," he agreed in the same soft tone as before, glancing carefully over in time to see Bertie's shoulders drop. Arthur wondered if he'd been expecting another argument, but he didn't say anything. Just waved again to indicate that he didn't care what the food was when Arthur tried to get his preference.

He simply took his new book and curled up on the floor in front of the fireplace, where Arthur had a feeling a roaring fire would be crackling soon enough.

Arthur watched him for another moment, thinking about the idea of selfish, jealous, miserly dragons and where it had come from. Then he got up to feed them both before he could ask Bertie. He had no doubt that Bertie could tell him; he just wasn't sure he could make it through the explanation without embarrassing himself even more.

CHAPTER 6

THE rain continued to fall for the next week and into the week after that. It meant late fall was starting in earnest, and earlier, darker evenings. It also meant more people ordering food in, which meant more work and more tips for Arthur on busy weekend nights.

The money was good. He rode fast so the food was always hot, and people appreciated that, but he wasn't sure how much longer he could keep doing it, especially in the rain. It helped that Bertie insisted on feeding him whenever he got the chance, but the rain had soaked through his jackets last weekend and riding around in the damp ones was giving him what felt like a permanent chill in his bones.

Kate was not happy with him but did her best to dry his clothes out, even wasting quarters in the laundry room using the dryers. They were only going to get wet again, but there was no reasoning with her. It was like trying to convince Bertie that a cup of noodles was an adequate lunch.

It turned out dragons, or at least his dragon, had a lot in common with his mother and weren't able to stand watching people go without a meal. Arthur would have felt worse about it, but it was hard to feel guilty on a full stomach; and there was something about the sight of Bertie wearing an apron, of all things, and humming in the kitchen that shut Arthur up before he could protest. Bertie loved to cook but didn't like to cook for just himself, or so he claimed. Arthur didn't believe him at first, but after seeing him in the kitchen, he changed his mind. It did make him wonder what Bertie did for food, or would have done in his dragon form when he wouldn't have been able to reach the countertop.

Bertie also insisted they take time out from working to eat properly, setting up plates around the island in the kitchen while explaining that he'd converted the dining room to another room to hold his books years ago and there was no other place to eat. Arthur considered trying to convert some of the books to an electronic format, but he had a feeling Bertie used only the technology he had to and would ignore any eBooks. He was as old-fashioned about that as he was about eating rituals like dinner.

Of course, after eating he'd stay chatting in the kitchen forever if Arthur didn't eventually get up and insist on washing the dishes or putting them in the dishwasher before heading back to work. Bertie would sigh but agree with him, slipping back into his study with long, forlorn looks in Arthur's direction.

He also took to clearing his throat before entering the main room and glancing at Arthur before removing any book from whatever temporary pile Arthur had it in. It was as if he didn't want to disturb anything and feared Arthur's response if he did. Arthur couldn't figure it out. He had never yelled or even snapped at him. They were Bertie's books. He could mess up Arthur's increasingly complex system of stacks if he wanted to, and Arthur had no right to comment at all. It wasn't as if Arthur would have shouted at him. He'd really only ever gotten furiously angry once in his life and it hadn't been over books, yet if he turned to see which book Bertie was taking, maybe raise an eyebrow as he considered where it might end up later, he'd get a quick "I just need to borrow it for a bit. Sorry, Arthur" every time.

It would always be returned by the next day, too, which was better than however Bertie had put them away before. Now if only Arthur could convince him to switch temperature controls to something more reliable and steady than the fireplace—or whatever was going on with the heating that kept the house so hot. It might be a losing battle. If Bertie owned socks, he had yet to put them on that Arthur had seen.

In any event, the antique books were definitely getting moved to a better room as soon as Arthur cleared this one. He had the shelves clean and a rudimentary system for keeping them organized that was, of course, dependent on the other books he was sure to find in the other rooms. He was going to wipe the layers of dust off the knickknacks he'd collected as well, as soon as he had time, because it was worth it to do the job thoroughly.

And maybe there was a part of him that wanted Bertie to see it and call him something sweet again. Any of his terms of endearment would do, though "pet" and "pearl" were the ones that haunted Arthur's dreams.

He took his time finishing Bertie's second book, mostly because as he read it now, he heard Bertie's voice reading it to him. Arthur had it bad and he could admit it, though it was probably just because he hadn't had any kind of dating life in years and he happened to be working for someone who was incredibly hot. It didn't help that Bertie's books were fascinating in their own right.

The first had been large and ambitious in a dissertation-gone-out-of-control kind of way, a sprawling exploration of the witch and werewolf hunts carried out by humans, mostly on other humans, though Bertie had documented a few cases where some Beings' lives had been lost too. It must have taken him years, though when Arthur finally finished it, he found himself wishing it had gone into more detail. The ultimate conclusion wasn't terribly original; the more scared and abandoned humankind felt during the darkest of their dark hours, the more they turned on anyone different or with a perceived power they did not possess. But the way it was described was unlike anything Arthur had read before. It was no wonder the book was epic in length: Bertie brought everything to life.

After knowing Bertie two days, Arthur had expected to find sympathy for the victims, most of them innocent of any real crime, even the real witches that might have been considered something like doctors today. He was surprised to also find sympathy even for the humans doing the persecuting, the torturing. Their ancestors had destroyed their books, their centers of learning, and they lived in isolated, perilous conditions with pestilence, war, and famine lurking around every corner; and those in charge told them that the very ones who might have saved them, or at least helped them, were the causes of it all. It was tragic to think of what could have been.

Not that the beauty of the lines had blinded Arthur to the ridiculously packed index and bibliography that indicated exactly how many texts Bertie consulted in his research. Whoever "organized" it had not had an easy job. Arthur could only imagine the mess, which made him resolve to go through the notes he'd already typed up and footnote and tag every source he could, to save time later.

He jumped into the second book after the first, wondering why someone like Bertie would choose such a serious subject matter, but unable to stop reading. *The Blood of Wolves* was a study of the massacre of wolves, and the subsequent flight of all werewolves from England during the Anglo-Saxon period. It had a detailed explanation of where many of them had ended up, with a few chapters at the end about the shifter Beings among the Native Americans and how they'd been mostly wiped out along with their human relatives before those European weres could ever really encounter them. It was a tragedy, and Bertie's sympathy was with everyone; from the early farmers in those primitive forests who had encountered fearsome, giant wolves; to the weres who had faced first slaughter and then the slow deforestation that took away their homes.

This must have been what Bertie meant when he said dragons tried to look at the larger picture. There were no sides Bertie didn't try to understand, though Arthur detected some anger in the later chapters that hadn't been in the first book—anger at those who killed the wolves and weres and then tried to claim their power and strength by taking their names and wearing their pelts. It made Arthur think about dragons being hunted for the power in their body parts. People frequently compared dragons to weres, but Arthur had never really thought about why.

Bertie's book or books on dragons had to be in the house somewhere. Arthur just hadn't found any copies yet, and he was afraid to snoop around too much. Not that he'd encountered any locked doors. What he *had* encountered was dust in every room but the two most used, the kitchen and Bertie's study, although the study was a mess too.

When he peeked into the study, he saw a desk with a large, obscenely comfortable-looking chair, a laptop, another couch, and the only TV he'd seen in the house. The couch and TV were both low to the floor—really low, as if Bertie watched TV in his dragon form. Arthur remembered Bertie's dragon legs as being shorter, so Bertie probably couldn't climb up onto a regular-size couch without difficulty. It still seemed decadent somehow, like a pile of pillows on the floor of a palace or something similar. Bertie would probably have worked that way too, if he could have used his laptop with those claws, but Arthur somehow doubted he could. It might be part of what took him so long to write, but perhaps he thought more clearly in his natural form.

The curtains were drawn, leaving the room dark except for the electric lights, and instead of bookshelves, there were end tables covered in magazines, journals, and paper notebooks. Arthur half expected to find a quill, but instead there were costly pens sitting next to dishes and jewelry boxes that had been used as ashtrays. Arthur emptied them and put everything but the dishes with the other knickknacks he intended to clean, and then stopped on his way into work the next day to use the leftover money from his trip to the herbalist to buy more toilet paper and two cheap ashtrays.

He did it for the sake of cleanliness and his sanity first, and for the smile he got at the sight of them second. It didn't take much to get a smile from Bertie anyway. Arthur just had to walk in the door and Bertie would be grinning and talking and giving him confusing orders that Arthur couldn't seem to make himself mind.

He resolved to get more information on dragons before his own smiles got any more out of control. Though so far a deeper Internet search had only gotten him facts on reptiles and information from the last census. He mentioned that one to Bertie, asking why the U.S. population of dragons was so small compared to other countries—not that any country had a population of dragons that could be called large, unless he counted the Firesnakes in Finland—

although in proportion to the population of the country, the numbers were about the same. Bertie stopped fretting over some bread he was making to huff at him.

"The numbers reflect those dragons who identify as 'pure-blooded', Arthur, which indicates how flawed that census information is." It was a surprise to watch Bertie pop his dough into an electric oven: Arthur had expected to find something less thoroughly modern and more like charred bricks and wood fire. "Not that there isn't some concern amongst my kind about losing our species completely to interbreeding with humans. Dragons used to be much larger."

It made Arthur pause. He'd been asked to slice onions, so he was slicing and trying not to cry. That idea was a new one. He hadn't realized dragons were capable of having children with humans. A few of the Beings were; he didn't know why it hadn't occurred to him before.

"It's a short-sighted, almost human view, since in my opinion survival of DNA means living forever, but I suppose it's an understandable fear. Nobody wants to disappear." Arthur wasn't able to look over, not with his eyes stinging, but he had the feeling he was being carefully observed. "Soon enough my parents.... You haven't met them yet, Arthur, but they are darlings. Perhaps not darlings.... They are quite difficult and concerned with the family name, and they think of me as their hopelessly fanciful son, throwing away his potential by not dominating some university with my genius, and they definitely identify as 'pure-blooded'. Not that they hate humans, not at all. Of course not. They'll love you... once they get to know you." Bertie cleared his throat. "They're both professors. I'm sure you can understand when I tell you their standards are high?"

Arthur nodded without looking over, mostly because he wasn't sure where Bertie had been going with that, but he wanted to hear more.

"Soon enough, Arthur, my darling parents are going to start throwing willing, pure-blooded females my way to at least ensure that the line continues.

"We're a very old family on both sides," he went on when Arthur must have visibly reacted. Arthur couldn't be sure; his vision had suddenly gone blurry and wet. "And as long as I don't have to marry the girl, I admit, it's not entirely objectionable. I might enjoy being a father."

Bertie wasn't smoking, but Arthur imagined him drawing on a cigarette anyway, exhaling a moment later in a long, lazy spiral. He went on in a quiet, casual voice.

"What would you think of a houseful of little hatchlings, Arthur? Are you fond of children?"

"Children?" was the only word Arthur could manage for a moment. Maybe it was the image of Bertie with a female of his own kind that rendered him speechless. "I didn't know you were... that you liked women." He'd been thinking that dragons must be like fairies, open to any gender and experience, or that Bertie's flirting was merely habitual after all. Bertie started coughing and wasn't able to stop until he had some water.

"Lovely creatures," he whispered at last, and then shuddered so much that Arthur saw it from the corner of his eye. "But *yech*, no. No, pet, I do not like women. At least, not when they're naked. You have no worries on that score."

"Worries?" Arthur wasn't able to deny it, not that Bertie gave him a chance to.

He slid back over to stand next to Arthur, scoop up his onions, and then drop them in a pan to caramelize them.

"Arthur," he began almost hesitantly, then stopped himself. A moment later he handed Arthur a cool, wet towel.

"For your eyes, love," he explained with no sign of a grin, and then turned back to stir the onions.

About the only thing to be grateful for about the whole conversation, aside from confirming where Bertie's interests lay, was that the overwhelming scent of onions and fresh bread must have hidden any trace of the momentary confusion and hurt Arthur had been feeling. Imagining how terrible he must have looked with red, watery eyes was bad enough; Arthur didn't need to know if he'd smelled pathetic too.

He wasn't sure if he could ask Bertie anything else about dragons now, not when one answer had left him more confused than ever and pretty sure he'd made his crush even more obvious.

If he wanted to keep this job for as long as he could, he ought to stop fantasizing about his overly flirtatious boss and find someone else instead. If Kate got that job, he could quit delivering food, and then maybe he'd have some time where he wouldn't feel too exhausted. He didn't think his crush on Bertie would go away, not with Bertie being the smartest, kindest, sexiest thing he'd ever seen, but at least it should be manageable if he got laid once in a while.

It all seemed reasonable enough to think about, right up until Arthur fell asleep, then it was Bertie kissing him, sucking him off, fucking him, and then he'd wake up and imagine it all over and over again with cheap, bedside lotion on his fingers and his knees bent so he could push in and think of Bertie. Then he'd come into work and catch a glimpse of that tongue before Bertie would beam at him and wish him a "Good morning, Arthur" as if he'd been waiting impatiently for Arthur's return, and Arthur couldn't help smiling back at him until he remembered himself and what he'd been doing just an hour before.

He honestly had no idea what to say when Professor Gibson e-mailed him to ask how the work was going and to let him know he'd sent Bertie a copy of his thesis. When Kate asked, her eyes narrowed, Arthur could barely resist the urge to tell her… if not everything, then enough of it. It would only alarm her, he told himself, and anyway, so far his feelings hadn't interfered with his work.

That was what he should focus on, the work and keeping this job. It might lead to more work in this field, and he needed the experience if he was ever to go back to school. That was what was important, that and providing for Kate. Anything else was something that Arthur should leave to his dreams, because it wasn't going to happen to him in real life. Nothing that amazing ever had, or not for long anyway.

AS IF to prove him right, he felt weak and got a scratchy throat on the last weekend of his first month in Bertie's house. The rain had been coming steadily down for two days, and he'd been working seven days in a row and biking back and forth across town until late the night before. It was only a matter of time until he got sick, he knew that, but he'd tried to stay home and rest last night, bundling up next to Kate to keep warm and drinking as much water as he could.

It hadn't mattered. He was still so weak the next morning it took him twice as long to ride to Bertie's part of town, and when he got to Bertie's house, he was shivering despite his efforts to make himself stop.

He almost fell in the door and had a moment of relief that Bertie wasn't there to see it, or to see him quickly stumble to the couch and put his laptop on his lap. He was fully prepared to work, whatever Bertie was going to say about it when he saw his pale skin and the dark circles under his eyes.

He should have stopped in for tea, but he realized his mistake too late when Bertie came out of the kitchen. The room was as warm as ever, but he couldn't stop shivering.

"Arthur? You're late, is everything— Dear." Bertie came to a halt, and Arthur frowned dizzily in his direction and saw the absolutely stunned expression on his face. Arthur was tired enough to want to laugh at it, but too tired to actually laugh.

"I'm sick." He stated the obvious, but only because he knew he looked awful and possibly a bit green. He hadn't eaten much except for a piece of toast the day before. He shouldn't be surprised that he looked awful. He only hoped he didn't look too pitiful; if Bertie sent him home, he wasn't sure he could make it back across town right now, not without a rest first. This house was so warm and Bertie's couch was so soft, if he had to get up now, he might pass out—or cry. It was another horrifying thought he was too wrung out to react to. At least not until Bertie said something.

"You look terrible." Bertie let his hands fall to his sides for a moment. He was wearing that university sweatshirt again, the one that always looked worn and comfortable and that Arthur had vague fantasies about wearing someday. Arthur belatedly realized that he was still in his damp jacket and moved to shrug it off, and when he looked back up, Bertie was scowling at him.

"Did you ride here on your bike?" he demanded. "In the rain, feeling like this? What did your sister think of that?"

Arthur had known he was going to regret telling him more about Kate the other night during dinner. Bertie looked ready to call her and ask her himself, and probably would have if he had her number. He picked up Arthur's jacket and then tossed it aside with a shudder when he saw how wet it was.

"She wasn't happy," Arthur sighed. "But it's okay, I can work on your notes."

"She wasn't happy," Bertie repeated with a snort. "Look at yourself, pet. Your sweatshirt is soaked too." Arthur turned his head to look too fast and saw stars. He put a hand up as Bertie shot forward, but it didn't hold him back. Warm hands landed on Arthur's shoulders and tugged at his clothes.

"It has to come off, Arthur," Bertie insisted softly, which Arthur knew, but he shook his head and squirmed anyway. Even sick, the idea of Bertie undressing him was enough to make him burn. "Off," Bertie said again but let go at the same time. Arthur shivered as Bertie moved away and then felt the sudden whoosh of air and heat as the logs in the fireplace caught fire.

"*Arthur.*" He'd never heard Bertie's voice so stern, so Arthur shut his eyes and pulled his sweatshirt off, shaking in just a damp white T-shirt until something heavy was thrown on top of him. He opened his eyes to the same blanket that Bertie covered him with before and pulled it closer without thinking. He let the laptop slide to the side.

"Do you want to go home?" The rumbling, angry question drew Arthur's attention back to Bertie, and for a second he thought he saw him as a dragon again, with a flicking, furious tail, but whatever expression was on his face made Bertie pause and his imaginary tail stop flicking. "It's raining, Arthur," he went on before Arthur could answer yes or no.

"I know." He meant it to be sarcastic, but it came out on an exhale. Those big dark eyes turned to liquid again.

"Oh, pet." For a second, Arthur thought Bertie was going to cry and quickly sat up, but Bertie sat down next to him instead, so close Arthur shut his eyes again. Later, when he wasn't sick, he was going to think about how close they were and cringe to think of what he looked like. At the moment, however, all he could think was how warm Bertie was and how close and what it might feel like to lean into him and fall asleep.

He wanted to *fall asleep* on someone who looked like that? He must be sicker than he thought.

"We really should try to work today." Arthur wet his lips. "I mean, you should. There's no reason *you* can't work today. I can rest and then go home—"

"As if I could concentrate with you so unwell." The instant response made Arthur open his eyes to slant a look sideways. Bertie probably just wanted to get out of work. Arthur struggled to look as earnest as he could.

"You're teasing me, but I'm going to let it go. I think I'm too tired to frown," he announced, not sure why, and Bertie's eyes went wide. His hand, no the inside of his *wrist*, was suddenly pressed to Arthur's forehead.

"Arthur." His voice shook. "It must be serious if you can't frown at me." He made a *tut* sound and pulled his wrist back, though how he would know if Arthur was too hot, Arthur couldn't begin to guess, and when he asked, he got another worried look. It only lifted when Arthur heard himself trying to explain.

"But you're already so *hot*," he mumbled but gave up when Bertie choked on a laugh and his name.

"Arthur, do stop arguing, please. Just lie there and feel better. Really, there's no need for this level of sacrifice on my account."

"But…." The pay… the food… Bertie… Arthur was already enjoying this job too much. He wasn't doing nearly enough work to demonstrate how much. Another impatient sigh shut him up.

"I'd ask when was the last time you rested, Arthur, but I have a feeling I won't care for the answer."

For someone who wasn't asking, he managed to make Arthur feel guilty anyway, as if he'd done something wrong when he hadn't.

"I have to make money." He gritted his teeth and hoped the pounding starting behind his eyes wasn't going to get worse. "And don't say I can't do that if I'm dead. I'm sick, I'm not going to die of a cold."

"*Is* it a cold? You don't look well." Bertie abruptly stood up. "Your little human nose and cheeks are red, the rest of you is so pale that I can see the blue of your veins. And those shadows…." He reached out, not quite running a dark fingertip under Arthur's eye. He pulled back before Arthur could remember to and then he looked away. "I'm going to bring you tea and perhaps some medicine if I have any."

"I don't need you to—" Arthur could frown after all, but only as he tried to chase down the distracting thought. "Medicine?"

Bertie ignored his protest and misunderstood his question. Arthur wasn't sure if he was imagining the gray smoke that Bertie exhaled, but even with his mouth dry and his nose and throat raw, he could feel the searing realness of it when he inhaled.

"Try not to be a pain, Arthur, and let me do this, please." It was a hoarse rumble, like the dragon voice that had first called Arthur into this house. Bertie's eyes were intense, and after a second, Arthur gave up and looked down. It got him another sigh, but Bertie's tone grew less fierce. "When was last time you let someone take care of you?"

"Years," Arthur answered without thinking. "When my parents were alive." He swallowed after it came out and glanced up again, unsurprised to see the shining light in Bertie's eyes but captivated by it anyway. He was in no condition to fend off his feelings for his tenderhearted employer. He should never have come in today.

The steady, soft-eyed stare held him still, made him try to control the faint tremors running through him as if he wasn't warm enough even in this house with a blanket over him. He knew what would make him warmer and right as he pictured Bertie curling up with him, climbing over him, pushing closer, he saw Bertie's lips fall open and that pink tongue dart out to taste the air.

Arthur wondered if Bertie was having the same thought, but he must not have because he suddenly took a deep breath and seemed to push himself away and toward the kitchen.

"Pull your blanket closer, Arthur, for my sake if not yours," he shouted from behind the swinging doors, and only once they stopped swinging did Arthur let his shoulders sag.

Okay, he was more exhausted than he'd thought, and sicker too, too sick to deal with the concern in Bertie's voice. He should go home, where he wouldn't embarrass himself. If only he could make himself move.

He pulled the blanket closer, up to his chin, and sighed at how pathetic he must look, though Bertie said nothing one way or the other as he hurried out of the kitchen and went up the stairs.

Arthur stared at the fire, at the fire he didn't remember Bertie starting with any kind of match or lighter, and thought about heat and smoke until his eyes closed. The kettle whistling from the kitchen started him awake, and he reached for his computer without thinking and waited for it start up before he pulled up the file he'd labeled with numbers so Bertie wouldn't accidentally find it. Then he stared at it.

Facts About Dragons

1. They have existed since before the first written human records in almost every human culture.

2. They "came out" around the turn of the last century when the other magical Beings started to emerge from hiding both during and after the First World War, though many did not come into public view

until the mass exodus of Beings from the countries torn by war and strife during the Second World War. This includes Russia, China, Northern Africa, the islands of the Pacific, and most of Europe.

3. Like fairies they are said to possess powerful magic.

The numbers after three had been added recently.

4. They like to flirt. (Possibly unique to Dr. Jones.)

5. They often give their children powerful names.

6. They can, and will, intermingle with humans, up to and including sex, marriage, and children.

He skimmed over his notes about possible new list entries at the bottom and quickly typed in three, his fingers flying over the keyboard so Bertie wouldn't catch him.

7. They often have a "type" when it comes to human lovers ("bold of purpose, fair of face, pure of heart"... pure of body as well?—see: legends of maidens sent as sacrifice)

8. Like werewolves and other weres, they can shift form at will.

9. Might breathe fire.

He closed the file, his face still flushed from thinking of how Bertie had described him the other day.

Bertie came back downstairs only to go into the kitchen. He came back out minutes later with a cup of tea and a saucer with a spoon on it. He set that on the table and then pulled a bottle of bright orange syrup out of his sweatshirt pocket and shoved it at Arthur.

Arthur took it to squint at the label but accepted the spoon when it was also shoved at him. The taste was horrible, but cold and flu medicines always tasted like that. He twisted up to put them both back on the table and to get some tea to take the taste out of his mouth, and Bertie made a noise.

"Your T-shirt is damp too, Arthur. I can...." For a moment it was as if Bertie couldn't finish his own thought. "I can get you something to wear if you take it off. If you like."

Arthur's eyes flew up. Either dragons couldn't be embarrassed or they couldn't blush, not that Arthur had seen, but whichever it was, Bertie looked warm and uncomfortable for a moment, as if he wished he *could* blush.

"Not that I will object if you choose to remain shirtless." Bertie looked back at him, and Arthur looked down at the blanket covering up the wet cotton clinging to his pale, skinny chest. He licked his mouth and wrinkled his nose at the lingering medicinal taste.

"You can get sick?" He changed the subject clumsily but didn't care. "With human diseases, I mean. I thought dragons were like fairies...."

"Fairies probably could get sick if they didn't regenerate so fast. Someday a disease is going to catch up with their overactive immune systems and it won't be pretty." Bertie took a moment to look pensive, and Arthur thought about wriggling free of his T-shirt and what Bertie's possible reaction would be. He didn't seem the type to worship from afar like the courtly love poems he liked to tease Arthur about, but then again, Arthur wasn't the type that was worshipped.

"You're saying fairies aren't really disease proof."

"I'm saying they are as resistant as one could ever hope to be. Like with demons, viruses and bacteria simply don't stand a chance against their unique physiology, which sees and responds to changes faster than viruses can evolve. Dragons, like most Beings who can shift, are also capable of rapid physical changes and response, but most of us spend our time as dragons, and dragons *can* catch one or two things from humans or other animals, though influenza is the only one I'd consider serious. The flu can pass to almost anything, Arthur. It's quite a nasty bug."

Arthur opened and closed his mouth. "I just have a cold."

"You're still shivering, pet," he was told as a rebuttal. Arthur shook; there was little else he *could* do. "And yet you insist upon working." Bertie gestured down at the laptop. "What do you plan on doing?" His tone was a mix of irritation and something warmer.

Arthur stared at the computer screen, which seemed to be getting less clear. "I could take notes. Or edit."

"Edit?" Disbelief was all over Bertie's face, but he huffed a second later. "Very well." He slid gracefully around the couch and out of sight, and when Arthur didn't hear the swinging doors, he assumed he'd gone into his study. He reached under the blanket and yanked his T-shirt up and off.

He draped it over the arm of the couch and tried not to make any noises about the feel of the velvet on his bare, chilled skin or to think about what Bertie's clothes might feel or smell like, or how warm they would be if he asked for them. He had a feeling Bertie might literally give him the shirt off his back.

"Here you are, you mulish dear, two chapters for you to—" Bertie stopped, as Arthur had kind of thought he might, by the end of the couch to stare at Arthur's T-shirt. Something inside of Bertie rumbled like thunder. Arthur wasn't sure if it was a laugh, but somehow he didn't think so, not when Bertie inhaled before finally swinging his gaze over to Arthur. "You dreadful tease," he announced slowly and Arthur realized, right as the medication hit his empty stomach and his vision started to swim, that Bertie's hand was clenched tight on a sheaf of papers. He shoved them at Arthur.

"Take these, Arthur, and give me your thoughts. I'm going to the kitchen for a minute. To get myself some bloody tea," he added under his breath as he pushed the swinging doors out of his way.

Arthur scanned through the pages of typed words, his heart beating a little faster and out of rhythm, though that could have been due to the medication. He couldn't tell what part of the book they were supposed to be in; possibly neither could Bertie. They looked like background, a history of Wales and a discussion of dragon artifacts from the same era.

"The dragons there were writing regularly long before the people of this area were," Arthur commented out loud, not really asking, and Bertie grunted as he came back into the room. He had a tray and put it on the table, then topped off Arthur's tea and insisted Arthur drink it down before he took the cup back.

"Yes. It's unfortunate that they were fond of flowery imagery. It makes it difficult to follow their exact meanings at times. And of course, etching symbols onto metal doesn't really give them a chance to tell a complete story. Are your jeans wet as well?"

"I… yes." Arthur kicked off his shoes, shifting as he shivered and sweated at the same time. He blamed the tea. Bertie took the laptop from him and closed it before setting that aside too. Arthur thought about wriggling out of his jeans and then wondered if that was the cold medicine or his own fantasies taking over.

"Arthur, there is no way you are leaving this house any time in the near future," Bertie rasped, just to make Arthur want to moan. He gave up and leaned back and to the side, falling against the cushion and hiding his face in his T-shirt. His shoulders and part of his back were visible but he didn't care.

"You don't have to sound so pleased about it," he mumbled but turned onto his side when the papers still in his hand crinkled.

"How little you know of dragons, Arthur." Bertie's response was oddly slow. Arthur dared a glance up, but Bertie turned at the same time to go over and use a poker to stab the logs in the fireplace. "You may put your feet up too, if lying down to read is easier for you. I shall read with you." He slid around the many stacks of books and picked one, at random as far as Arthur could tell.

It hardly counted as working. Arthur scowled, but he was so tired that his bones seemed to ache, and there was a headache behind his eyes and it was definitely getting worse. He sighed.

"Okay," he agreed, settling in to try to read sideways, only to jump when Bertie sat down at the other end of the couch, hotter than hot even through the blanket over Arthur's cold feet. "You'll get sick too!" Arthur objected, though it wasn't what he meant to say at all. The area around his knee was patted as if Arthur was slow in the head.

"Someone of my lineage?" Bertie scoffed while staring intently at his book. "Don't be ridiculous. And I can read that scowl, Arthur. You are thinking that those are famous last words."

"I was, actually." Arthur's face felt weird, as if he was smiling and not scowling. He tried to fix that and couldn't seem to. His feet were so very warm.

"There are some gestures, Arthur, that will never be considered over the top, and this is one of them." Bertie was still studying his book, idly flipping pages without reading anything.

Those words sounded familiar. Arthur tried to focus through the haze of heat and achy bones and his swimming thoughts, but he couldn't quite place them.

"You drugged me," he accused sleepily, and Bertie gave a small laugh.

"That's hardly a secret." He patted Arthur again, creating new kinds of shivers. "Just read, pet. Read and rest." He seemed to notice Arthur's tremors. "Are you cold?"

"With you on me? No." It was Arthur's turn to laugh. Bertie shot him a startled glance. "I read that Neruda." Arthur's tongue couldn't quite keep up with him. "I think you used the wrong line for dragons. You should have said…." He concentrated. "*As if you were on fire from within/the moon lives in the lining of your skin.*" He met eyes like melting volcanic rock and thought he might burst into flames. "I would have said that. It… it made me think of you."

Bertie's lips were parted as he caught his breath, but he seemed to have no interest in any scents in the air. He was staring at Arthur and kept staring until Arthur's stomach flipped and his heart pounded in that irregular, drugged rhythm. Arthur dropped his head back down to the arm of the couch.

"Chilean love poems seem an odd choice for someone interested in courtly love," Bertie commented after a long pause, so long that Arthur had tried to read again and gave up when his eyelids could not seem to stay open.

"I thought so too," Arthur whispered back, not sure how much time had passed since either of them had spoken, and exhaled when Bertie let him kick out and bury his feet deeper underneath him. Then he shut his eyes and kept them closed.

He was in a low mound of pillows, all of warm and soft velvet, and a hot voice was bidding him to wake up. Arthur wasn't sure if he was dreaming or awake, or even where he really was, until he opened his eyes and saw Bertie leaning over him and realized he was still lying on the couch and that he must have fallen asleep.

He'd pushed the blanket off at some point, too, because Bertie dropped it back over him and pushed him gently down when he tried to sit up.

"I don't think you'll be riding anywhere today, Arthur, much less across town in the rain." He put Arthur's cell phone on the cushion next to his face and it took Arthur much too long to realize that it was so he could call his sister or anyone else he needed to in order to let them know where he was. He wished dizzily that he could remember Bertie's hand in his pants, as it must have been to get his phone. Then he tried to sit up again but stopped, not at a push but at Bertie's low, coaxing voice.

"Won't you stay just a little longer?" he asked, rough and hungry, and Arthur shivered into the blanket and didn't move.

IT WAS Bertie's own fault that he got sick too. Two days after Arthur finally went home—driven home in the luxury car that, of course, Bertie owned—he came back into work drained from the bike ride over but feeling better, only to find Bertie on the couch in his study, snuffling into three blankets.

He must have needed them because the house was colder than it usually was. No fire was going, and Bertie must have forgotten to turn the heat up, if the heat could even be turned up. Arthur was starting to think the heat was coming directly from Bertie, not that he'd asked yet.

"I told you not to come in until you were well," Bertie immediately barked at him and used the remote to turn off the TV as if Arthur hadn't already seen him entranced by some kind of cheesy procedural show about the FBI.

Arthur's nose was red and his throat was still scratchy, but the lack of smoke scent around Bertie was a worry, not a relief, so he didn't say anything about his choice in shows.

"I'm not arguing with you," Arthur told him. He didn't feel up to arguing anyway. "Do you want me to get you some tea?"

"You pearl," Bertie said, which Arthur took to mean *yes, please* and nodded before heading slowly to the kitchen. He looked through the fridge while the water was boiling, but Bertie hadn't had any more groceries delivered recently. So he sighed and looked through take-out menus until he found a place that made soup. He placed an order for later and then dug around until he found the tray Bertie had used for him and put the tea and teacups together in a way he thought looked right.

He'd never served tea before, but right or wrong, no explanation or apology was necessary. Bertie's eyes just turned to him with a grateful sort of hope, and he exhaled noisily over his tea as he drank, not seeming to notice its scalding temperature. Arthur thought about his notes on dragons again, but didn't feel like going for his laptop just yet. He studied Bertie instead.

He wouldn't have said Bertie was sick, not just from looking at him, though the gleaming beneath his skin seemed more obvious, as if his skin was getting lighter, and his eyes didn't exactly focus on Arthur the way they usually did.

"I told you not to come in until you were completely well." Focused or not, Bertie apparently could see that Arthur was still weak.

"Lucky for you I did." Arthur tossed his head. "I ordered you some soup for later."

"Oh, Arthur." Bertie beamed at him for a moment, as if he couldn't imagine anything better than Arthur spending more of his money without waiting for permission first, and then abruptly turned an alarming shade of white, his black hair and nails standing out starkly. "Soup?" His tone said he might throw up.

Arthur hurried forward, but Bertie dropped back to the couch without vomiting, leaving his cup and saucer on the floor.

"Is it worse for dragons?" Arthur hadn't thought of that, but an immune system not used to getting hit by every malevolent virus out there might not react well to the ones that finally got past its defenses.

He reached out carefully, so carefully, to run his fingertips over Bertie's forehead. Fine, fine hair tickled his fingertips, feeling almost like feathers, as Arthur had imagined. But he stopped and pulled his hand back when Bertie grinned.

"Oh," Arthur realized out loud. "You're just being a baby."

"Baby?" Bertie pouted. "I've been working, I'll have you know."

Arthur spared a moment to look pointedly at the blank TV screen. Bertie pouted for a bit longer and then lifted his chin as he dug around the pile of blankets to produce his laptop. He held it up like a banner advertising his diligence and then moved, not quite sitting up, but no longer laying down. He put it on his lap and opened it up.

"I got cold," he explained with some dignity, and Arthur leaned against an end table to consider that.

"Do you want me to turn up the heat?" He regretted it as he asked. Bertie gave him a pitying look that seemed to confirm Arthur's suspicion that there was no heat to turn up, that the house was heated by Bertie himself after all, or at least that any man-made heating system wouldn't compare to his own internal fires.

Arthur considered those, the flames that must rage in Bertie's belly, the heat that must run under his skin, and wasn't as scared as he probably should have been. He did look away, but only to catch his breath without Bertie's eyes on him.

"Don't be cruel, Arthur." It wasn't until Bertie spoke again that Arthur noticed the warm, wavy silence between them and how long it had gone on. He looked back and shifted from foot to foot.

"Is there anything you want me to do? To help you?" He had to offer. He could blame his slow responses and wild thoughts on his own lingering illness. "Do you need to shower or…?"

The look Bertie gave him was probably meant to be sexy. Fortunately for Arthur and his stupid imagination that had made him say those words, it was more pitiful than anything else.

"A cigarette?" he amended his own sentence, and Bertie let out a breath. His wrinkled nose said a smoke was not currently appealing to him, but he didn't remark on Arthur's offer to help him shower, so Arthur stepped closer. "More tea then?"

"Yes, dear. I will need my strength to get this section done." If he hadn't been so pale, Arthur would have said Bertie was faking it for attention, but up close the unhealthy lack of color in his skin was even more startling. His eyes were too bright.

"You're going to work?" Arthur blinked in disbelief. "You try to wiggle out of working to hover around me at every opportunity and now you want to? You're sick. You told me that I wouldn't get better if I insisted on pushing myself too hard."

"Yes, well, I have a deadline after all, Arthur." Bertie's gaze swung away and he straightened wearily. Arthur saw the bottle of orange syrup fall out from behind a pillow and hit the floor. He didn't see a spoon. The image of Bertie gulping flu medicine straight from the bottle made him put a hand to his stomach.

"Bertie." Arthur crossed his arms and ignored the stunned stare in his direction, though he was aware that he'd avoided saying that name directly ever since he'd pictured himself saying it against Bertie's skin. "You are sick."

Bertie shook himself, then wet lips that for once actually seemed to need it.

"If you can work while unwell, Arthur, so can I."

Arthur remembered waking up later on the day he'd been sick to a blazing fire and the blanket tucked around him. Bertie had been nowhere to be seen, but he left his chapters on the table, along with crackers, and Arthur had munched a few while he did his best to read and gather his thoughts. At least it had been a mild flu, only lasting about a few days. With some rest, Bertie would feel better in no time at all.

"You don't need to prove you're stronger than a human, you know." Arthur kept his voice stern, because it really didn't need saying. Obviously, he couldn't measure up to someone like Bertie.

Bertie frowned back at him.

"No, just that I'm at least as strong as you, my Arthur," Bertie huffed, his tone so haughty that Arthur almost missed the content of his words. He stared and leaned harder against the end table while he thought about that, and only once he had filed that idea away to contemplate later did he come forward.

He knew he was flushed but couldn't look over while he picked up the cup and saucer and the bottle of medicine and the scattered bits of paper that had probably been on the floor for days. He scooped them into his arms and then rushed out of the room to deal with them and give his face a chance to cool.

He came back in with his laptop and sat down on the couch as nonchalantly as he could, which wasn't much. It was so low, he mostly fell into it, not that Bertie objected. He did open his mouth when Arthur took his laptop away from him and set it aside but said nothing as Arthur opened up his own and stopped with his fingers poised over the keyboard.

"Okay, go ahead. Work." He kept his eyes down until Bertie rumbled and purred.

"Thank you, treasure." He spoke softly and then moved. Arthur stiffened as Bertie slid against his side and exhaled down his neck.

He swallowed. Bertie's breath smelled like artificial orange flavor and black tea and smoke, and yet it was still hot for him to be this close.

"You're going to get me sick again," he warned unsteadily, but Bertie must have been high from too much medicine because he whined into Arthur's shoulder and didn't move. Arthur had fallen asleep under the influence of that syrup. It was strong stuff. That was all it was, he told himself, just the drugs. "Okay, just don't breathe on me, then," he added to save himself all the wet, warm breath on his neck, only to yelp when Bertie nodded and moved again.

"Yes, Arthur," he agreed as he slid his head down to Arthur's thigh. Arthur moved the laptop without thinking, and Bertie took that as permission to settle in. He pushed his legs out and then curled up, dragging the blankets back over him as if he really was freezing. There was no way he should have fit on the couch with Arthur there too, but if parts of him were on the floor, the blankets hid them. Once he was comfortable, he let out a long, long, tired breath. There was no sign in his easy breathing that he'd noticed Arthur's tension.

Arthur finally looked down, although he couldn't see much but the vague outline of a curled-up body. He put his hands back on the keyboard and pulled up the notes for Bertie's book, not that his mind was on it.

"So, dragons," he began in a voice a little bit too high. "This house wasn't built for them, though this couch obviously was." Or had been altered for one.

His thigh was burning up, a lot like the rest of him. He wanted to put a hand down and didn't dare.

"No, the house was built by humans, for humans." Bertie's rumble was making its way through Arthur's body, up and then back down his spine. Arthur shut his eyes, although it wasn't as if listening to Bertie's smoky voice had ever calmed him down. "I work with humans, so a human house in a human town makes that easier, and they have yet to build a keyboard suitable for claws, so I have to be a man if I want to get my work done faster."

Arthur had suspected that much, but it was good to hear that he'd been right.

"I also like to cook, as I've told you. Dragons, like weres, will eat their food raw or roasted, though anything high in sulfur will do, but I have found I also enjoy the rituals of cooking. A human kitchen is more suited to that activity as well."

"Activity?" Arthur didn't mean to repeat it, he really didn't. "How about your bedroom?"

He hadn't meant to ask that either.

Bertie let out another pleased, fiery sound, a soft roar or a big purr, as if he were just a big cat after all.

"Asking to see my bed, Arthur?" But the hand he pulled from the blanket waved weakly in the air, as if he wanted to flirt and couldn't really manage it. Arthur nearly swallowed his tongue when Bertie dropped that hand to his knee. His pulse was racing. He didn't see how Bertie could be missing it, even if he was stoned.

"My bed is also low to the ground. I am mostly... myself... when I'm upstairs. Those stairs were not built for shorter legs. It's ungainly to see me walk down them as myself and I refuse to let you."

"You're worried about how I see you?" Arthur tightened his mouth to keep anything else stupid from coming out. Bertie's fingers curled around his knee, nervously maybe, or perhaps just flexing, Arthur couldn't tell but changed the subject instead of asking. "Is it painful for you, shifting? They say for werewolves it isn't a comfortable experience."

"No, no, it's not painful. Though you'd think it would be." Bertie seemed thoughtful, taking long pauses before speaking. "It does make me dizzy, however, as if I've stood up too fast. I suppose it helps that I'm small for a dragon."

"Really?" Arthur wasn't typing anything and didn't think he could have at the moment anyway. "You seemed big to me."

It was another perfect opportunity for Bertie to flirt with him, but he simply sighed and patted him. "Thank you, Arthur." When he didn't add anything else, Arthur opened his eyes. Bertie's hand didn't pull away.

"Was there anything else you wished to know about my body?" Bertie finally got back to flirting in a low, wicked voice that Arthur distantly recognized as meaning he must be feeling better. Not that it mattered, with Arthur wanting to squirm and being unable to. His jeans felt tight, and he was getting totally, embarrassingly hard under his laptop. There was nothing he could do about it, and if Bertie smelled *that* in the air right now, Arthur was in serious trouble.

"Uh…." He couldn't think of any words.

"I mean, about dragons' bodies," Bertie corrected himself and sounded so sincere that Arthur had a strange urge to apologize. As if this was his fault somehow and not the sexy man-dragon's who was trying to sprawl across his lap and kept whispering suggestive remarks against his thigh.

He continued thinking that Bertie might be attracted to him, but he couldn't be nearly as attracted as Arthur was to him. If he was, he wouldn't be doing this to drive them both crazy, and there was no way he would have sat so close to Arthur on the other couch when Arthur had been sick without feeling what Arthur was feeling now.

Arthur raised a hand to rub at his forehead and then dropped it to Bertie's back without thinking. Bertie twisted into it, letting out a moan that had to be deliberate.

"Be a dear, Arthur," he begged, as if Arthur was going to rub his back now after everything he was putting him through.

"This is…." Inappropriate didn't begin to cover it, but it was far too late to protest about that now. Bertie had the flu. He probably ached all over, that was all it was. Arthur already had his hand spread out at the thought so he could absorb that heat while he pushed the heel of his thumb into the tense muscle over Bertie's shoulder blades.

There were too many blankets and probably clothes separating him from Bertie's skin, but he imagined it anyway, what it might feel like, what it had looked like, nearly stopping as those shining scales popped into his mind.

"*Now* I feel like a personal assistant," he murmured instead, because a murmur was as loud as he could get at the moment. Bertie let out one gentle laugh but didn't move.

"Am I that spoiled?" he mused. Arthur couldn't tell if he meant it or not. He dragged his fingers up to Bertie's neck for a light scratch and shook his head. "I didn't think I was," Bertie went on as if he'd seen Arthur do it. "I don't feel spoiled. I feel…."

He trailed off without finishing, which was good because the only way Arthur could finish that sentence was "incredibly frustrated" and that was answering for himself, not for Bertie.

"So humans can help dragons too." Arthur kept his palm flat for a moment and then ran it slowly down Bertie's spine, feeling every shiver and thinking he'd like to make it better. He thought of the other day and wishing Bertie would climb over him to keep him warm but only wet his mouth without voicing that particular thought. "It's not all a dragon's wise guidance on us poor, helpless people, I mean."

"Don't be ridiculous, of course they can." Bertie pushed against his hand, urging it lower for another scratch. "Did you think it wasn't mutually beneficial? That we got nothing out of it?"

"What did you get?" Arthur wasn't sure if they were talking about ancient or modern dragons. He wasn't sure if Bertie was either.

"Beauty. Music. Stories. Jewelry. Art." He tightened the hand on Arthur's knee and then moved it, stroking Arthur gently, petting him without seeming aware that he was following Arthur's motions. "Someone to listen, to make our own, someone to spoil, someone to protect. Sex," he went on dreamily, making Arthur twitch. "Companionship. A treasure never to be shared. We got the best of it, if you ask me. It wasn't all kidnapping virgins, you know, not that that doesn't hold a certain appeal."

"What does that mean?"

"What it sounds like. Scritch me again please, pet." For a proud, if small, dragon of ancient lineage, Bertie didn't seem to mind begging. Arthur kept his eyes tightly shut but scritched as he was told, scratching gently over and over again until Bertie's shivers finally stopped.

"I…. My mother used to do this for me when I didn't feel well." Arthur said it to distract himself from his burning skin and hard dick. "She hadn't for years, I was in college when she, when they, when my parents died, but yeah, she used to do this. It always made me feel better."

This wasn't the same thing at all, actually, but Arthur wasn't exactly thinking clearly. He was grateful that the same could be said for Bertie, who seemed ready to fall asleep until he spoke.

"I am very sorry for your loss, Arthur." His fingers momentarily curled around Arthur's knee and squeezed before letting go. His hand smoothed down over Arthur's jeans again in the next second. Arthur's eyes started to sting, but he blinked back the tears.

"I had no idea." Bertie whispered mournfully. "You and your sister must miss them terribly."

Arthur sucked in a shaky breath but still couldn't speak. No one but Kate had mentioned his parents to him in years. He hadn't told anyone at school, and he'd lost contact with the extended family. He'd never thought of what he'd have to say when confronted with warm, sincere concern.

"We do," he managed at last and blinked back the tears. Sometimes he wondered if the freak car accident that killed them was the reason Kate had done the stupid, reckless things she'd done in cars while high or drunk, but so far he hadn't asked her.

"Would you like to talk about them?" Bertie called him from his dark thoughts. "Share more happy memories? I don't mind. I'd love to hear more."

"More?" Arthur's mind spun for a moment, and then he said the first thing that came to mind without thinking about why. "They were kind of rebellious hippies despite having boring, traditional day jobs. They didn't get married until Kate was four. We were both in their wedding." He had the pictures packed away in a shoebox.

"Dragons rarely marry. They think it's a useless and purely symbolic human ceremony, but I can imagine that to make that sort of commitment meant they truly loved each other." Bertie's breath was hot and calming for all that Arthur burned where they touched. He exhaled loudly and Bertie patted him again. "It sounds lovely,

Arthur. Your family, your parents, their love story. Tell me more, if you don't mind."

"We're...." Arthur's throat tightened with the urge to cry, something he decided to blame on being exhausted from the flu and working two jobs, though he knew it was that the room was so warm and Bertie's voice was so soft and understanding. He'd never been able to talk to anyone about those kinds of memories, not even Kate, not when she'd reacted by disappearing into vodka. "We're supposed to be working."

"Arthur." The hand petting his knee stopped, a heavy, steady weight. "Haven't I taught you yet that everything is connected?"

"*This* will help you understand a lost race of dragon?" Arthur had to clear his throat to ask. Bertie nodded.

"Yes, Arthur, yes it will. It will help me understand many things," he answered earnestly then stretched against Arthur to remind him to keep rubbing his back. Arthur frowned, uncertain, but licked his lips and felt forgotten words rising up even before Bertie went on, quiet and encouraging and impossibly content.

"Tell me a story, Arthur love. Stay and tell me a story."

CHAPTER 7

DRAGONS, Arthur had discovered, were fond of stories in all forms: myths and anecdotes, TV shows and movies, songs and history books. There was a long history of dragons either telling stories or demanding that humans entertain them with songs and tales in some sort of exchange of information.

At least, that's what Arthur decided to call it after he finally found a book on dragons to explore. It was another book written by humans, and written in the fifties to boot, but its intention hadn't been to frighten people, and Arthur found that encouraging. In fact, when he spotted it in Bertie's study and dragged it over with his foot while Bertie slipped in and out of a dreamy, fitful sleep, he thought it was one of Bertie's because of its intriguing title, *The Dragons of Mankind*.

He considered what Bertie told him during one of their early meetings, that dragons collected things with eternity in mind, while he scanned through the glossy black-and-white photos and lithographs that filled the book, and saw picture after picture of dragons sitting atop piles of jewels and gold with tiny humans wrapped in their coils. The artists' depictions of what an encounter with a dragon could be like dated far back into the Middle Ages and featured more European-looking dragons and beautiful, brave humans with musical instruments in their hands or with their mouths open as if reciting a story. Some of the drawings were clearly sexually charged—tightly bound, beautiful youths laid out before panting dragons, with the imagery of fire all around them.

The artwork from Asia that the author had used in the book didn't show dragons with humans much, but then that artwork tended to show the dragons as powerful and god-like as they guarded rivers or chased after pearls. Those haughty, commanding dragons probably wouldn't have needed to kidnap anyone. There probably would have been volunteers lining up to spend time with them. Arthur wasn't sure he wouldn't have been among them if he'd been alive back then and living somewhere under the control of a dragon king. They were definitely known for their generosity, more so than the human emperors who eventually grew jealous of their power and imprisoned them. It would have been an honor to serve creatures like that.

Arthur wasn't even entirely certain that he wouldn't have done the same with a European dragon. He'd noticed in the stories about them that the author of the book had dutifully recounted that there were plenty of knights and maidens who *chose* to go to the dragons. The explanation in the stories was always that they did it to save their people from the dragon's wrath but the author, and Arthur, had still wondered.

The stories were only written down or drawn decades, sometimes centuries later. More than that, the power of the dragons was evident in every flexing muscle and curling bit of flame. Power had always been an aphrodisiac and always would be. Even if it wasn't, there was still something alluring in every strange, sinuous body.

Arthur had stopped reading the book when he found himself tracing the drawings and photos of artifacts with his fingertips and becoming even more aware of Bertie's head on his thigh. He'd taken the book home to read without the risk of Bertie catching him and then spent the next few days flushed and avoiding Bertie's eyes.

The fact that he had to read it alone as if it was porn was embarrassing, but not embarrassing enough to keep him from finishing those romantic stories in one night. He added to his list that night too, writing that dragons liked back rubs and stories about devotion before waking up flushed and panicked and deleting both entries.

He couldn't help but wonder if those stories were the ones that Bertie found so romantic, the way he'd said before. Kidnapping people didn't sound romantic, but then, even the artists who tried to depict dragon encounters as monstrous hadn't quite managed to. The pictures made it seem incredible, awesome in the strictest sense. In any culture, the humans who had been around dragons and survived were considered fortunate, if not blessed.

That those same humans then chose to kill the dragons and glorify themselves for it made no sense, not that Arthur could tell. The explanation the author had gone for, that in order to prove themselves masters of the world they lived in, the humans felt the need to conquer *all* of it, made Arthur think of the Romans, though he couldn't exactly say why. He did read the stories from Asia of warriors and nobles who slew dragon kings to gain their power; he read them until they made him feel sick and he finally skipped ahead to another chapter.

He had nightmares that night about long, black dragons cut into pieces, like elephants harvested for ivory, and woke up sweating and tense. After a few days of distracted thinking, he'd come to the realization that stories about dragon slaying appeared most when cultures or dynasties or countries were on the rise and needed to assert their strength and power. The author hadn't come to that conclusion, but it seemed obvious to Arthur. So obvious that he hurried into work even earlier than usual to ask Bertie about it.

He also wanted to slip the book back into the collection without Bertie seeing because somehow he knew he would blush if Bertie saw him with it. But he did that and straightened some more and emptied ashtrays, and still there was no sign of Bertie.

The house wasn't cold, though the warmth Arthur felt when he walked through the door slowly faded as Arthur passed the hours cleaning up the study and glancing alternately at the clock in the kitchen and the one up the stairs, hoping that Bertie was just sleeping late.

The first time he shivered from the cold, he accepted the fact that Bertie wasn't home, but no matter where he poked around, he couldn't find any of Bertie's usual scribbled notes to him explaining where he was or when he'd be back. There wasn't even one instructing Arthur on what to do.

He did find the temperature controls, which were on and set to low and which included air conditioning. That would be good for the summer if Arthur was around then. Bertie's presence would make the house stifling on hot days.

Arthur turned up the heat while he dusted Bertie's study and checked his cell in case he'd missed a call somehow, then gave up and went to the kitchen to make himself some tea. Tea was starting to grow on him, though he still preferred a strong cup of coffee, thick with cream and sugar.

He finally found a note from Bertie in a used teacup by the sink, smeared with water and almost unreadable. All it said—that he could make out—was "Precious" and "I'll be out today."

Arthur opened his mouth while he stared at it, full of questions that he had no one to ask. Bertie was gone for who knew how long, and anyway, the time had long passed for Arthur to object to being called pet names. He really should have put a stop to things before Bertie fell asleep on Arthur's knee, seemingly unaware of Arthur's hard-on, and he definitely should have said something in the days afterward while he'd been watching Bertie's skin go back to its normal color.

Maybe he would have if Bertie had gone back to his usual flirtatious ways, but he hadn't. Instead, once he woke up for real, he sat up and tried to work, tossing out the names of books Arthur should find for him—including some Arthur would have to get at the university library—and then getting up to find a flash drive with some new sections on it for Arthur to go over.

If Bertie had wanted to keep Arthur busy while he recuperated, he'd succeeded, not that he'd seemed happy about it.

Arthur frowned over his sweet, milky tea and went back into Bertie's study to sit on his pillowy couch and consider. Actually that "precious" was the first pet name Bertie had called him in several days. Ever since he'd been sick in fact. Arthur hadn't really noticed until now, probably because even the way Bertie said "Arthur" with that rumbling voice and posh accent was enough to make him warm.

He went back to his list of dragon facts, typing in "disease-resistant" and then pointedly re-adding "They like stories of all kinds" but wasn't sure about the pet names and so left them off. He also forewent mentioning the back rub again, though the memory was sharp and fresh, as if it had just happened. If that wasn't a dragon thing, if that was a Bertie thing, then like the nicknames, it had to mean something, and Arthur couldn't think of a way to ask that wouldn't give too much away.

Maybe he should be grateful Bertie had kept him busy while maintaining his distance. He definitely saved Arthur from himself.

Unless... Arthur had the horrifying thought that Bertie had been aware of Arthur's hard-on after all and stopped flirting with him to spare Arthur's feelings.

It was something Arthur couldn't think about. If he did, he'd succumb to the humiliation and never return to work, and he loved this job. He should just get on with his work, pretend it never happened, and act calm whenever Bertie was around, if he even could.

Of course, he'd need Bertie around to do that, but that was okay. He could spend the hours while Bertie was away thinking of ways to avoid Bertie when Bertie *was* with him, and then when Bertie reappeared, Arthur wouldn't act as stupid and obvious as he must have been acting, and things could go back to the way they were.

But Arthur's feelings for Bertie must have been *very* obvious since their time on Bertie's couch, because Arthur waited for hours, finally giving in and eating lunch alone, and then a few more hours, until there was no sign of Bertie and no word from him and it was either leave and get across town before rush hour started and things got more dangerous, or wait another few hours.

Since he didn't want to think about what he'd look like, staying late in Bertie's cold, empty house waiting for Bertie to come back, he finally cleaned up his notes, did the dishes from his lunch, and then turned the heat back down before he forced himself out the door.

IT HADN'T been completely dark when he left, but it was late enough that Arthur assumed Bertie finally came home shortly after he left. Seeing that Bertie hadn't turned off the alarm Arthur set last night made him stop halfway in the door and look up, as if he could see upstairs into Bertie's bedroom.

The beep of the alarm system and his own shivers from the cold both in and outside of the house finally spurred him forward. The chill told him Bertie wasn't home, that he probably hadn't come home at all, but Arthur looked around for him anyway before turning up the heat and then falling onto the couch to glare at the dead, empty fireplace.

He knew where the logs were—outside, underneath the covered walkway that led to the garage—and went to get some to give himself something to do. Once they were in the fireplace, it took him forever to find a way to get a fire going. Bertie didn't believe in matches—not that Arthur could fault him for that if he didn't need them—but Arthur had to use an antique cigarette lighter from the study and some old *National Geographics* to finally get his fire lit.

It didn't roar and it didn't blaze the way Bertie's fire did, but it let Arthur smile a little. He wasn't quite out of his mind enough yet to light up an herbal cigarette for the smell, but he did open the silver dish to count the remaining cigarettes and make a mental note to head out to the herbalist again soon so Bertie could roll up and restock his supply.

Groceries had been delivered again a few days before by Ravi, who turned out to be a chubby, short man with the kind of sunny smile that Arthur had to return. There was plenty of food in the house. Arthur made a new grocery list anyway and stuck it on the fridge, including instant coffee just because, then gave up on waiting for the front door to open and made himself some tea before heading into the room next to the study. Whatever the room's original purpose—Arthur suspected a sitting room or a morning room because of the position of the high ceiling and tall windows—Bertie had built in more shelves and used it to store his knickknacks. Or objets d'art. Or whatever they were. Probably more tarnished silver like the cigarette lighter that Arthur was going to give in and polish soon.

It might be a good activity for a day like today, a lot more soothing than hauling in all those dusty books and wiping them down before sorting them. Not that Arthur needed soothing, exactly; it was just that the organizing wasn't having its usual effect on him. The dust was making him itchy and irritable all over again, and instead of being charmed by Bertie's eclectic choices in reading material, he heard himself remarking on it, talking bitterly to himself the way he had during long overnight shifts by himself at the gas station.

"This is the third copy of *The Prince and the Pauper* I've found in here!" He was starting to think that whenever Bertie couldn't find something he wanted, he went out and bought a new version. Thinking about that didn't improve his mood.

He had Bertie's cell phone number. Bertie might even have his cell phone on him, since Arthur hadn't found it anywhere downstairs. Arthur could call him. The thought had occurred to him more than once. He didn't, but only because Bertie probably didn't want to be bothered. This distance was probably on purpose, some way to give Arthur time to get Bertie out of his head and accept that the flirting wasn't personal. Arthur could accept that, he really could, if only disappearing hadn't been the first thing his sister did after moving in with him following the death of their parents. She started going out and staying out later and later, until she'd finally been *gone*, and since she was over eighteen by then, there wasn't anything Arthur could do about it.

The trouble she got into had been bad, and it easily could have been so much worse. Arthur wasn't in the best frame of mind then either, but he tried to keep it together for her, be what she needed. It wasn't enough, not then, and she ran off to do some truly stupid things, and just thinking about it now made Arthur toss down the book he was wiping clean.

Bertie had better not be doing anything that dangerous. It was bad enough that he didn't have the sense to lock his doors or set his alarm. Imagining what he might do out with the general public, with humans interested in selling pieces of him to the highest bidder, something Arthur knew more about than he should, made his stomach clench.

His frown at the fire in the fireplace got lost for a moment as he heard the front door open, and then came back with a vengeance when he heard a familiar sleepy note in Bertie's voice as he gave someone else instructions to the downstairs bathroom.

"Just down the hall there."

The instructions were followed by a deep, male voice with an accent Arthur had never heard before.

"Leave it to you to choose a house with stairs, Jones," the voice said, and Arthur turned in time to see a tall, blue-scaled man— a tall, blue-scaled *dragon*—disappearing past the kitchen. He was wearing a loose shirt and tight pants and a hat, but Arthur caught the sapphire gleam of his scales before he turned back to get a look at Bertie.

Bertie met Arthur's gaze, then his head went back almost defensively.

"Arthur!" he exclaimed brightly and made a vague, nervous gesture when Arthur only continued to stare at him. "Trust you to have the place blazing warm for me, you dar—you dear boy."

Arthur felt frozen despite being close enough to the fire to singe the hair on his arms if he reached out, but he rolled his shoulders and then went back to wiping down books and stacking them.

He stopped again when he heard the bathroom door open and watched Bertie from the corner of his eye until the other dragon returned. Then he twisted to get a good look.

The new dragon was considerably taller than Bertie and thin like an athlete. He looked like a fencing foil wouldn't be out of place in his hands, which, Arthur noticed, had fingernails as blue as the scales shining from beneath his skin. He was holding a cigar, a real cigar of tobacco and not herbs, that he must have lit in the bathroom. His hat was a fedora, which he pulled low. His eyes were azure blue. He had a small white mustache, as white as his hair, but he didn't seem old at all.

He glanced at Arthur for a moment and then took a puff from his cigar.

"He's a fierce one, isn't he?" the new dragon drawled, and it took Arthur several shocked seconds to realize that the dragon meant *him*. Bertie's mouth went soft, just enough for Arthur to see a hint of his tongue as he wet his lips.

"Zeru, this is Arthur. Arthur, this is Zeru, an old friend."

"Hello." Arthur felt that was all he had to say after such an introduction and went back to staring at the books. He was pretty sure his ears were red because he *felt* flushed, just like he was sure they could see it. It only made him tighten his jaw, and he continued stacking and restacking books whose titles he wasn't even reading anymore. Bertie hadn't even introduced him as his assistant. Not to his "old friend."

Zeru, Arthur thought to himself. He'd bet it was a name that meant something powerful. This dragon was beautiful and exotic, and unlike Bertie, he had no problem conveying what he thought of humans, of Arthur. He wasn't rude, but he clearly didn't regard Arthur as anyone important. In fact, from the way Zeru was looking him over, Arthur felt a bit like Bertie's dog. Like his *pet*.

"Hello," Zeru greeted Arthur politely and then kept talking to Bertie. "*Arthur*," he said significantly, as if his eyebrows were raised. "Even with that Being-bait right in front of me, I will never understand your taste."

"You don't have to as long as you recognize that it's mine." It hardly made sense, but then, these were two dragons talking to each other. Arthur probably wasn't meant to understand. He shoved some of the less valuable books into a pile while he wondered if Zeru was from an ancient and noble family. He probably was; he certainly acted like it.

Arthur should be using this opportunity to ask him questions about dragon families and their different cultures, but his mouth stayed firmly shut as he listened to them bicker about something and then walk away as Bertie gave his old friend some of his hand-rolled herbal cigarettes to try and then went with him into the study. When they came back out a few minutes later, they were talking about something else. Art, Arthur assumed, though he didn't comment or join in.

He was an assistant, that was all. He'd speak when spoken to and that was it. He looked up only once it was clear that Zeru was on his way out the door. Zeru, who was beautiful and noble and *dragon*.

"We must do this again, and soon, if your boy won't mind." Zeru adjusted his hat and Bertie opened the door with a loud sigh. Arthur couldn't tell if it was exaggerated or not.

"I'm afraid that what Arthur says, goes," Bertie told him, though he couldn't be serious because he added a "Call me" before he closed the door on his friend.

Arthur's shoulders were stiff with expectation, but there had been no long farewells or kisses. There hadn't even been an exchange of nicknames, and he thought faintly, distantly, that he was glad he took "Dragons use nicknames" off his list—unless it was only that they used nicknames on humans.

As if humans really were their pets. He coughed out the smell of cigar smoke and glared at the fragile collections of books before him.

He still wasn't seeing the titles, but Bertie was hardly going to notice. He stared at Arthur for a minute before jumping into sudden, excited motion. He seemed oblivious to Arthur's mood as he went into the kitchen and then came back out. He was babbling.

"As I was saying before—" He coughed too, as if he also had cigar smoke stuck in his throat. "—it's quite chilly suddenly, isn't it? I mean the weather of course, darling."

Arthur did not glance over. Bertie continued talking, his words picking up speed.

"Don't know how you ride in it. We really should get you a car, pet—er, Arthur. I thought of you all the way home, wondering what you'd been up to in my absence."

"Working." Arthur kept it short and was pleased by how calm he thought he sounded.

Calm or not, the single word made Bertie stop short, and Arthur glanced to the side to watch Bertie untangle himself from a long red scarf and peel off a wool jacket. He looked tired and somewhat pale, and there were wrinkles in the dress shirt he was wearing. As Arthur didn't see any luggage, he assumed that Bertie was wearing the same clothes he wore out yesterday.

He pushed out a tight, startled breath. Bertie made a fretful noise.

"Dear. I know you're going to think I was shirking my responsibilities, Arthur, but I can assure you I wasn't. In fact...."

"You're only my boss. You don't have to explain yourself to me," Arthur told him, finally noticing that he was creating a pile that included Mark Twain, *The Scarlet Pimpernel*, *The Constant Gardener*, and a book on the Underground Railroad but not correcting his mistakes. Bertie was wearing the same clothes he had on yesterday. So much for Arthur's nightmares about his body being hacked to pieces for black market magic sales and poor, helpless Bertie in the hands of someone heartless. Whoever's hands he'd been in had apparently been enough to make him completely forget about Arthur. Arthur was an idiot, mostly because now when he imagined Bertie in the hands of someone heartless, he was picturing blue hands, holding a cigar.

"Only your boss?" Bertie's confused exhalation made Arthur's stomach flutter in a way that made him wish he'd stopped to eat something before he sat down. There was a long pause where Arthur didn't comment and then the soft sound of Bertie stepping onto the rug. He stopped before Arthur would have had to look up at him.

"Arthur, is something wrong? You aren't sick again? You ate while I was gone, didn't you?"

Arthur almost shut his eyes at the concern. If he was flushed, it could be blamed on the fire, but if he gave a little sigh, Bertie would definitely notice. It had been so stupid, expecting all that attention for himself, especially under the circumstances, but he couldn't help how nice it felt. That wasn't Bertie's fault, and he shouldn't be taking it out on him.

"I'm fine," he said at last with a small shrug to let Bertie know it *was* fine even though Arthur's twisting stomach kept insisting it wasn't. "I ate yesterday. I've been busy this morning." He shut his mouth, then wet his lips and heard himself saying more. "I suppose you were busy too, too busy to let me know you were all right."

Arthur really was stupid. He winced and risked a look up, but the sight of those eyes fixed on him, round and dark and intent, made him swing his gaze back to the fireplace. He wasn't ready to beard the dragon in his den, not yet. He felt bad enough as it was. There was Bertie, a hot, rumpled presence, safe and sound and looking only in need of a nap, and here was Arthur, sitting on the floor, red-faced and dusty and irritable from worrying about nothing.

He probably looked terrible. Not exotic or beautiful or anything even close to it.

"It's okay," Arthur walked back his words, then scowled at the fire. "But I wasn't sure if I should worry." If only he could stop talking, or at least keep that hum of tension out of his voice. "It's nothing." He shook his head and wiped a hand through the air. "Never mind."

That never worked on his sister and it wasn't working on Bertie.

"Were you worried?" Bertie took a step forward with such energy and delight that Arthur was surprised into looking up again. The open throat of Bertie's white shirt did as much to scramble Arthur's brain as Bertie's wet, full lips did, until Bertie inhaled sharply and forced Arthur's eyes higher. His slight frown was troubled, like something had pulled all his earlier delight right out of him.

"My apologies, Arthur. I'm so sorry." He knelt down, and Arthur wasn't sure if he was kneeling or if he was going to sit down with him; he was just suddenly, overwhelmingly hot. Bertie's breath on him, unusually minty, didn't cool him down any. "You see, yesterday Zeru popped into town, and I don't see him nearly often enough, so I offered to show him around. Breakfast became lunch, lunch became dinner, and the whole visit ended up in a bar by the campus, and then I couldn't very well drive back in the condition I was in. He followed me back here this morning so I could give him a copy of one of my books he'd expressed interest in and then, well...."

Dragons could get drunk, Arthur noted absently, though the information wasn't surprising. Not nearly as surprising as learning that they could spend all day with a "friend" and forget how to use a phone.

Bertie leaned in closer and raised his voice when Arthur didn't respond to his explanation. His gaze was so intense that Arthur finally stared back at him. He knew he was frowning, but he didn't feel like suppressing it.

Bertie cleared his throat but continued on with an eager light in his eyes. "Anyway, he'd been to the Asturias region in Spain, and he had a tapestry I *had* to see. You should see it, too, Arthur. It has a xana and a dragon."

"A tapestry," Arthur repeated, nodding for the sake of agreeing. He didn't ask what a xana was, or even how it was spelled, and Bertie developed a line between his eyes that Arthur couldn't look at without feeling terrible. He pushed back and stood up, almost losing his balance as he stepped onto the fireplace stones. "Well then I shouldn't have worried."

He wiped his hands on his jeans and hurried away, going for the kitchen mostly because eating gave him an excuse to leave. "I should eat something."

The kitchen doors swung open behind him as Bertie followed. "Arthur, I didn't expect I'd be so long coming back, but he insisted on buying me breakfast this morning and...."

"I don't need to hear this," Arthur snapped and opened the fridge too late to hide his expression. He ducked behind it anyway. "I mean…" He sucked in a shaky breath and hoped Bertie wasn't smelling any of the jealousy that he was definitely feeling now. The anger about worrying all night was still there, but right now all he was thinking was that Bertie had sat down to breakfast with someone else, some old friend dragon with tapestries, and Arthur couldn't compete with that no matter how many books he cleaned. "You… you don't need to explain it to me."

But when he turned, shutting the fridge door too hard behind him, Bertie was staring at him with his mouth open and his tongue sliding, moist and pink, along his bottom lip.

"Shit," Arthur said out loud and really, really wished he could blame it on being sick or malnourished again. Shiny black pupils swallowed up everything but thin rings of pale brown as Bertie regarded him, and then his posture changed, shifting into something smart and compelling and so powerful that Arthur's knees went weak.

"Arthur, pet." Bertie was almost purring as he spoke, and Arthur tried his best not to shiver, but hearing himself called "pet" again burned him up inside in ways the fire never could. He should hate it. He didn't at all. Thinking about it, even now, made him half-hard. "Arthur." Despite the pleasure coming through loud and clear in his tone, Bertie was speaking slowly, carefully. "Arthur, are you jealous?"

It knocked the anger right out of him. Arthur might have been a potential thief, he knew that, but he wasn't any good at lying. There was no way he could answer that question.

Maybe he didn't need to, he thought faintly with an edge of hysteria, one more inhale and swipe of Bertie's tongue and he was done for anyway.

Arthur's stomach felt cold with nerves. He moved back instinctively, only processing *why* the moment his back bumped into the center island and Bertie stepped directly in front of him. He was still talking, blowing soft words at Arthur as if he had to be careful not to stoke any embers back into a raging fire. Arthur opened his mouth to defend himself without knowing what he would say, but then what Bertie was murmuring sank in.

"He's truly just an old friend, pet, and not my type even if I were his—which is female, I'll have you know."

"You don't need to explain." Arthur pushed up, looking up once quickly while he had the strength and then down to preserve what he could of his pride. His heart was racing, and his skin was still so hot that it felt tight. His entire body felt tight. Shaky. Restless.

He could hear the grin in Bertie's voice.

"But I want to." He was either inching closer or Arthur was. "I want to." Bertie's breathing was heavy, deep, and fast, like he couldn't get enough air, or enough air with the scent of Arthur in it. The sound was drowning out Arthur's heart, his own breath. It was like Bertie was lapping up the oxygen around him, consuming it. Arthur thought of fire again but couldn't move to run for cover. "Arthur," he was called back, as if his thoughts were all over his face. Arthur raised his eyes and thought that he must be dreaming again because now Bertie looked like he was dizzy and feverish too. "Even if that hadn't been the case, Arthur, I wouldn't have touched him."

Arthur pushed back against the island, but only to stay on his feet. When that didn't work he raised a hand and put it on Bertie's shoulder without thinking. Bertie's dress shirt was thin. Arthur unfurled his hand and felt the heat of skin just out of reach and thought of flesh that looked like ink and the scales that meant more magic than he could ever comprehend.

Maybe *this* was magic. He'd have no way of knowing, though he didn't think Bertie would ever stoop to this kind of spell. He wouldn't have to. He might be a dragon, but Arthur was here of his own free will. Arthur, who wasn't powerful and who wasn't magic and who definitely wasn't another dragon who was both of those things.

He frowned at the thought, because what Bertie had said didn't make any sense.

"Why not?" He blinked and raised his chin to aim his frown at Bertie, only to stop at the complete surprise in Bertie's expression. His eyes were wide and unfocused a second before they focused again, narrowing on Arthur as if he'd never laid eyes on him before.

Bertie stared at him, looking the most serious that Arthur had ever seen him, and then quirked a small smile.

"Because…." He was still breathing heavily as he seemed to grow so hot that he burned to the touch. Arthur nearly flinched when he raised his hand, gasping instead when Bertie seemed to change his mind about whatever he had been going to do and only let his palm graze Arthur's jaw. "Because I wouldn't hurt you for worlds." He sighed it, some epiphany lighting his eyes before he flashed another deliberate grin and took several steps back.

He coughed and moved toward the fridge, too, not looking back to see Arthur's lost shudder.

"Don't look so frightened, Arthur. You'd think I was going to devour you." It didn't have his usual flair, but Arthur scowled anyway out of habit because Bertie knew statements like that were alarming to humans and said them to be funny.

"I'm not scared." His chin was still up, but Bertie pulled out cream for tea he must be planning on making himself and didn't turn back to him. It was better that he didn't. Arthur was shaking weakly, cold without Bertie so close to him.

Whether or not he could smell it, Bertie didn't call him on the lie as he got out some tea.

"Perhaps I am, Arthur." Which didn't make sense either, because Bertie had nothing to fear from Arthur. Arthur was pretty sure Bertie only had to say his name and he would come running no matter how furious or jealous he might be. He certainly wasn't any sort of physical threat. Bertie couldn't think that.

But he moved when Arthur did, glancing over with too much warmth in his eyes for someone who was just making tea.

"I wasn't expecting it to be like this. I feel quite disgustingly weak. Grovelly—you will have to check to see if that word is correct, Arthur. I want… things… but I can't move without thinking, *would Arthur approve, would he smile?*"

"I don't understand." Arthur had never had trouble controlling his mouth before. Of course, he had the vague memories of Professor Gibson's patient expression as Arthur had asked yet another question in a long series of questions, but those questions were nothing to the things he kept blurting out in this house.

Bertie snorted and Arthur caught a whiff of smoke.

"I know." In the time it took Bertie to fill the kettle with water and put it on the stove, Arthur's heart hadn't slowed. Bertie seemed better though, almost calm as he peeped over his shoulder at Arthur. "Are you still angry with me?"

Arthur flattened his mouth and resisted remarking that Bertie must be recovering from his late night to offer him that fake meek look. He just sighed.

"No." He wasn't angry anymore. He was a lot of things at the moment—frustrated, horny, confused, hurt—but not angry.

"I'm glad." Bertie beamed at him for another second that became two, then three, before he tossed his head and glanced away. "Now." He moved as if he didn't know his way around his own kitchen, pausing before finally finding the right drawer to get a towel to dry his hands. "I'm going to shower and change." He paused again when he was finished. "You'll be here when I come back?"

Arthur nodded before he could speak because he kind of thought now that he'd do anything Bertie asked him to. He even kind of thought, or hoped, that there was something that Bertie wanted to ask him to do. But when Bertie only continued to wait, Arthur nodded again.

"Yes." He was aware that his tone was still defiant and angry, as if Bertie was the foolish one for asking, but Bertie didn't seem offended. He only snorted again before shooting Arthur one last look as he slid out the doors.

CHAPTER 8

THERE were scones and a china coffee set waiting for him on the table in the living room when he came into work the next few mornings. Arthur assumed Bertie had seen the note about instant coffee, the same way he assumed that the coffee was some sort of peace offering from a guilty dragon.

"I do forget things at times, you see," he explained to Arthur the day he'd come home late, after he showered and came back downstairs. Arthur hadn't fully recovered from that strange, tense moment in the kitchen, but he felt comfortable enough to raise an eyebrow at the statement, because after finding two novels' worth of notes scattered among Bertie's library, if there was one thing he knew, it was that Bertie "forgot things at times."

He *had* left a note. Arthur finally reminded him of that to stop the awkward explanations, though when he added that it had been too soaked to read, Bertie looked at him with such wide-eyed guilt and horror that Arthur sighed and realized he'd already forgiven him. It was no use being angry, not with Bertie already torturing himself.

Next to the scones was a note, because Bertie left him notes for everything now. Arthur couldn't decide if it was endearing or annoying that Bertie took the time to write him a note wishing him a good morning and letting him know he was in the study. He was going with endearing, but only because the scones were good, not because Bertie had addressed the note to "My darling Arthur" or had been thinking of him. That's what he told himself, because even if Bertie wasn't trying to put distance between them anymore, there was still something different about him now, and Arthur didn't want to upset anything else by obsessing over Bertie any more than he already did.

In any event, if he said anything about it, Bertie would only bat long eyelashes at him and say, "I will gladly give you coffee if you stay with me a little longer, Arthur," as though it was nothing. It was a lot like when Arthur finished up for the day and Bertie would catch him putting his laptop and some books in his backpack. Then it was "Oh, are you going now, Arthur? But it's so cold and dark out. Wouldn't you rather curl up on the couch with me before the fire?" As if he could read Arthur's mind and knew that each night Arthur was finding it harder and harder to leave.

Arthur looked back in the direction of the study, where he thought he could detect movement, and took an orange scone with his coffee before he set to work getting his laptop out and placing some books on the table. Bertie had requested them, and Arthur had needed to put a hold on them at the library, but they finally came in the day before.

He added a packet of herbs to that and then a new cell phone charger, because of course Bertie had lost his somewhere upstairs, or so he thought, but Arthur hadn't offered to go up there to look.

Arthur shrugged off his jacket as he finished his coffee and ate another scone with a quick glance around for any audience. Then he gave in and went to the kitchen to get a damp towel for the job he'd given himself today.

For the moment, he was done with books. There were more to be found upstairs, but he wasn't sure how to ask permission to go searching for them, and in the meantime, before he could figure out how to best put them away, he had to deal with the rest of the clutter from the bookshelves: all those dust-covered odds and ends.

He decided to simply wipe them down first and see what was valuable and deserved a proper cleaning, or a polish in the case of anything silver, and then see what actually belonged on display and what didn't. Knowing Bertie, there would be awards and statues or a solid gold umbrella stand all jumbled together.

He didn't think Bertie's former housekeeper quit because of the nudity. He'd bet she quit because of the mess in here. It would take someone very determined to keep these shelves spotless and in order. Even Bertie couldn't, and he loved his books. It would take someone who didn't forget things like dusting because something else had occurred to them.

Arthur smiled at the thought, a smile that he caught sight of in the shiny side of the toaster and quickly wiped from his face. All he needed was Bertie to see that and say something about it, probably something else about *dimples*.

Kate saw that same smile on his face last night, and her eyes almost popped out of her skull before she made a tiny sound and looked away. She eyed him for most of the rest of the night and flipped through the books he'd brought home to read.

"You shouldn't change yourself for a guy, Arthur," she warned him. She still seemed too young to be warning him about anything. But Arthur took her as seriously as he could. She'd been in high school when she met her asshole boyfriend, and confused and hurting. Arthur wasn't any of those things.

Not that Bertie was his boyfriend. Anyway, Arthur would never say "boyfriend" because it would never compare to "treasure" in an introduction.

"I'm not," Arthur answered her but followed her stare to the book on the Welsh language he'd been picking through. "The spellings are killing me." The explanation happened to be the truth—he'd wanted to get a better handle on the language before he typed up anything for Bertie. But the way she then pointed to the other book, a translated *Tales of the Dragon Kings*, said more than one of her sarcastic comebacks.

He put down the language guide and tried to put his feelings into words that wouldn't freak her out. He couldn't say she'd understand if she met Bertie, though he felt she would. Everyone had to see how fascinating he was, how amazing. It was unbelievable that his cell phone wasn't constantly ringing with people asking him out. Arthur was sure that if Bertie had chosen to teach he would have had grad students and TAs throwing themselves at him.

Arthur finally settled for extending one hand and looking directly back at his sister. His face felt hot, but that didn't matter, not between them with everything they'd been through.

"I just want to know more. I want to know everything," he whispered, because it was true; he wanted discover everything—about dragons, but also about this one dragon. His....

His boss, Arthur reminded himself sternly at the memory and crumpled up the towel as he headed into the main room and the collection of Bertie's tchotchkes.

He knelt in front of the pieces he'd left sheltered under an end table and pulled out one of the heavier ones. He wiped with his finger across the surface of the dust, looking for anything that the water on the towel might damage more than at the thing itself. He was going to need a good polish for the silver and some soft gloves and natural oils for any of the older wood items he found.

Arthur made another mental note to pick up what he needed either tonight or tomorrow and then froze and stared hard at what was in his hands and saw, really saw, what it was he was holding. After several minutes, he put it carefully back down, though it was still caked in dust, and picked up something else.

He flicked a dust bunny from one corner and pursed his lips to blow away the dust down one side. The color struck him first, what he could see of it, and then the intricacies of the carvings. He realized what it was and what it was made of, and his heart stopped as he almost dropped it.

Shock made him clumsy, and he didn't trust himself. Arthur got it back to the floor in one piece, something he was grateful for only distantly because his mind was racing. He peered at the other things he'd set aside to clean while he was focused on the books, and then glanced up toward the second floor and the treasure he hadn't let himself imagine in any kind of detail.

"… believe in eternity through the accumulation of beauty and knowledge…." That's what Bertie had said. Arthur looked over at the growing selection of antique books and thought about how just the other day he'd joked that he expected to find a stack of scrolls like in the ancient library at Alexandria, and how Bertie had given him a blank look and then a puzzled frown, almost as if he was surprised Arthur *hadn't* found a collection of scrolls in the kitchen alongside the first edition *Mastering the Art of French Cooking* or among all the back issues of *National Geographic* in the bathroom.

Arthur jumped to his feet at the thought, leaving the towel behind as he moved around the table and stalked past the kitchen to the downstairs bathroom. Once inside he ignored the magazines, shoving them aside until he found the heavy piece of stone he noticed in there the other day.

He pushed out a breath before he picked it up to set it on the sink, and then he watched his shaking fingers wipe away cobwebs, though he already knew what he'd see carved into it. It was what he'd seen before, he just hadn't been paying attention, hadn't thought it was real.

It was a depiction of a Dacian dragon, the weapon of war and intimidation used by the Dacian people before the Romans conquered them and took the symbol as their own. They had probably carved this stone. Romans, *ancient Romans*, had probably carved this stone. It was probably a piece of some destroyed monument. It was…. Arthur didn't know enough about stone to tell the age of the carvings just from looking at it, but it was old. More than antique. More than priceless. It *was* history.

He turned on his heel and stormed back into the main room, stopping to fall to his knees in front of the collection of what he'd thought were pretty, possibly expensive knickknacks. Things he'd been planning on wiping down with a *kitchen towel*.

The first was a trick dog piggy bank from the late 1880s. The second, the one he'd almost dropped, was a horse carved from chicken-blood jade, carved in a style Arthur was no expert on, but which looked Chinese and was smoothed and worn by time. A very long time. He was scared to touch the rest without gloves, but couldn't resist running a fingertip over a brooch showing a smiling wolf, shiny and heavy enough for him to assume it was real gold.

They had all been on the same shelf as two marbles and a painted, wooden top that, now that he thought about them, could have belonged to a child a few decades ago or a century ago.

He couldn't look at anything else yet. He might actually faint. Antiques and artifacts were collecting dust in Bertie's living room. Priceless pieces from history most likely forgotten about the way he forgot his notes. He could see the yellow globe Bertie liked to spin in his hands sometimes when he was thinking, and was suddenly certain that it had cost a fortune.

He twitched at the sound of padding footsteps behind him and the rattle of dishes as Bertie probably added his teacup to the coffee set next to Arthur's empty cup.

"Good morning, Arthur," he murmured in that pleasure-filled voice that made Arthur shiver even when he could barely see straight, he was so upset. "I thought I heard you."

"You're rich, oh my God, are you crazy?" Arthur demanded before turning around, clawing his way to his feet only to stay where he was and gesture at the room. He'd known Bertie had money, but he hadn't *known*. Not even at his most comfortable during his childhood had Arthur thought to own anything like that horse statue alone. It had probably been in Bertie's family for generations, and Bertie probably thought nothing of it. No wonder he left it on a shelf next to some pulp novels.

"This room isn't even remotely temperature controlled enough to preserve any of these things!" Arthur added, his voice cracking dryly. Bertie looked stuck to the spot, his eyes round, his jaw slack, his attention entirely on Arthur and the breakdown Arthur was sure he was having.

"There's a depiction of a *Dacian dragon* on that stone in your bathroom. Did the Romans carve that?" His voice kept rising. He might be slightly hysterical. But the bathroom was the last place he'd ever expected to find a piece of the ancient world.

"Really?" Bertie seemed taken aback, but not for the reasons Arthur thought. He made a face and glanced behind him. "How did that end up in the guest bathroom?" His tone of mild interest was not helping. Arthur huffed out a breath so hot he was surprised that *he* didn't have smoke coming from his nostrils, and Bertie shut his mouth.

Arthur couldn't break eye contact and Bertie didn't seem to want to, but after a few seconds he furrowed his brow and somehow the one tiny motion made the air crackle.

"Arthur." Arthur didn't know that tone, but he knew it was dangerous; his pulse said it was dangerous, that something in his attitude was unwelcome. Bertie was standing tensely still, frowning imperiously, like a king, like a dragon king, like Arthur was the human peasant foolish enough to question him.

Arthur couldn't see Bertie's teeth but he could see black nails and shimmering skin, and with every second his pulse was roaring louder and louder in his ears. He didn't have anything, not even a shield, not even the right to say what he was saying, but he scowled and heard himself talking anyway, his voice loud and rough and more than a match to Bertie's rumble.

"You told me I could clean," he said it plainly, meaning to be defensive and failing because if any room deserved to be cleaned, it was this one with these incredible things in it.

Bertie's head went back as if that wasn't what he'd been expecting to hear, and Arthur saw him draw in a breath and then relax a fraction as he exhaled.

"You were cleaning…," Bertie went on slowly, not asking, but easing his posture to put a hand on the table. He looked wary. Arthur couldn't tell why, but he pointed to the items at his feet anyway and then his voice went right back up.

"These are real, aren't they? You can't just leave them lying around," he jumped in before Bertie could get a word out. "They should be cleaned and displayed and safeguarded."

"Don't talk to me about money, Arthur." There was no "pet" or "darling", just his name, bitten out. But even the way those dark eyes narrowed couldn't make Arthur stop.

"Money?" Arthur asked in confusion then shook it off. "The only money should go into their care. They should be *revered.* These things *are* history. Do you even know what you have here?"

The barked laugh from Bertie startled him and almost made him fall back, but Arthur concentrated on Bertie and the relieved, huge grin on his face that shouldn't be there when Arthur was mad at him. Arthur hadn't said anything to calm Bertie down.

He itched with sweat he was only beginning to notice, nerves and fear leaving his clothes damp, but Bertie was languid again and shaking his head gently, as if Arthur was precious and anything he did now was more than fine with Bertie.

Arthur didn't want any scales tipped in his favor. He didn't want any scales. He wanted Bertie to take this seriously. But the man was waving a hand at him.

"Of course I do!" Bertie insisted with dignity, then peered behind Arthur. "What is that?" Arthur didn't turn to see what he was staring at, but it didn't matter, Bertie figured it out. "Oh yes, right, I remember. I haven't seen that in ages. Did I leave it downstairs? No matter."

"Is this your treasure?" Arthur's voice was shaking and he curled his hands into fists at his side. Bertie gave him another considering look and slow frown before shaking his head in a way that explained *nothing.* Arthur's irritation must have been on his face. Bertie stopped to lick the corner of his mouth before narrowing his eyes again.

"It's mine, yes," he answered at last, and Arthur realized he was clenching his hands, too, but Bertie was doing it over and over again, as if he wanted to grab the items in question and was barely restraining himself.

"But is it your treasure?" Nobody should treat their treasure like this. Then it wouldn't be special, it would just be *stuff.*

Bertie opened and shut his mouth and then spread his hands wide.

"My treasure?" His voice rumbled and then he moved, coming forward with a determined expression on his face but stopping abruptly just in front of Arthur.

That close, Arthur could feel all that heat and uncertainty in front of him, the silent stare, the hunger at the talk of treasure, and he dropped his gaze before he got caught staring.

"Is it all like that?" He imagined rooms full of paintings left exposed to the elements and chipped marble and shuddered. "Because that... that stone piece alone should be in a museum. You can't deny the world that."

"The world?" Hoarse disbelief brought Arthur's eyes back up. Bertie's jaw was stuck out in a petulant, stubborn expression. He crossed his arms. "I don't like to share, Arthur. Not what's mine."

Arthur's heart kicked hard against his ribs as his face flushed with heat.

"Dragons don't or you don't?" Arthur had never been this demanding before or so out of breath. Arthur felt like he'd been riding uphill for miles and miles. He got a huff for an answer, a huff he could only describe as pissy. "Well you should," he insisted over the rush in his ears and his spinning thoughts and the tiny sparks bolting down his spine. "Think of who it would benefit. Think of what other historians might learn by examining a collection of items, gathered by dragons over the centuries, that have never been seen before." Bertie had looked at other collections for his books, been to museums, seen other treasures. He ought to understand.

"No, Arthur. It's mine."

"I didn't think a dragon of your blood line would be so pouty." Arthur didn't even know where the words came from, but instead of roasting him or tearing his head off, Bertie gasped in outrage and flung his hands wide.

"It's *mine*." He said it like the word alone explained everything. "I can't have strangers around it. They'll touch it. They'll try to steal it." He fixed his eyes right on Arthur. "I don't want to lose it to greedy, stupid people who won't know what it is they have."

He probably didn't mean *people* to mean *human*, but Arthur flinched just the same. He lifted his chin in the next second, because despite his talk, Bertie wasn't caring for what he had either.

"You aren't even looking at them. You forgot they were in here!"

"But they're *mine*." It was nearly a growl. Arthur knew he should back off, but if he didn't explain it now he was never going to.

His armpits itched with more sweat. He could feel Bertie's frustration like a shockwave rippling through the air.

"Collecting isn't the same as preserving or sharing. You should know that." Arthur was pretty certain Bertie did know it. Some of the artwork in the books Arthur had been reading was from dragon collections. Other dragons had learned to trust. Bertie could too, even if it was only other historians.

But Bertie wrinkled his nose and flicked his gaze away as if Arthur was being slow. Arthur's mouth tightened.

"What's the big deal? If it's all cleaned and catalogued and protected, if people ask to see them, they couldn't steal without you knowing. That stone in your bathroom alone—"

"Is mine," Bertie finished for him. No one so hot should ever sound so cool. Arthur snapped, stepping in closer until Bertie looked back at him

"Aren't you proud of them?" He couldn't understand it and didn't try, not even when Bertie suddenly wet his lips uncertainly and then echoed him.

"Proud?" He was whispering. "Arthur, you have no idea how much, even at this moment."

Arthur looked away from all that warmth and tried to keep his focus.

"Then why don't you take better care of them? Do you know what the heat and moisture in the air in here does to the paper and wood alone?"

"Arthur!" It came out as a shocked shout before Bertie lowered his voice. His hands came up in a gesture that was almost pleading, brushing Arthur's sleeves. "But who out there will care for it as I do? Who will love it?"

Arthur almost said it. Arthur opened his mouth to insist that he could, that he would, and stopped himself just in time. He didn't even have his degree. Who was he to make that offer? He didn't have the experience, and if Bertie's treasure was as amazing as Bertie's tone said it was, then he should have the best.

He stepped back, moving around the jade horse and walking to the fireplace. There wasn't any fire so he moved on, going for coffee that was probably cold now.

"Sorry." Now that he thought about it, away from all that smoke and fire, he couldn't believe the things he said. "I won't mention it again." He reached for a coffee cup and saw the dust on his fingers. "I'll just go wash up," he offered without looking up and turned to go back to the bathroom.

He had to lower the heavy carved stone back to the floor to use the sink, but he left it on a pile of magazines to protect it the best he could and then splashed cold water on his face without caring about the mess he was making. He dried himself with toilet paper, because laundry wasn't high on Bertie's list of things to remember either, especially not the towels from the guest bathroom.

Arthur thought about doing it for him and then thought of his last offer and worked his jaw before opening the door and stepping back into the hallway.

He stopped short at the body in front of him and jerked his head up at the scent of herbs.

"Arthur." A low, cultured rumble tenderly saying his name…. Arthur shut his eyes but Bertie didn't stop. "Arthur, I'm sorry."

"No." Arthur shook his head and made himself look at Bertie again, at those incredible eyes. Bertie was a dragon, Arthur reminded himself. He was different. He was some kind of aristocrat, though he hadn't come out and said it directly. He was a doctor and a historian and brilliant. Arthur should remember all of that. "I didn't mean to… infringe on your heritage or anything. I just…."

"You love history, Arthur, and you love preserving it," Bertie interrupted him with a serious frown. He leaned in, blocking what little light from the main room made it down the small hallway, and Arthur put a hand up to Bertie's shoulder just as he'd done before.

He put his other hand to the wall and swallowed, because he couldn't exactly deny anything Bertie was saying. Bertie studied him for a moment and then glanced down at the floor. He was unusually hesitant. "If I… if I allowed that, would you stay?"

Arthur blinked, not sure what he was hearing. He stared at the feathery black fringe of Bertie's hair as it fell forward into his face and didn't fight his scowl. He hadn't known he'd been going anywhere.

"You can't bribe me to stay," he remarked after taking a breath, in voice so level he surprised himself. Bertie's head came up, but Arthur looked away this time, down the hallway. "If you don't want your treasure available to the public then you shouldn't do it." *Just to make me happy*, he thought, but it seemed too unbelievable to say out loud.

He turned back, but in the low light he couldn't make out any of the brown in Bertie's eyes. He couldn't tell if he was being studied or what Bertie might be thinking. All he *could* tell was that Bertie's mouth was open, and that his breathing was fast and shallow.

The sound was almost too much. In the dark like this, it was worse than waking up from one of his dreams. He was so much hotter, and so was Bertie, burning up through the cloth that was keeping Arthur from really touching him.

"I don't want to lose it." Bertie whispered it like a confession, drawing the oxygen out of Arthur's chest. Arthur couldn't breathe but he didn't care. "You don't know what it is to hold it."

Arthur supposed he didn't. He'd never held a treasure, or anything like a treasure, unless he counted the antique books in the university's collection. But touching Bertie's books, touching that stone, that horse, had all felt the same once he realized what they were. Awe and electricity traveling up his arms, leaving him almost giddy, then weak.

"It's wonderful. It was…" Arthur couldn't think of the word. "I'm grateful I even got to touch them for a second. That they were…" not his, but something like it. "The weight of them. They were… precious."

He blushed the moment the word came out of his mouth. He was spared by the dark, he thought, but then again maybe not, not with Bertie's wet breath against his cheek.

"Yes. Yes, Arthur. You do understand. You felt it too."

"Felt it?" Arthur was close to falling forward, adrenaline and desire leaving him dizzy. He thought he might be leaning on Bertie already, but if he was, Bertie wasn't pushing him away. He was only speaking more softly.

"So you see I will do anything to keep it, Arthur." It was practically in Arthur's ear, and Arthur couldn't control his shiver of reaction. He wasn't sure what to say to that, and he couldn't think with Bertie so close. He thought maybe Bertie was still upset at the idea of possibly losing his treasure, and slid his hand up over Bertie's shoulder when he couldn't find the words to apologize again.

His thumb brushed the skin of Bertie's neck. This time Arthur couldn't tell who shivered, but he pulled his hand back, kept it safely on fabric and not on skin.

"Okay," Arthur agreed blindly, then tracked back to their argument and thoughts that weren't about the texture of that skin, the burn of it, the rasp in his voice as he tried to answer. "But you should think about it," he suggested, because he had to. "Someday. Maybe only show some of the pieces to—" He turned his head. "—to people you trust."

"You ask difficult things of me, Arthur." Bertie growled, but he didn't sound angry, and he didn't appear angry when Arthur looked back at him.

"I do?" Arthur paused. Bertie had already been too nice to him. "I didn't mean to. I wouldn't ask anything of you."

"I know, pearl." Bertie sighed again, regretfully this time, before he backed away and let Arthur's hand slide away from him. "I know." He left Arthur in the cold and dark and then surprised him by turning back. "You...." Arthur wanted to say Bertie was being shy, but that seemed impossible. But Bertie glanced down again before asking his question. "You loved them, didn't you?"

"They were amazing." Arthur didn't try to keep the awe from his voice. "But I don't need to see more," he added quickly. Bertie instantly tossed his head, giving Arthur the impression of him shaking his mane, like a dancer in a New Year's parade.

"Arthur." In much the same way, he got the impression he was being teased now. "You have only to ask me."

"Now *that* sounds like a trick," Arthur answered back quietly, trying to make it a joke. "I'll probably find singed suits of armor from foolish knights, and I don't want to end up a bunch of bones alongside them."

There was a moment of silence before Bertie let out a small, unsteady laugh and then continued to put distance between them.

"I assure you I'd hate myself with every bite." He stepped into the main room, his body lit from above and tense, and then he walked on, almost out of sight. Arthur followed after him, putting his hands to his face to judge how red it was.

Bertie was standing still when he got there, holding the wolf brooch in one hand and staring hard at it. Arthur cleared his throat to ask the question he had to ask.

"Should I keep going?" It didn't sound like he'd been fired, but maybe it was something else he didn't understand. Bertie twisted to give him a sideways look and actually rolled his eyes.

"Love, asking you not to organize would be like asking a siren not to sing."

Arthur wasn't entirely sure that was a compliment. Before he could think of a response, Bertie held up the brooch. "Lovely isn't it? I know a were who would love to examine it." He huffed and then set his shoulders. "I will think on what you've said, Arthur."

"You don't have to."

He got another dramatic and obvious eye roll.

"I know." Bertie put it down on the end table and fixed Arthur with another long, searching look. "In any event, they won't do anyone a bit of good covered in dust and lost in this room, will they?"

Arthur took a very noisy breath and met Bertie's gaze.

"I'll just…" Arthur's head was swimming and he was smiling, he knew from how transfixed Bertie seemed. "I'll just make you some more tea first," Arthur got out, and the bright, happy grin he glimpsed on Bertie's face before he turned around to dash into the kitchen was going to keep him up late tonight and every other night for a very long time.

CHAPTER 9

"WHAT do you mean 'how can I forget what he is'?" Arthur unlocked the door and made a face, though Kate wouldn't see it over the phone. Kate was worrying on the other end, once again under the impression that Arthur was the one who would need her advice about anything man-related. "I know what he is, he's a historian," he hissed as he pushed his way inside, lowering his voice so at least Bertie wouldn't know he was the topic of conversation.

He had no idea what brought on Kate's surge of protectiveness but figured she must have found one of the books on dragons. Probably the one with the lithograph of a mythical wyvern surrounded by very human bones.

"He's more than that, Arthur." Kate sighed as if she thought Arthur was dense. Arthur knew what she meant and chose to ignore it as he put down his backpack and closed the door.

"My boss?" Arthur didn't exactly play innocent, but Kate snapped at him anyway.

"A Being and a dragon, Arthur. They're different and they have different rules and you don't even know the human ones."

"Beings aren't that different," Arthur whispered furiously, glancing up and around to make sure that despite the heat in the house, he was alone. He considered telling his sister that he'd been with a Being before—not that he was *with* Bertie now—but she'd probably say he had a type and his type was Beings, and Arthur really couldn't think of an answer, except to point out that Bertie would probably find this funny and that he didn't like *all* Beings because he hadn't liked Zeru at all.

"Just be careful." Kate wasn't backing off. It could have been her anxiety, or it could have been because she hadn't seen Arthur much in the past few days and it was making her worry more. But she should know that he'd been working. He had a busy Friday and Saturday night delivering food and spent Sunday at the library tracking down books and the e-mail address of a particular author Bertie wanted to contact.

Arthur stopped at the thought, knowing exactly how it felt to worry like that, and smiled into the phone so she would hear it in his voice.

"I love you too."

Kate made a startled noise at Arthur's unusually honest statement, but Arthur didn't hear if she said anything back. She probably didn't: things like that tended to freak her out. She described it once as the sudden return of emotions she'd been too numb to feel when she was drunk, but Arthur was only distantly thinking about that when he heard the sharp cough from upstairs and looked up to see Bertie frowning down at him from the landing.

"Do go on, Arthur, don't mind me." Bertie's tone said he very much would mind. He sounded absolutely *forlorn*. It was especially strange when he was scowling so fiercely that Arthur was surprised that the room wasn't bursting into flame. Arthur hadn't done anything wrong, but he went motionless anyway, only moving again when Kate spoke in his ear.

"Okay, I admit he sounds hot."

"You have no idea," Arthur told her seriously, if faintly, because he didn't think Bertie had ever looked at him in quite this way before, disappointed and saddened and hungry enough to leap over the railing to grab Arthur that very second.

Arthur straightened, not sure what else to do, with sweat prickling under his arms.

"That's not the fairy, is it?" Bertie turned to come down the stairs, leaving one hand on the railing as he did in a way that seemed sophisticated and ridiculous at the same time. He must watch soap operas in secret too.

Arthur let out a small breath because Bertie wasn't any less upset than he'd been a minute ago; he was just pretending that he was. Arthur met his gaze the moment Bertie was downstairs with him and thought about how it would be nice if that melting stare meant Bertie was jealous.

"What fairy?" Kate was still on the phone. Arthur almost hung up on her but controlled the impulse in time.

"I'll talk to you later, Kate," he said instead and *then* hung up on her before she could add anything.

"Kate?" Bertie stopped for a second's thought before his frown faded away and he swept forward. Arthur had the fleeting thought Bertie was going to grab him again, or at least hug him, but he stopped again before Arthur had to think of what he'd do if he did. "Your sister? You didn't need to hang up on her on my account, Arthur."

"I know." Arthur was only just starting realize that he hadn't been breathing normally. He sucked in air, because he had a question to ask. If Bertie hadn't been jealous, he'd been doing a good impression of it and that was almost unbelievable. "But, um…."

"Is she well?" The anger, if it had been anger, was completely gone from Bertie's expression and voice now. He was just softly rumbling concern far too close to Arthur's space. "You two are close, aren't you? I could hear it."

"We are. We kind of had to be." Since he hadn't meant to say that, Arthur looked away. He put his phone in his pocket and then went back to his bag to get his laptop out. "I mean, she's fine. She was actually worried about me." He realized what he'd been about to say and cleared his throat. "She worries a lot these days. That's all."

"And you worry about her." Bertie didn't make it a question and Arthur turned to glance at him.

"She's had some problems, mostly with alcohol," he admitted carefully, watching Bertie's expression go thoughtful before he went around the table to sit on the sofa. He was studying Arthur with that same curious look he got for any story. For a second, Arthur wondered if that was all it was, and then Bertie exhaled.

"The poor thing. And you, too, because you took care of her. Don't deny it, Arthur."

"I wouldn't." Arthur blinked and lifted his chin. He wasn't ashamed of anything. "But it wasn't so bad." Bertie made a small sound of protest, so Arthur shrugged and fussed over his laptop as he brought it to the table. "So I skipped a few meals. If you saw how she's improving, you'd see it was worth it."

When he dared a glance up, he got a doubtful stare complete with pursed lips, but then Bertie leaned forward.

"I should like to meet her, Arthur." He was so warm Arthur was almost sure he meant it, but he knew his frown was still in place. "If you would ever allow it." There was something so careful in his words that Arthur looked down at himself. His hands were in fists at his sides, as tense as his shoulders.

He opened his mouth, shocked to realize how protective he still felt about Kate, and forced his hands to relax. Not that he was any kind of threat to a dragon, but he felt the need to apologize anyway. Bertie waved at him when he tried.

"You should never apologize for protecting what you love, Arthur." Bertie's approval washed over him. Arthur put his head down and took a moment before peeking in Bertie's direction. He was sitting quietly, looking for all the world as if he had nothing better to do than sit and listen to Arthur talk about his sister. As if Arthur was going to talk about his sister with him.

He didn't know what Bertie would say about Kate's history, but he could guess now that he'd read some of Bertie's books, where the sympathy he seemed to feel for everyone always came shining through. Maybe it was his delicate tone or the careful way he circled ever deeper, down toward the truth, as if the whole story had to be told, no matter how unflattering or ugly.

Arthur bit the inside of his cheek as he debated and then tossed his head and gave in because he wanted to know what Bertie would say.

"I, uh, haven't done anything like that since my sister's ex showed up at our door a year ago," he confessed after a moment, going on when Bertie held his breath. "He was abusive and had, well, she had—has—a drinking problem too, but his was worse. He was the reason she even started. She doesn't like it when I say that. Don't tell her I did."

"Of course not," Bertie promised solemnly. Arthur shivered but looked over again.

"He hit her a few times that she told me about. She wanted out by then. She *was* out, living with me and going to meetings, and she didn't want to see him and he didn't want to leave." He rubbed his cheek. "So I hit him. Punched him, really."

He'd never punched anyone before. He hadn't even fought anyone since elementary school, and that had been play fighting. He was just grateful that it had scared Ricky off and he hadn't broken any of his fingers. That punch had hurt for all that it also felt so satisfying and right.

"I knew it." Bertie sat back and blew a smoke ring into the air though he didn't have a cigarette. "My warrior." He looked back at Arthur and let his pleased expression fade somewhat. "Is she better now?"

"She is. She's been looking for work, which hasn't been easy for her. She barely made it through high school," Arthur elaborated when Bertie looked confused. "That was when, well, when my parents died. I was in school and I wasn't there for her enough."

He hadn't anticipated having this conversation ever, much less early in the morning without any food or caffeine to bolster him. Bertie exhaled, without a ring of smoke this time.

"Sometimes the lost have to find their own way home." He spoke as delicately as he wrote. "And I imagine you were also lost at the time."

Arthur had been younger, living at the university, far from home and Kate, worrying about finals and his sex life when he got the phone call.

"Arthur," Bertie gently called him back from the memory. "Was there no one else to help you? Friends, family?"

"I…." Arthur worked his jaw, but he still had to clear his throat again before he could talk. "People offered. They always offer. Most of them just"—Arthur shrugged—"didn't really mean it. They had their own problems. I—you shouldn't expect them to give up a lot for you, and anyway, work gave me something to focus on." Something that wasn't how his parents weren't *there* anymore. His voice caught on the last few words, and Arthur quickly scowled down at his laptop.

"You mustn't be too hard on them." Bertie seemed to be picking his words carefully. Arthur glanced up but only for a moment.

"I know. Being or human, it's a lot to ask. I don't blame them."

"Oh, Arthur." It was lighter than a feather and it made Arthur swallow. He could tell Bertie was going to offer to help and didn't look up when he did. "I assure you I mean it when I ask if there's anything I can do."

"You already do enough," Arthur managed, thinking that he ought to offer to make tea and leave the room to end this conversation. "More than enough." He tried a smile to help disguise the force of emotion in his words, but he didn't think he was fooling anyone.

"Hmm." Bertie wasn't indicating that he wanted tea. He wasn't doing anything but watching Arthur. "Is Kate the reason you leave at night?"

Arthur's mouth fell open. Maybe he just hadn't been expecting that question, but he couldn't think how he was supposed to answer it. In response to the vague shock Arthur was certain was all over his face, Bertie let out a little roar and shook his head. "It's silly and dangerous for you to ride home in the dark and the rain when you're only returning here in the morning."

It didn't make Arthur feel any better to know that Bertie was honestly asking him to spend the night for his own health and safety. It should have, but it didn't. He raised his head.

"I can't ask that of you. You already feed me and overpay me."

"Perhaps I'm just fattening you up." Bertie attempted a leer but when Arthur kept his expression serious he sighed and got serious too. "Arthur." He lifted one hand toward Arthur only to drop it a second later. "Arthur, you ought to ask. I am sure there are many out there dying to be kind to you, many who would have been kind to you when your parents died, if they had known how." His rumble got lower as he went on. "I know you're stubborn and determined and everything Gibson warned me about...."

Arthur gave a start, because he couldn't imagine what Professor Gibson would have had to warn anyone about him, but despite how Bertie's eyes wouldn't leave him, Bertie didn't stop to explain.

"But you *should* ask someone for help." For the first time in several tense minutes, Bertie finally glanced away. "I'd prefer it be me, of course, but it doesn't need to be."

Arthur kept his gaze on the side of Bertie's face, noticing the straight line of his nose again as if he hadn't already memorized his facial features. Bertie looked like he always did, rough with stubble, pale and dark at the same time, powerful even with the full force of his personality aimed at the fireplace instead of at Arthur.

The clothes he was wearing looked thrown on and probably had been, but they still probably cost more than all of Arthur's clothes combined. Bertie had a ton of money and treasure somewhere. Maybe he meant it when he said feeding Arthur was nothing; it probably was to him, but Arthur wished it wasn't. It was a stupid thought, wanting someone to give up more for him when they already gave him more than so many others, but he couldn't help wishing for it for a moment.

"Really?" He didn't know his own voice, it was so quiet. Bertie looked back at him.

"Very much. I can't tell you how much. Damn this lizard brain of mine."

Arthur didn't think Bertie was joking; there was no trace of the Cheshire cat grin. He frowned.

"I don't know why you treat me like this," he pushed out, since he was obviously dreaming this conversation. "I'm not anything special. I'm just an assistant. I'm years away from ever running a library or a collection, if that's ever even possible. And when I came here I—" He closed his mouth as his eyes went to the shining scales just beneath the surface of Bertie's skin. "I have no money." He stated the obvious instead of confessing the truth. "I have no achievements."

He couldn't tell if the noise Bertie made was a laugh or something rude and disbelieving.

"Achievements, Arthur? I am reasonably certain that even if you could pull a sword from a stone, you wouldn't want to. It's remarkable, really. It's the reason people like you are chosen to lead."

Arthur didn't move because he couldn't, as his mind was stuck trying to understand that remark, but that just made Bertie sigh. "At the risk of sounding like a fairy, you, my darling boy, are quite shiny." Bertie closed his eyes and let his mouth fall open. When he licked the air, he let out a sound that was almost obscene.

Arthur shifted and Bertie's eyes opened back up.

"More than that, I am not the kind to sit back and watch another suffer, even humans who seem to enjoy it at times."

"Hey," Arthur protested weakly, but it was a welcome distraction. He put his hands up to his warm face and then jerked them back down when he realized what he was doing. "The moment I learn more about dragons…." He trailed off deliberately, expecting a comeback from an offended dragon and unsurprised when he got one.

"Do you want to learn more now?" He had no idea why Bertie kept waiting for Arthur to ask, when he was only too happy to lecture about other things freely and without asking, but the brightening of his expression helped Arthur relax a little bit more. He nodded.

"I still can't see exactly where your book is going. I know it's about a family group that no longer exists...."

"Or so it seems, Arthur. So it seems. There is quite a bit of evidence to the contrary. Children born after the Norman conquest that had unusual abilities. A lingering reputation for magic and mysticism in those mountains, and an unusually high number of children accused of being changelings despite how the fairies have long denied that they ever snatched a single child. If you look a few centuries later, there start to be reports of miners so good they can see in the mines without a lantern."

He was implying that those human children had had some Being blood, and not just a little, but enough to give them powers that went beyond the usual skill with magic that accompanied human and Being children.

"Can you see in the dark?" Arthur interrupted, coming closer until he could sit down on the opposite end of the couch.

"No," Bertie tutted but carried on smoothly, "but I can light my own way."

"What happened to them? The children?" Arthur thought of his laptop but didn't turn to get it. He wasn't going to forget, and he didn't want to miss anything.

"Burned, I imagine," Bertie snorted. "They would have been burned as witches or shunned as outcasts or sent away, often to America to be the Colonies' problem. The fey weren't supposed to exist in the New World. But think, Arthur, a century later and they might have ended up in a sideshow or a hospital. A century after that and they might have been recognized for what they were. Sometimes I think Beings should never have taken to the shadows."

He didn't say what a tragedy it was, but it was in his face, in the slow gesture he made at Arthur with his hand out and his palm up, as though he wanted Arthur to fix it. Arthur realized that he was frowning and shaking minutely with a very real fury, because he *wanted* to fix it and couldn't.

He swallowed and moved on, because Bertie would see that on his face, and whatever Bertie thought, Arthur wasn't any kind of warrior. "Is that what it's about?" He was glad he hadn't read any pieces about that yet. It was going to upset him even more. It might even be why Bertie had been putting off finishing certain chapters.

"In a way. You see… I think they still exist, Arthur." Bertie jumped to his feet with sudden burning, restless energy. "In those children. Through them. Other groups of the same time start telling stories of besting the dragons—and of the Vikings trying to conquer them for that matter, but also dragons. But not this culture. This culture, as several groups did elsewhere in the world, became the People *of* the Dragon. The people of the *red* dragon. They embraced their dragons, and not only for their power. They didn't just revere them, they implied descent from dragons and worship of them in the very name they gave themselves. They loved their red dragons, and I can only think of one good reason why."

"A big, over-the-top gesture?" Arthur guessed, though it wasn't a totally blind guess. Bertie spun back around.

"Exactly. I knew you'd get it."

Bertie had hinted about those gestures before, but Arthur still didn't completely understand what he meant. But he held still as Bertie slid back over to get himself a cigarette and then exhaled a small stream of fire so the end of the cigarette caught. He took a small puff from the other end in the next second and only then looked up to see Arthur staring at him.

Bertie looked apologetic. "In my human form, that's close to the best I can do," he explained, as if the small size of the fire was why Arthur had been startled. The precision in the little jet of flame was impressive. Arthur had to wait a second for his heart rate to slow back down and then absently revised his mental list of dragon facts to add *can definitely breathe fire.*

"Back to the red dragons?" he croaked. It wasn't the herbs making him dizzy anymore. Bertie began to walk as he continued his lecture.

"I can only speak for myself, of course, but I've talked to others of my kind all over the world. If we have one weakness, it's our *treasure*." The word itself shook with meaning. The smoke seemed to get heavier. Arthur shivered where Bertie couldn't see.

"Is this about your possessiveness?" His voice was low and dry, but Bertie didn't seem to notice that either.

"It's not greed." He shook his head and made a sad, disappointed noise. "Not like you mean it."

Arthur tried to keep up, but if Bertie did that fire trick again while Arthur was standing up, he was probably going to fall to his knees and ask him to do it in his real form. He had no doubt it would be terrifying and exhilarating at the same time.

"I didn't say that," he protested slowly, but Bertie still wasn't looking at him.

"Cold blood doesn't mean without feeling. Dragons actually fall in love quite intensely." He was leaning over the fireplace with one hand on the mantle. Arthur was hypnotized. "We fall in love with a passion and reverence to match any human. It is another reason we are often discussed in tandem with weres. Weres mate, and it's a quick, instinctive process. We don't, not in that way, but our attachments are just as deep." He turned abruptly, with no warning at all, and the best Arthur could do was blink and sit up. "There is nothing, you see, that we would not give to our beloved once they are discovered."

Those eyes were fixing him to the spot. Arthur wet his lips.

"So you're saying they lost their treasure? They just… gave it away to someone?" He put a hand to his chest then wasn't sure why and dropped it to his leg, only to suddenly become aware of how hard his blood was pounding. "That's surprising, even as a romantic gesture." He stumbled over his words when Bertie's tongue made an appearance, darting out to the corner of his mouth. Arthur did his best to think clearly. "The stories always said it was hard for dragons to let anything go. And that's a sacrifice anyone would hesitate to make."

Bertie gave him a long, sharp look before taking an equally long drag from his cigarette and then exhaling to let the smoke circle Arthur. Arthur remembered the drawing of a tiny human wrapped up in the coils of an attentive serpent.

"Not exactly." Bertie's gaze was heavy. "I'm saying that humans by far outnumber dragons, and unlike weres, we possess considerable magic. There is magic in my fingernails, in my blood, in my every so-called golden scale."

Arthur bit back a noise but Bertie's stare didn't waver.

"Magic enough to make us a threat to some ancient governments or to make us worth more to many dead than alive, to fools who don't understand the greater magic is in what we give freely. Magic enough to make children possible, as it is for fairies, in addition to our changed physiology when we're… like this. What I think, Arthur my pearl, is that those red dragons took the beliefs of our culture to heart and intermingled with their humans, the humans who understood them, who loved them in return, until the only parts of them living on are in the genetic code of their descendants and the names of villages, even of the people themselves."

Bertie took another pull from his cigarette and Arthur took the opportunity to look away into the fire. It didn't slow Bertie down. "There isn't much difference between your genetic code for example, Arthur, and that of your ancestors. In a very basic way, they are still with us. It's very romantic."

"It could have been for survival," Arthur commented to the flames, in a faint but reasonable voice. He sensed that Bertie was going to give him another lecture on how unromantic he was, and he let his body slide down on the couch cushions. Arthur wasn't going to argue what was romantic and what wasn't. "But why would they do that? I don't understand. Other dragons didn't, or not to that point of extinction."

"In my notes—" The amusement in Bertie's voice was very close. Arthur turned just as Bertie insinuated himself onto the seat next to him. "—I remark that they were living much closer to humans than many other groups. In addition, throughout this time, there were many outside attacks and invaders. Dragons are long-sighted; they knew changes would come, yet they chose to stay. Only one thing would make them. They wanted to ensure their treasure… their humans… would live on."

"But wouldn't the invaders take their treasure?" Why else would they even go there, except to take everything the land and the people and the dragons had to offer? Someone should have stopped them.

"Arthur." Bertie's rare, gentle smile flashed across his face, silencing Arthur before he could say anything else foolish. But it was a brief smile, and then Bertie's shoulders fell. "You still don't understand." He paused and then wrinkled his nose. Arthur almost lifted his chin at the insult, but whenever Bertie was hesitant like this, Arthur found himself leaning closer instead, hoping for more information, and this time was no exception.

Bertie straightened, getting to his feet and looking down at Arthur without a trace of a smile.

"Would you like to see something, Arthur?" he asked coolly as gray clouds filled the space between them. "It might help."

He looked like a king, and though he phrased it as a request, Arthur wasn't sure it was; the tilt of Bertie's chin was regal, making his words formal. Arthur glanced away from the steady stare and then back when it didn't leave him.

"I'm not afraid," he insisted, because Bertie was talking about his treasure, he had to be, and that was serious, "but…."

"You see?" Bertie's smile returned and Arthur could move again. He wanted to reach up, take the hand Bertie offered him. "Anyone else would know I meant gold and jewels and the like and would be leaping from their seat to get a closer look, but not you, Arthur. Not you."

Bertie's palm was dry though his hand was hot. Arthur felt it close around his and then he was on his feet and following after an impatient, anxious dragon. He kept his eyes on their hands because he wasn't sure where else to look, at least not until they were up the stairs and he was somewhere he hadn't been before.

He looked around as they moved down a dark hallway and noticed stacks of books on the floor and a few dishes, but then returned his attention to Bertie, who kept turning to look back at him with a question in his dark eyes. They passed a few doors that Arthur doubted had ever been locked, but he barely glanced over and then forgot all about them when Bertie stopped at the end of the short hallway and pushed the last door open.

It wasn't locked either, Arthur noted, and inhaled with a loud gasp when Bertie let go of his hand and stepped aside so he could enter the room on his own.

It was a bedroom, Bertie's bedroom. Arthur recognized that much from the large, custom-made bed. It was of a cherry-colored dark wood and low to the floor, surrounded by the kind of heavy velvet curtains that people in past eras had used to keep warm in cold castles of stone. The curtains had been pushed aside to reveal a multitude of pillows spread out over the bed, and the wall beyond the bed where an antique, full-length looking glass was resting by a chest of drawers of the same dark wood.

Arthur took in all of that between one blink and the next, and then he turned his head to look over the rest of the room, what was filling up the rest of the room.

It was impossible to see it all in one glance or even two. He stared until his eyes were burning and then stared some more. Bertie turned on the light, but he didn't need to. Everything was so bright that it was blinding with it on. Even the reflection in the mirror was just another light among so many.

"This is...." Arthur couldn't finish, and though he lifted his chin when he felt Bertie move behind him, he couldn't quite tear his eyes from the treasure piled high in front of him. It was a scene from the Arabian Nights, or exactly what anyone would think of if asked to describe a dragon's hoard. He could see coins of many sizes and metals from countless regions, each one probably just as valuable for its historical significance as it was for the gold or silver or bronze it was made of. There were some precious stones cut and set into jewelry—tiaras, crowns—and others with raw, jagged edges, as if they'd been torn directly from the walls of a mountain cave.

He counted seven swords before he stopped counting, and one suit of armor without even a hint that black smoke had ever touched it. Rolled up rugs, bolts of fabric, busts, and books were just more things to stare at, to try to calculate their value, their age, their significance. There *were* scrolls, obviously fragile even from a distance and set atop the stool beneath a large harp. There was another crown dangling from the top of the harp.

Arthur swallowed and then slowly turned to find Bertie. He found his gaze instead, hot on him in the reflection from that antique mirror, watching Arthur react to the sight of his treasure.

If this was even all of it, Arthur thought, just slightly hysterically, like he'd been to find similar items collecting dust downstairs. He wondered if there was a basement somewhere filled with heavy gold, and swallowed again.

"Why would you show me…? It's incredible, Bertie, incredible…. No, I mean, look at all of this." He stopped and forced himself to breathe and then say it again. "Why would you show me this?"

What had Kate said about the treasure when he told her he'd be working for a dragon? She made a joke about stealing it, because that was what most people thought of. Most people would have come into this house looking for this. They would have leapt to see it, just like Bertie had said. It hadn't even occurred to Arthur. He'd been focused on the chance of finding a discarded scale.

He looked into those eyes, intensely black even at a distance and mirrored in glass.

"I know I said this before, but others need to see this." Now that he had found his voice again, there was no stopping him. "The historical value alone"—he gestured blankly—"is incalculable."

He would have held his breath if he could have, to wait for that raging stillness that meant earthquakes or Bertie upset, but it wasn't there this time. Bertie had heard; he *had* to have heard, standing as close as he was, but he wasn't moving away.

"You shouldn't give this away," Arthur was not entirely aware of what he meant, only that he could tell that Bertie loved it, that he slept in the same room with it, his treasure. He kept it close to him, and the expression on his face was all pride, so bright with love and pleasure that Arthur wanted to shut his eyes to it because all of that was for some gold. But it was spectacular, remarkable, unlike anything else he'd ever seen, short of pictures of King Tut's tomb. "You can't give this away. You can't and you shouldn't, not for anyone."

"Oh, Arthur." Bertie's happiness sang through his words and slid lovingly down the back of Arthur's neck to warm him beneath his clothes. "If you say so."

Arthur frowned at him, as fiercely as he could with so much greed and hunger staring back at him and breath like hearth fires leaving him flushed. The rest of what Arthur had been going to say stuttered out.

"But if you want to share your knowledge, if you want others to see this, we could find someone to help you preserve and display it, if you don't trust me."

The heat at his back grew stronger, closer, but Arthur didn't move when he felt and then saw Bertie's hand curling carefully over his hip. His breathing stalled, but he kept still, even as Bertie gently pulled him back.

"Should I not trust you?" Bertie rumbled softly just above his ear. Arthur wondered distantly if that old, wise dragon look was in his eyes, if he could see everything Arthur didn't want him to know. He had to feel Arthur's shivers.

If he did, there was no point in denying it. Arthur should tell him everything, about his stray thoughts of possibly finding an old scale someday and using the money to pay off the last of Kate's legal bills from her teenage DUIs and to get back into school. He hadn't thought it would hurt him at the time, and he'd never go through with it now.

But he had already taken so much from Bertie, who had enough faith in Arthur to show him his treasure. What if he confessed to everything and Bertie demanded that he leave?

He loved this job and this house, and he'd never met anyone like Bertie. The thought of being without them made him shut his eyes and fight to breathe.

"Arthur?" The prompt came in a rasp, like a reminder that Arthur ought to move, as if even Bertie couldn't believe that Arthur would shut his eyes to all that glory in front of him.

He opened his eyes and let out a wounded sound to see Bertie's gaze shining at him.

"I don't want to leave," he gave in enough to whisper and felt the earth shake at his back as Bertie shuddered. The world seemed to steady as he inhaled.

"Then don't."

It came out so simply that Arthur froze, not sure he heard it right, but Bertie released him and stepped back and turned away from their reflection all in the same moment. He was breathing hard, just as hard as Arthur was, but he didn't look over when Arthur stepped after him.

"The sofa, a guest room, even this bed, Arthur." He gestured at the room. "Whatever you need, you have only to ask. You can borrow the car if you like, and drive to your apartment."

It was a strange thing for him to be uncertain about, and Arthur thought of Kate trying to remind him that Beings were different. They weren't that different, not where it counted. Some of them were better than any human Arthur had ever met.

"You'll worry?" The question slipped out but Arthur knew the answer before Bertie nodded.

There was a room full of treasure behind them, a room full of treasure in a house probably filled with treasure, and Bertie was worried about Arthur riding his bike in the dark and the rain. And Arthur was... Arthur was tense to think of Bertie worrying. He didn't want him to worry, not ever.

He licked his lips and then nodded.

"Okay," he agreed. "When it's late and the roads are wet, I'll stay." It made no sense when he'd be out riding his bike in the same weather every weekend evening, but Bertie went still. A moment later he was smiling widely.

He probably meant it to be victorious, or maybe like a leer, but it looked so *relieved* that Arthur smiled back until he realized that they were both standing and staring and smiling at each other.

He didn't want to think about how dumb he must look and made himself glance down to the stacks of books and dishes that he still had to attend to. He coughed as he bent down to pick up a stack and didn't look at Bertie as he headed downstairs. Bertie's heat stayed close behind him, but Arthur didn't comment, not about that, not with his face and body on fire.

"I wouldn't need a bed." He stumbled over the words, only realizing how they might sound after he said them. He left the books on the table and risked a look at Bertie as he turned. "I mean, the couch will do," he added. Bertie huffed a soft laugh and winked at him as if he knew what Arthur had really meant and was just fine with it.

He took another second to eat Arthur up with his eyes and then grinned.

"Whatever you wish, pet, as long as you stay," he was still there, grinning, when Arthur came back from the kitchen with tea.

CHAPTER 10

IT DIDN'T rain for almost a week after that. Arthur was disappointed in ways he knew he shouldn't think about, not that it stopped him from imagining what it would be like to wake up and see Bertie smiling at him or to feel the warmth of his presence even before he opened his eyes.

Not that he didn't love Kate and spending time with her at home, but the first night, it had been difficult to look at her and not tell her about what Bertie had shown him. She guessed something, he could tell from how she looked at him, but it wasn't what she was probably thinking.

He still couldn't believe Bertie had shown him that room, but Arthur wasn't going to shatter his trust now by telling everyone about it. He wanted to—the world needed to know about it, what Bertie had given him—but he'd never risk hurting Bertie now.

He turned his phone off after Dante sent him another text and only turned it on to call Kate. She always acted surprised to hear from him, as if Arthur hadn't been around, when in fact he worked hard to be there for her. She was starting to do the same thing when Arthur walked in the door at night, feigning shock to see him spending a night at home.

He hadn't told her anything, but he had a feeling there were lights still reflected in his eyes. If Kate could see them, then so could Bertie, but so far Bertie hadn't said anything, not about that. Not unless Arthur counted the invitations to stay and watch TV with him at the end of each day, which were blatant attempts to get Arthur to stay longer.

The FBI show was apparently one of Bertie's favorites. He also liked channels about cooking and telenovelas and reality shows about New Jersey.

He didn't mind talking during TV shows either, or any questions Arthur might suddenly be compelled to ask in the middle of the news, like why he and the one other dragon Arthur had met both smoked, which turned out to be a self-conscious habit most dragons had about the smell of their breath due to how early humans had perceived their heat and dangerous, smoky auras. There *had* been quite a few references in many early stories to a dragon's foul breath, but Arthur found that he didn't mind the smoke scent. He was used to it, so Bertie didn't need to continue smoking around him if he didn't want to, but Arthur hadn't worked up the courage to say that yet, so instead he'd asked more questions.

"Have you been to all those places you write about?" It seemed strange when Bertie had everything delivered so he wouldn't have to leave his house. But Bertie nodded and patted his knee without looking over.

"Of course. You know, you really ought to get your passport in order." He'd taken a moment to register Arthur's silence and then finally glanced over. "Well, you are my assistant. You didn't think it was just for the one book, did you?"

Bertie probably didn't mind because he had his own questions. He would sit down next to Arthur while Arthur was typing and then reach out, letting his fingertips graze Arthur's shoulder to get his attention, as if Arthur wasn't very aware of whenever Bertie entered the room, and then sigh questions about lunch or dinner that would somehow evolve into conversations about Arthur's favorite foods and what his mother had used to make him.

He was very interested in Arthur's parents, or didn't mind when Arthur began talking about them, but Arthur didn't think Bertie would fake interest if he didn't have any. He sat and listened and occasionally smiled and would only get up when Arthur finally remembered that they had work to do or the doorbell rang with a food delivery.

Sometime around five every day was when Bertie would stop and come out to cook or reheat something, or make scones for the morning if the mood struck him, and if Arthur didn't watch out, he'd end up talking over dinner or watching television until close to eight. He could tell Bertie was waiting for him to say something, to protest or frown or get mad, but Arthur couldn't. It was too nice.

It was better than nice, if Arthur was being honest. It was almost perfect, and it was getting harder and harder to leave every night. He wasn't even sure why he was still making his way across town. There was no reason he couldn't stay. He knew that. Kate even knew it. Bertie had told him he only had to ask. Arthur ought to ask. He knew what the answer would be.

But today there was no Bertie to ask in any case. Arthur came in to find a cool house and a note stuck to a flash drive on the table for him. The note simply read, *Good morning, Arthur*. The drive had several files in it, the first being titled "Wouldn't some rain be exquisite?" and which turned out to be another note detailing how Bertie had been asked to replace a guest lecturer at the college a few towns over and had needed to leave early to get there; otherwise, as he was at pains to explain, he would have brought Arthur along with him. He was also going to visit their antiquities collections and didn't expect to be back in time for dinner.

I don't like to think of you eating all alone, but at least you will eat, won't you,. pet? the note ended, after another wistful remark about how coming home to a house without Arthur was markedly unappealing.

If he could have, Arthur would have printed it out and maybe folded it and tucked it into his pocket. As it was, he read it twice and felt stupid and then got up to work off his disappointment at not seeing Bertie by lighting a fire, bringing in more wood, and then turning up the heat.

He made a sandwich for lunch with the bread Bertie made over the weekend, which was only a little stale, and thought about Bertie eating with a bunch of professors and eager students while he brought down books from upstairs.

Of course Bertie was going to be popular: he was sexy and brilliant and exotic. Arthur wasn't surprised by that. It didn't matter anyway, not if he really did want nothing more than to come home to Arthur. Just the idea had Arthur restless.

By the afternoon, he decided he was going to take all the books out of the main room and put in more shelves in the other rooms, rooms without fireplaces, with air vents that could be controlled to regulate the temperature, but he dropped down on the couch before he could actually consider moving them all yet and opened up his laptop to go into the new files Bertie had left him.

Getting new shelves in the other rooms was asking a lot, but he had a feeling Bertie would agree to it if Arthur explained how it would be better for the books. He could even have cases put in to display some of Bertie's relics and protect them from the elements.

It would make Bertie happy. Maybe not ecstatically happy, not like Arthur agreeing to stay the night, but it should make him smile, and Arthur wanted that.

He opened the new files, which turned out to be several chapters, and immediately dove into the first one, reading more than editing because the story was so compelling.

Bertie told it backward, starting with the English conquest of Wales and then going back over the Roman and Germanic tribes' conquests in less detail. It was entirely different from the chapter he spent describing the culture and literature of the region. It was violent and bloody and full of treachery and scheming, and if Bertie had wanted to show exactly what the people and the dragons had been facing, or what had driven them together, he succeeded.

Arthur went back over the chapter a few times to add in his notes and leave questions he, and probably Bertie's future audience, would have, and then he settled back on the couch to read the next chapter.

The difference in tone was startling. First, the quote to start the chapter, another Neruda quote but not the one Bertie had thought he would use: *To feel the love of people whom we love is a fire that feeds our life.*

And then the writing itself, which began like a fairy tale, the old kind of fairy tale, the kind kids used to hear before the world knew fairies were real.

"Once upon a time," Bertie had written, and Arthur could hear him as if he was reading it out loud from the seat next to him. "If you will allow for so trite a beginning, once upon a time there was a village where the people were frightened because the mountains above them trembled every night. No one in this village could rest because they knew that the shaking of the earth was the rage of a dragon.

"They did not know why the dragon that lived in their mountains was angry; the ways of dragons were strange to them, and no one dared to approach such a creature to ask. Dragons lived among the gold and gems in the darkest caves of the mountains, and it was an unlucky human who dared interrupt their solitude.

"But the shaking would not stop until it seemed the mountains themselves might tumble down, so the villagers asked their lord and his bravest warriors to confront the beast and find the source of its anger, but the lord and his warriors refused. So the villagers searched for the loveliest maiden to offer up to appease the monster's hunger, because dragons coveted beautiful things, or so they had heard.

"The maiden wept to know her fate, until her brother stepped forward and offered to take her place. The boy had no sword because he was not a soldier, but he was braver than those who did, and he was as beautiful as his sister, and so no one stood in his way as he left the village and took the path into the mountains.

"It was a perilous journey, but as the sun was setting the boy made his way into the crevasse where the shaking seemed the greatest and the scent of dragon smoke was strong. He trembled because he was afraid and had no sword, and the dragon would likely eat him for coming near its treasure.

"But the boy, who was as smart as he was courageous, pressed on until he heard a great roaring and felt a heat that nearly made him turn back, but he walked on. He walked until the ground rose up beneath him and knocked him from his feet, and when he looked up, he found himself face to face with the dragon of the mountains.

"It was an awesome sight, a dragon as red as the setting sun, with eyes that pinned him to the spot and teeth sharper than any sword. The boy got to his feet and asked unsteadily why the dragon had been shaking the mountain. But even as he asked, he could see the cause: a large boulder had fallen and crushed the dragon's tail and had trapped it in its own cave among all its treasures.

"The fearsome dragon was really a lonely creature in pain with no one to save it, howling furiously as it tried to free itself. If the boy waited, the dragon would die of hunger and then the people would no longer be troubled by its presence. It was then, with that thought, that the boy also realized the dragon could have roasted and eaten him and lived a bit longer, but it had not. It had merely watched him, pitiful and powerful both, until finally the boy made up his mind that no creature deserved to die in such a fashion and pushed at the boulder in an attempt to move it.

"There was still danger, but the boy ignored it to offer the dragon its freedom, a gesture that was not lost on the dragon. The amazed Being demanded to know what the boy was doing, as the stone was much too heavy for one dragon and one human to push together. It was too heavy for even an entire village to move. The dragon was going to die, he told the boy. No single human could save him.

"But the boy insisted that he try, and pushed at the rock again, and when it didn't budge, he sat down to think. This intrigued the dragon even more than the boy's beauty until it stopped shaking long enough to ask the boy his name and where he had come from. The dragon asked the boy so many questions that it was morning before the boy realized that they had passed hours in conversation, and that the earth-quaking tremors had stopped because the dragon had grown weaker during the night.

"The dragon, smiling though it expected death to come soon, grabbed a large ruby and gave it to the boy to thank him for the stories during its last hours, but the boy tossed the stone away and beseeched the dragon to try to push the boulder away one more time.

"He wept when the dragon asked him to go, for the sunset-red dragon was kindly and gentle and the boy did not wish it to die, but the dragon insisted, and so the boy returned to his village to tell them he had learned why the mountains had been shaking.

"His tale of the dragon's plight moved the people, who had not thought a dragon could feel pain. The description of the treasure moved others, until they followed the boy's path back to the dragon in order to take it. But when the boy learned of their plan, he raced back to the mountain, and there the villagers found him, lying alongside the dragon and begging it one final time to rise.

"Pity overtook the greed in their hearts, and they worked with the dragon to push at the boulder. The great rock at last gave and the dragon was freed.

"The dragon became their protector, as the village itself became the village of the sunset dragon. They had saved him and most importantly, they had given him his boy, the brave, beautiful peasant boy who had refused a fortune in order to save the dragon's life and to whom the dragon gave its love instead, which was a gift the boy could accept. He came to live with the dragon in his lonely cave and served him well until the end of his days."

"A pretty story," Bertie had added at the bottom. "And I am quite certain they lived happily ever after, though the story doesn't say. Dragon tales rarely do, either because they feel the happy ending is implied or because they don't feel one was truly possible and don't wish to say. Personally, I prefer to believe in those two. They are a classic example of the kind of love story dragons in this region carved into their artwork in this period. Stories like this are also a strong example of the kind of human/dragon cooperation that used to exist, and the belief among dragons that cooperation was the *only* way to survive.

"The bond between a dragon and its beloved, particularly when it chooses a human to love, is without a word in any tongue, ancient or modern. In fact, the dragons were convinced that to name it would be to cheapen it, for it was beyond value and to define it as we might attempt to do today would destroy it.

"It's clear from most of the surviving stories that the humans were there to serve the dragons and that the nature of the relationship was almost always sexual. It also seems, from the surface at least, that within the human/dragon relationships in particular there was a distinct power imbalance. Dragons were and are far more powerful than most humans could ever hope to be. But upon closer examination, the relationship seems more like an *exchange* of power. Dragons see their primary roles in the world as protectors, as guardians, but they have their weaknesses, weaknesses easily exploited by anyone ruthless enough. Even peasants in the Dark Ages could see what a dragon wanted, and beautiful young knights and maidens were offered up more than once as traps to capture a dragon.

"Within this story, it's clear that the dragon is the weak one. He is completely at the mercy of the boy, even when the boy is depicted in the story as his servant. This, of course, puts a spin on their relationship that a modern scholar couldn't help but notice, but to call it that of dominant and submissive would be inaccurate. It may have been that for some of the pairings, certainly, and I won't deny that the idea doesn't have a thrill of its own, but that would miss the other point to these love stories.

"As seen when it was shown in their art and stories, as in the case of this dragon and his boy, love itself, between two dragons or a dragon and human, was essential to the dragon's survival. It seems a strange thing when the dragon is the creature of greater strength and wisdom, but to this very day, the idea is ingrained in most dragon cultures that a dragon requires a treasure, a treasure like the boy in the story, to guard and admire. It was why dragons the world over looked among the purest maidens for the one who would stay by their side; a dragon without a treasure was weaker than one with all the gold in the earth."

Arthur took a moment to breathe, to blink, and then read through the story again, suddenly understanding why Bertie had called the dragons of this time period "romantic little darlings," and then remembering that Bertie had said his parents thought of him as just as romantic and old-fashioned. Even his friend Zeru said something, hadn't he, when he called Arthur Bertie's boy. Bertie didn't deny it, either.

Arthur hadn't understood what those words meant to a dragon, but he could recall the number of times Bertie called him "his boy" after that. His boy. Or "pearl," the treasure dragons were shown chasing more than any other. Darling. Treasure. The only thing

Arthur had understood was how warm those pet names always made him feel, how rare and special and valued.

His heart was pounding. His thoughts were spinning around and around the same idea. He was as hot as if Bertie was sitting next to him. He wished Bertie was because he wanted to turn to him and ask. It couldn't be true, but he wanted it to be.

If it was... if it was, he had no idea what to do. There had to be some answer that would be understood, even between Being and human.

Arthur couldn't think clearly. His pulse was like thunder in his ears and below his waist, and he blindly skimmed through the rest of the file without reading a single word.

There was an image file attached to it, showing a series of photographs of images carved into a cave wall, probably by a dragon claw. Arthur could see the boy, the dragon trapped under the boulder, and even the weeping virgin sacrifice. But it was the pictures of the dragon and the boy curled up together that left him breathless.

"Bertie," he whispered at last with his fingertips on the computer screen, and then he shut his eyes. He forgot about editing, the books, the shelves. That could wait.

He closed his laptop without reading any more and felt his skin grow hot though the fire had been getting low last time he had looked at it. There was no response to that story that he could type up into notes. Arthur couldn't write down that his heart was racing or how shaky he felt.

He looked at the door, and then at the time, and then put his laptop aside to get up and throw another log on the fire, and when that didn't make him feel any less edgy, he grabbed his computer and flopped down on the couch to read the story again.

HIS dreams were about searching for something, something red and gold and black that he couldn't find. The loss stayed with him as he moved, but he stopped and frowned when someone whispered to him. Without looking he knew the singular heat that meant Bertie's presence, and he felt the weight of his laptop slip away as Bertie took it. He wondered if he was being tucked in, and then knew he was when he felt a gentle hand on his shoulder.

Arthur opened his eyes. Bertie was in what Arthur thought of as his "lecturing professor" outfit: black dress pants and a crisp, white-collared shirt, with his red scarf falling to the floor as he bent over to attend to Arthur. His shirt was buttoned wrong and probably had been all day. The fire was behind him, making him glow.

It wasn't raining and Arthur hadn't asked to sleep there, but Bertie didn't seem to mind that he had. He paused when he saw that Arthur's eyes were open, and then the dark, tender look on his face changed to a small, rueful smile.

"Arthur," he began in a careful rumble, as if he was going to step back, and Arthur frowned and sat up to slide his hand through Bertie's hair and pull him down.

He was burning already, his skin licked by flames and the startled, careful press of Bertie's fingers at his throat. Arthur pictured the flint-dark nails and felt the pad of each fingertip as it spread out instantly over his skin.

He should have taken his shirt off and not just his shoes before falling asleep, but Arthur shook the thought off as he struggled to sit up and bring Bertie even closer. For a small moment, when their mouths touched, all Arthur could think about was the *heat* sinking into his bones and shooting down his spine. He slowly curled his fingers into Bertie's hair and moaned into Bertie's mouth as he tipped his head back. Bertie's answer was a soft, pleased growl that got Arthur hard. And he was still so hot, he wanted his clothes off. Bertie's too. Now.

He took his hands out of Bertie's hair for a moment to tug at his shirt collar, and Bertie pushed toward him, putting one knee onto the couch. He made a muffled plea against Arthur's mouth, and Arthur shifted to make room for him.

Bertie's hands slid to his back, skimming down close to bare skin as Arthur's shirt rode up. Arthur shivered and tried to arch into it, but when he moved, Bertie let out a rough sound and pulled his mouth away. Arthur shivered again as Bertie's mouth vanished and then opened his eyes, *really* opened them, though he already knew he wasn't dreaming. He breathed out, fast and shocked, at the way Bertie was staring at him.

Bertie's eyes were all pupil, gleaming volcanic rock above his parted lips. He was breathing as hard as Arthur was, and Arthur moved forward involuntarily at the glimpse of his tongue only to stop at the force Bertie put into his name.

"Arthur?" He said it as if taking the second away from Arthur hurt him, but he had a question he *had* to ask.

Arthur wet his lower lip and watched Bertie watch him do it. Bertie's lips parted on a soft breath, but he didn't say a word when Arthur carefully leaned forward to eliminate the distance. He stopped when their faces were close together and let his lips brush over the shadow at Bertie's jaw, hoping as he did that it would leave them swollen and mark his skin. He felt stupid and brave like the boy in the story. He hadn't asked, he *still* wasn't asking, but when he ran his trembling hands down over the back of Bertie's neck to keep Bertie from moving away again, Bertie took a sharp breath.

"*Arthur*," he said again, a smoky expression of longing that made Arthur's hands shake so much that Bertie had to see it. Arthur held his breath and let his fingertips trace over the top of Bertie's spine, over the start of wicked black scales that remained just out of reach. His throat tightened, preventing a real answer, but when Bertie angled his head down to let Arthur explore under the collar of his dress shirt, Arthur forced the words out.

"You're hotter than I imagined," he admitted, and Bertie gave a slightly tense chuckle, though it changed into a gasp when Arthur undid the buttons at the top so he could slip his hand further underneath the fabric.

"I'm gratified to know you thought about me," Bertie answered with another laugh but made a quiet, aroused sound when

Arthur dared another button. "Arthur." Arthur stretched out and almost shut his eyes. If Bertie kept saying Arthur's name like that, Arthur was going to come in his jeans.

He stretched again, shuddering under all that heat and pressure, and then frowned because though Bertie was slowly climbing onto the couch next to him, over him, and he was sticky and damp with sweat, he still wanted more. He twisted, needing their clothes gone without having to take his hands from Bertie's skin, and rocked up as urgently as he could with Bertie's weight holding him down. He was so much heavier than Clematis. It was just what Arthur wanted. He wanted to feel it and know Bertie wasn't going anywhere.

His jeans hurt, they were so tight, and every breath left him flushed and hotter, harder. "You couldn't tell I was thinking about you?" he demanded, knowing that wonder was in his tone. He thought he'd been obvious and besides, Bertie was *magic*.

Bertie lifted his head.

The kiss was fierce and unexpected. Arthur was pushed back on the couch by Bertie's mouth and then by his hands, careful and strong on Arthur's shoulders, relentless at his back. Arthur arched toward him without thinking, offering up his hips, his throbbing dick just as Bertie's weight shifted over him. *Magic*.

As though to prove him wrong, Bertie grunted. "I am not omnipotent, Arthur," he chided roughly between kisses. Arthur panted at his mouth, trying not to think about how *hard* he was, how hot, or how long it had been. But this was Bertie and the name slipped out of him in whispers against Bertie's mouth.

If Bertie heard, there was no sign as his hands pushed Arthur's shirt up and spread wide on Arthur's skin. Arthur's skin buzzed in response, his heart pounding under his ribs. He pushed up and met Bertie's magnificent body in a quick slide. He licked his lips and looked up, then down between them. Bertie was hard too, his dick stretching out his dress pants. He felt big, looked big. Much, much bigger than Arthur's fingers.

Arthur couldn't vocalize anything for several moments, and when he finally could, it was just a "please" that didn't explain what he wanted at all. He frowned and tried again, shifting until Bertie was between his thighs, and even that wasn't enough. Arthur heard himself whine just a little, and would have blushed if he could have made himself care.

Bertie didn't seem to notice any of it. He was acting strangely irritable for someone busy licking under Arthur's ear and making approving noises every inch Arthur arched back to let him. His hands worked underneath Arthur until he finally got Arthur's shirt over his shoulders. He threw it to the floor with a satisfied huff and then turned back to Arthur. Arthur brought his gaze up.

He had no idea what he looked like. Probably not as amazing as Bertie looked, his gleaming skin damp and darker where Arthur had kissed him, his shirt askew. Maybe Arthur just looked as stunned as he felt, because Bertie gave a minute shake of his head and glared down at him.

That fierce stare should have pinned Arthur to the spot. Instead he shuddered again, and then there was the velvet couch at his back and hot weight above him. He tried his best to bite back his helpless moan, but suddenly Bertie was crouched over him, peering into his face and staring at Arthur with a mix of pleasure and annoyance on his face. Arthur tried distractedly to think of why, but Bertie spoke before he could.

"I thought you had a Being lover before." Bertie bent back down to puff at Arthur's collarbone and made Arthur gasp. The skin there was still wet from Bertie's mouth, slightly raw from Bertie's stubble. Arthur put a hand into Bertie's hair so Bertie wouldn't move away or stop doing that, ever. Bertie's voice went lower. "Do I surprise you?"

At that shaky, uneven tone, Arthur opened his legs and grabbed at Bertie's shirt to try to pull him down. But Bertie put his hands under Arthur's ass and lifted Arthur partly up against the arm of the couch before sliding down over him. For one heartbeat Arthur was cold and shivering and then Bertie's fingers found the trail of blond hair at his navel and Bertie's mouth was on his chest. When

Arthur pushed up there was finally pressure, burning against his tight jeans and trapped dick. Bertie's body, everywhere, skin and bulk and fire.

"No. I did. No. What?" Arthur panted without any kind of thought. He wanted to defend himself, but he gave up the cause as smoky breath hit his nipples. He jerked and reached out until he found more of Bertie's skin. He touched the back of Bertie's neck, the line of his throat, but it wasn't enough, so he gathered up bunches of Bertie's dress shirt and tugged until the shirt was out of Bertie's pants. Then he pulled again until he felt more buttons give. He almost didn't hear Bertie's growl, but he felt it slip under his skin. He couldn't tell if the sound meant Bertie was pleased or angry, but at the moment he didn't care.

"What?" Arthur tried again, pushing up and getting a hand between them to get at his zipper. Bertie swatted his hand away and licked at him when Arthur moaned.

"The *fairy*," Bertie spoke shortly and put a hand to Arthur's hip to hold him still. Then Arthur thought he felt *teeth*. He almost blacked out when that made his blood pound harder, made it agony to move and know no relief was coming, but no matter how he tried Bertie didn't let him move up as he made his way slowly, too fucking slowly, down Arthur's chest. As if this was really, finally happening.

Arthur dragged his hands along Bertie's back where the skin was like silk. Bertie stopped. His roar wasn't quite a word, but Arthur thought he heard his name, like a plea that coiled up inside Arthur as tight as a spring. Bertie slid his mouth over Arthur's stomach and shifted over him again. Forget fairies, Arthur thought, breathing raggedly in and out, he had this.

"Clem—" He stopped himself before he said the name, somehow sure it was wrong to say it now, and then struggled to think of anything to say at all. "He… that was different," he insisted. Bertie growled anyway, the sound hitting Arthur deep inside, in a place dark and lonely.

It was dangerous to make a dragon jealous, but Arthur wet his mouth again because he couldn't do anything else, and he wanted Bertie to want him that much. "Clematis," he began to explain, though he was underneath a dragon without even a shield to protect him, and gasped because those *were* teeth against his skin. They were as sharp as Bertie's voice was soft. Arthur would come right that second if Bertie weren't careful.

"Please, pet. Please." But Bertie wasn't pushing inside him or holding him down, he was begging Arthur for information about Clematis, wanting Arthur to want him more.

Arthur's hand found its way to Bertie's cheek. "No, it was…" He tried to think of his ex and could only get flashes of glitter and giggles and the taste of sugar. "It was fun."

The second growl hit him in the stomach and traveled, white hot and heavy, down to his balls. He pushed up and groaned when Bertie continued to hold him down. Arthur shook his head and realized his voice was the barest rasp. "But this is…" frightening and intense and amazing. Deathly good and terrifying at the same time. If he could have, he would have fallen to his knees. He sucked down a breath at the thought of declaring himself as Bertie's boy so obviously. It didn't do any good. The thought made him writhe. "This is *serious business.*"

The low rumble against his palm and then his hipbone sounded a lot like "darling." But he had no time to wonder if Bertie had understood what he meant, because Bertie abruptly pulled away and knelt back, watching with all-black eyes as Arthur trembled. Then he slid one hand over Arthur's hip and put the other over Arthur's fly.

Arthur arched his hips up, frowning at Bertie when the glide of the zipper took too long and then inhaling in relief and pleasure when Bertie licked at his lips, probably to taste the precome in the air. Maybe he did, or maybe he smelled how close Arthur was to begging, because in the next second he shoved Arthur's pants down in one rough motion and pulled down Arthur's underwear with them. Bertie didn't give Arthur a chance to do much more than try to kick to get rid of the tangled mess, and then he settled back down between Arthur's legs.

He must have understood what Arthur meant by serious business, because the tongue that tasted the skin around Arthur's belly button took its time, and the nip that followed was gentle.

"Arthur." Bertie's body was mostly out of reach, but his mouth, his hot mouth, was close enough to make Arthur go tense. "Arthur, I wouldn't leave you." Contempt for Clematis left the air charred, but Bertie slipped a slow hand between them to tease Arthur's balls.

Arthur looked down at Bertie's sleek black hair, the rasping stubble almost at his thigh, and the full lips close to his dick. The room was trembling.

"I don't want you to," Arthur wanted to say, but he forgot everything when Bertie turned to taste the head of Arthur's cock before sucking it into his mouth.

It had been forever since Arthur felt this and it had *never* been Bertie, with his hands pressing into Arthur's skin like he wanted more and his curling tongue that could smell and taste everything.

Arthur reached out until his hands were flat at Bertie's shoulders, and he arched up the moment Bertie's hands slid to the couch. Bertie let him this time, breathing hard and drooling wetly around Arthur's dick. Arthur closed his eyes and tried, tried not to move anyway, but his cock was sliding into a hot, wet mouth, into a tight throat, and he was so hard that for a second when he heard the greedy sounds escaping Bertie, he thought he was the one making them.

He shifted up, just an inch this time, maybe less, and Bertie didn't laugh a delighted fairy laugh at his eagerness or impatience, he didn't do anything but swallow and take more and make choking, embarrassing noises that Arthur couldn't bear to hear because he wanted Bertie inside him too. That much, maybe even more. He wanted Bertie inside of him almost as much as he needed to come, to hear Bertie tell him to. Bertie would want him to, he'd purr it if he could. "Come, Arthur pet. In my mouth please, treasure." And the idea of the words was like the firm heat of his tongue under Arthur's cock, a soft stroke and a whispered request. Arthur would do anything Bertie asked, didn't Bertie know that?

"Bertie," it slipped out in that same raw voice, louder than Arthur had ever said it, and he shut his eyes tight and imagined Bertie's voice again, begging him, *pouting* at him for not spurting come into his mouth for him to taste. He thrust up and then came, sudden and hard until he couldn't do anything but twitch as Bertie swallowed around him.

He opened his mouth and left it open for a long time so he could catch his breath. He stared up at the ceiling until Bertie pulled away from his sensitive, soft dick and climbed back into view.

Arthur couldn't make out his expression. It was too like what his expression was in a room full of blindingly bright treasure, but he recognized the smug curve to his lips and the quick dart of his pink tongue.

"Arthur." The slow murmur against his mouth was deep and sweet and flavored with his come, which wasn't sweet at all. Arthur thought vaguely of fairies one more time and then put his hands back into Bertie's hair before he raised his head. With his mouth against Bertie's ear, Bertie wouldn't see his face.

"Sorry," he mumbled over his embarrassment at coming so quickly.

"I don't mind. In fact, I... thank you." Bertie surprised him again since Arthur was sure he was supposed to be the one saying that here. "It was flattering. Not everyone cares for dragon bodies when we're changed like this, and I thought... I wasn't sure about you."

"Not sure?" Arthur's voice was husky. He pulled back enough to watch Bertie blink awkwardly at him. Bertie looked like he wanted to blush again. "You couldn't tell?"

"Dilated pupils can also mean fear, dear boy," Bertie teased after clearing his throat, but the way he exhaled against Arthur's skin was warm. He moved his hips, just a little, and Arthur automatically inched his legs open wider.

"You couldn't..." Arthur hesitated and then tried a lick under Bertie's ear. His tongue couldn't detect the things that Bertie's could, but it felt good, and Bertie seemed to think so too. He curled into Arthur and grasped at him, so Arthur did it again before he scowled and thought about his next question. "You couldn't smell it?"

"Ah." Bertie either sensed his confusion or was just making sounds for what Arthur was doing to him. Arthur had never thought about rendering a dragon speechless, but at the moment it seemed like something he really should try. "That... oh, Arthur... that isn't how it works, as such. Arthur, please." Bertie's breathing hitched as Arthur dared more, licking at Bertie's jaw, spicy and clean, but he allowed Arthur to push him up and back onto the cushions and said nothing that didn't indicate acquiescence when Arthur straddled his hips. Arthur could feel the powerful, hidden strength beneath him when Bertie breathed in, his body rolling under Arthur as if Bertie *could* move mountains.

The air stuttered out of him, leaving him weak and wanting to apologize, but Bertie's eyes closed and his voice was quiet and eager. "Please, Arthur."

"How does it work?" Arthur asked to distract him from how clumsy he was with the remaining buttons, not that Bertie seemed to care. He shrugged his shirt off and then took Arthur's hand and pulled it to his crotch. Arthur instantly spread his fingers over the bulge, though he also scowled to himself, because he wasn't *completely* a virgin here. He didn't need *that* much guidance.

He bent down to suck a mark onto Bertie's shoulder and scooted up until he was in Bertie's lap. He wanted to move in time to Bertie's heavy breathing but he didn't want to take his hand away either.

"You cruel thing, asking these questions now," Bertie whined but eased up when Arthur pulled down the zipper to lightly touch the slick, wet fabric stretched over his cock. He paused to exhale and then opened his eyes. "*Arthur.*" Bertie was practically vibrating. "It's not about what I smell as much as it's what the scents trigger in me. What they make me want to do. Don't tease, darling."

"What...." Arthur's mouth was dry. "What do they trigger? What do you want to do?" He kept his head down but stared with wide eyes as he peeled away damp silk to look at Bertie's cock. It was normal. Uncircumcised, but big like he thought before, thick and flushed darkly. It was also hard—hard for Arthur. Just thinking about it made Arthur feel hungry. He swallowed as he bent down. When he slid back he breathed in to catch the scent, trying to think of how it might make Bertie feel. He knew how it made him feel. He wet his mouth.

Bertie whined again, then let out a small, unsatisfied roar.

"What I want?" he asked in disbelief. His eyes were riveted to Arthur's face. "I want to take you and keep you."

Arthur met his stare for one moment, feeling the heat spread through him, and then he ducked his head. He couldn't do what Bertie had done, but he could spread his fingers over Bertie's stomach and press down as he used his tongue to explore Bertie's foreskin.

Bertie's breath hissed out of him. "Arthur." He didn't push up, not much. From the corner of his eye Arthur saw one of Bertie's hands stretch over velvet, and then Bertie drew in another long, long breath. "Arthur," he started again, but Arthur shook his head mutely and adjusted his position to get more comfortable. His hair fell forward, but only for a moment and then Bertie was sweeping it back for him. It was like being petted, but Arthur didn't care. It was embarrassing how much he liked it, how much he'd like to be Bertie's pet, his boy, how much he wanted to be kept.

He moved his head forward until there was weight on his tongue and then tightened his lips. Bertie wasn't a fairy. There was no laughter, not like that anyway, though when Arthur stopped moving there was a strangled sound from Bertie that could have been a laugh. But it wasn't breezy and it wasn't light and it wasn't followed by teasing instructions or the kiss of glitter at his back.

Arthur took his hand away from Bertie's stomach and raised his gaze up to Bertie's face. Of course he was watching, but his eyes were dark and he wasn't moving, as if anything that Arthur wanted to do was fine by him. Arthur used his tongue, letting his spit and the satiny taste he lapped up mingle on his taste buds before he swallowed.

"Darling," Bertie purred with his head back, and the word shouldn't have been as dirty as it was. Arthur's hips pushed forward as he hummed over the taste difference between fairy and dragon. He wasn't hard, but the bitter taste on his tongue made him want to slide his body forward until he was on top of Bertie. He lifted his head and felt stinging hot at the sound of Bertie's cock popping free of his mouth.

Bertie made a noise too, low with loss and frustration until Arthur moved closer, shifting up to fit in his lap. Arthur ducked his head because he had no grace, not like Bertie, but when he rocked and settled himself over Bertie's legs and Bertie's cock slid against his ass, Bertie choked out his name.

Arthur couldn't resist moving again at that, shifting his hips experimentally after Bertie's groan and then one more time when Bertie panted at his ear. His hand pushed down between them and went to Arthur's dick, which was throbbing but not stiff, and then crept over to Arthur's thigh. Arthur opened his mouth wide, gasping over Bertie's throat. He felt muscles move when Bertie swallowed and almost, but not quite, scraped his teeth over Bertie's jugular and the path of those hidden scales. He felt Bertie's voice too; it trembled under his lips.

"Arthur." Bertie's other hand fell weakly through Arthur's hair, curving over his ear and then his jaw. Arthur turned his head without thought and sucked Bertie's thumb into his mouth. He just needed *something* inside him.

Bertie's hips left the couch. Arthur pushed him down by rocking against him. He didn't stop because Bertie begged him not to and because it felt right, the sticky pulse, the heat, the freedom to run his hands over the skin of Bertie's stomach, taut as a drum. He rolled his hips and grunted when Bertie rose up to meet him. Bertie's fingers dug into Arthur's lower back. It was only for a moment, and then his hand fell away and Arthur realized Bertie was biting back a growl.

He couldn't look up—he couldn't. He wasn't hot or very experienced but he could do this. He could make Bertie come, and right now that was all he wanted.

"Don't stop, Arthur." Bertie's praise was rough but intimate against Arthur's ear; it worked its way down Arthur's back and made him grind down, harder than Clematis had done to him. He wanted Bertie to come, wanted to ride him and please him, and he couldn't rain down glitter, but he could nip at Bertie's skin and twist against his cock. But he gasped when Bertie pulled his hand from Arthur's mouth.

"Bertie," Arthur protested in shock as the thick weight of Bertie's thumb slid out of his mouth. He raised his head, leaving his mouth open and empty and his chest heaving. He would have died of humiliation if Bertie hadn't been staring at him like Arthur was a dream come true.

"May I?" he asked as if Arthur knew what he meant, but when he ran his wet thumb along Arthur's lower lip, Arthur parted both lips wide to take in his fingers. He knew Bertie was watching and blushed hot but curled his tongue around Bertie's two fingers and drew them in to the last knuckle. He sucked until Bertie was groaning, his voice getting rough and strange. "You make me want everything." He was breathing heavily, his body thrusting up as Arthur worked his fingers. Then he inhaled sharply, cutting himself off as he pulled his fingers away.

Before Arthur could react, he moved that hand to Arthur's hip and then around to his ass. His eyes were steady on Arthur's face as he slid those wet fingers even lower.

Arthur exhaled shakily and arched back into the stroking touch. He glanced away, then back when Bertie whispered, "Arthur you don't know what you do." Arthur moved mutely against Bertie in reply, because if Bertie pressed in, Arthur *would* be hard again.

"Bertie." Saying the name was just like he'd thought it would be, longing and soft against Bertie's skin, along his neck.

Bertie pulled him close and held him there, pushing up to meet Arthur's every wild move and gasping out Arthur's name over and over, as if he was weak and wasn't digging marks into Arthur's hip or teasing him with two wet, hot fingertips.

Arthur bent his head to put his mouth over shining shades of black, untouchable unless he sucked them to the surface, like a bruise.

Bertie's hand scrabbled at his side and he moaned. Arthur used his tongue, his teeth, until Bertie was arching up and coming, coming hot and fast on Arthur's thighs, under his ass, possibly all over the velvet couch. Arthur rocked into him until Bertie fell back. It took him longer to pull his mouth from Bertie's skin, to realize that he'd marked Bertie while rubbing himself all over his lap, but when he started to sit back Bertie threw one arm loosely around him to keep him still.

"Arthur, won't you stay just a little longer?" he spoke in a sleepy, warm voice and sighed. Arthur looked up. Bertie's eyes were closed, though there was a slight grin at his mouth. Arthur glanced away from him and around the room, but there was no reason to get up. After a second he wiggled a little to try to get more comfortable, then gave up when Bertie put a hand between them without opening his eyes. He gave Arthur's dick one lazy stroke as if gauging Arthur's state and then smacked his lips.

"Just give me a few minutes, dear boy," he murmured and seemed oblivious to Arthur's wide-eyed stare as he shut his eyes. In seconds his breathing evened out, and Arthur realized that despite his words, Bertie had fallen asleep.

THE breathing in Arthur's ear woke him up and he turned toward it with only a partial awareness of feeling sticky and oddly contorted. There was soft velvet at his back and then something like hot silk, like *moving* hot silk, under his palms and against his chest.

It was heavy too, and he opened his eyes. Surprise almost stopped his heart. For one second as he realized that a dragon was asleep on top of him, he wasn't sure his heart *didn't* stop. Then he became aware of things like the unpleasant, gross feeling around his ass and how he was perilously close to the edge of the cushions.

The fire was dying but Arthur was itchy with sweat. Bertie must have gotten him onto his back at some point and fallen asleep half on top of him. Arthur couldn't say whether Bertie had been a dragon then or not; he couldn't recall.

He blinked and looked over at a peacefully sleeping Bertie, at the side of his neck, which was now covered in black scales. There wasn't even a hint of the hickey Arthur had given him earlier.

Carefully, Arthur lifted one hand and felt over the spot. It was almost like running his hand over an abalone shell and yet it was softer, alive and warm. Bertie snuffled in his sleep but didn't wake up. Arthur considered that, then traced a line down one of Bertie's arms to the end of the long claws that were curled over his chest.

He touched Bertie's feathery mane next and then his beard, though he couldn't reach the small spot in the middle of Bertie's back where there was a strange dull patch that seemed new. So he returned to Bertie's neck, to the point where the softer skin became hard and the scales got bigger. Bertie's head came up so fast that Arthur jumped and flailed and fell back onto nothing but air and then the floor.

Expensive though it was, the rug didn't soften anything. Arthur grunted in surprise and pain and looked up. For one moment a dragon as black as the night sky stared down at him and then the air shimmered and blurred, turning the dragon into something indistinct and then into Bertie, who slid to his feet to help Arthur up.

"So sorry, pet. I take up a lot of space as me and I didn't realize you were...." He paused once Arthur was standing and rubbing his back. "Petting me?" It was almost a question and Arthur wasn't quite ready to answer it.

"I thought it best to confront the beast head on," Arthur remarked smartly instead. He *had* been petting Bertie, but maybe that wasn't done. In any case, he had to look up eventually, so he took a breath and raised his head.

Bertie's expression made him warm to his toes. His very naked toes, Arthur realized abruptly, though Bertie's stare would have made him feel exposed even if he'd been fully dressed. It saw too much. He quickly lowered his head again as he fought the urge to cover up. Bertie was naked too, after all, he told himself. He just looked better that way than Arthur did.

Arthur could see a red circle on Bertie's neck now, already fading from the purple hickey it had been. Arthur couldn't think of a way to ask how long a hickey could be expected to last on Bertie without admitting that he wanted to give him another one, so he swallowed. Bertie licked the edge of his mouth.

"I could keep you like this for days," he growled only to quickly glance away when Arthur raised his head to stare at him. Bertie clenched his hands and then relaxed them. When he spoke again the dark, desperate note in his voice was gone.

"A wash up might be in order I think," he commented too lightly. Arthur glanced down again and saw the dried come on his thighs. He should agree, but he couldn't move, not with the memory of that comment, of Bertie's voice as he had said it making him feel slow and faint. Bertie took his hand. "Let's get you squared away."

They were at the staircase before Arthur realized he was being led upstairs. He didn't balk, but he looked back at the mess on the couch and shivered. It was one thing to read a story and want to take the place of a dragon's boy, to admit to wanting it in the heat of the moment, but it was another to live it afterward. He wasn't that boy. He had responsibilities: his sister, work, school. He *couldn't* be that boy. But Bertie would want it. He would want *everything*, he had said so. Everything, including keeping Arthur covered in his spunk for days.

Arthur couldn't breathe.

"Here we are." Bertie either didn't notice his silence or was nervously avoiding it. Arthur squinted as the bedroom lights came on and bounced off all the treasure but Bertie gave him no time to focus on it. "If I could trust myself...." He cleared his throat as if he knew how fierce his voice was getting. "Bathroom, my little human."

Arthur wasn't his, but Arthur didn't say a word about it as Bertie left him alone in his bathroom and closed the door. His reflection in the giant mirror over the sink startled him, and Arthur frowned back at the wiry muscles of his body, the flushed swell of his mouth, the deep, fierce blue of his eyes.

He was bruised too, marked with fingerprints and the soft imprints of Bertie's stubble along his chest, his stomach, even his thighs. He reached down to touch the hot, chafed skin and watched his pupils dilate at the memory of Bertie's mouth near his cock. He exhaled. Despite Bertie's doubts about Arthur's feelings, Arthur had never really been afraid, not of Bertie.

He jerked into sudden motion at the thought and looked through drawers and cabinets until he found a towel and then he let the water run as he cleaned himself up. The water was cool but he barely noticed it until he was done. Then he shivered and looked at himself again. He looked the same. Not beautiful, not exactly, not like Bertie, but like someone worth looking at.

"Are you all right in there, Arthur?" Bertie called through the door, and Arthur froze. "I haven't frightened you, have I? I didn't mean to this time. But you kissed me, you see."

Arthur dropped his gaze to the sink and then to elsewhere until something in an open drawer caught his eye. He identified it with a tiny laugh of disbelief even as he noted that the drawer was a mess and his mind replayed Bertie's words. Arthur *had* kissed him. And Bertie reacted like he'd been waiting for it for a long, long time. Arthur took a shaky breath.

"Yes. Yes, I did," he called back at last and reached into the drawer. When the lubricant was warmed and slick on his fingers, he leaned over the sink and thought of Bertie as he slid his fingers over his hole and then pushed in.

He held back his gasp, barely, and then shut his eyes and stretched himself as much as he dared, as much as he had in his bedroom at home while thinking about this, being this boy.

He worked his fingers in until it burned, until his legs were shaking and he didn't think he could wait to be fucked for real, and then he pulled them out and washed his hand. He didn't look in the mirror then, not wanting to see even the possibility that Bertie might reject him, then took the bottle and turned to the door. The small bottle fit right into his palm, and he held it at his side as he stepped out of the bathroom.

Bertie straightened up. He was still naked. "There you are," he said unnecessarily as his gaze moved over Arthur and then back down to Arthur's dick, flushed and half-hard. "And still looking scrumptious."

Arthur thought of teeth and bite marks on his skin, of the chafed, empty feeling inside of him, and *felt* scrumptious. He met Bertie's gaze and thought Bertie was reading his mind or smelling the changes in the air around him because his eyes went black.

Some small part of Arthur, some tiny, primitive part that sensed when he was being hunted made him shiver and widen his eyes, as if he was cold when he was anything but. He was hot all over, inside and out, and already panting though the chase was almost over. He turned with the last of his strength, turned his back on the predator who wanted him and walked on shaking legs to the bed.

There was heat at his neck like heavy breath as he sat on the edge of the mattress but it was only when Arthur felt the warm air across his chest and sliding down over him that he realized the room itself was hot and getting hotter. He felt the itch of sweat and patches of damp on his skin and flicked a look over.

Bertie was across the room from him. He was staring, watching Arthur with intent, narrowed eyes. His mouth was open, his tongue just visible. Arthur remembered it on his cock and let out an uneven sigh. He wasn't really made to be seductive, but his limbs were heavy and it seemed only right to place one hand on his thigh and slowly draw it upward.

He clutched the bedding with his other hand, his stomach clenching in fear and excitement when the room shook. Coins slid to the floor. A sword clashed into armor and nearly tumbled down. Arthur glanced at them and then quickly back at the large, dark shape of Bertie. He no longer seemed all the way human, though he stood on two legs and spoke in a rumbling voice.

"You look like a maiden waiting to be ravished." Bertie's voice wasn't quite his own anymore either, though Arthur recognized it as the guttural sound of a dragon using human words. He curled his fingers tighter into the bedding and looked up. Then he took a deep breath.

"What if I am?"

Bertie took two steps, two impatient, ravenous strides toward him before stopping abruptly. Arthur saw shoulders, hands, legs, cock, face—Bertie but not Bertie, not human, dragon—and made a small, hungry sound that drew Bertie forward another step.

"Do not say such things to a dragon, Arthur." There was no pet name, just fire in the words. Arthur should have been burned but he wasn't. He blushed and curled his fingers around his cock so Bertie could see how hard he was.

"I'm not afraid."

Dragons had eyes that could ensnare the soul. Arthur couldn't look away.

Bertie slid closer. "I would take you and keep you."

Arthur lost his breath. "Then do it."

He didn't see Bertie move. He only felt the mattress at his back and the whisper of sheets on his skin as he was pushed to the middle of the bed. Hands slid over him and Arthur went still as his mind caught up to the fact of Bertie pushing his hips up, his legs apart, pulling his hands up by his head and holding them down.

Bertie's fingernails were short, but Arthur could feel the edges pressing into him and thought of claws. He shivered for the pressure and the marks they would leave, and then for the wet tease of Bertie's tongue over his chest, smelling him more than tasting him. Arthur couldn't stop shaking.

He turned his head to the side and saw them, just for a moment, in the mirror by the bed, a tiny human wrapped in the arms of something greater. He looked up and shifted to feel Bertie's cock against him. Bertie's head was down, but his body heaved, his hands tightening to keep Arthur still.

"Arthur." Bertie said it as if speech hurt and Arthur imagined him struggling to hold on, to not simply take, the way dragons did. But Arthur hurt with how empty he was.

He brought his knees up as much as he could and opened his mouth as Bertie took one hand away from his wrists to lift himself up. There was light reflecting off his skin as if the scales were closer to the surface, but his eyes were dark.

Arthur moved his hips, the small roll all he could manage with Bertie holding him down. "I'm ready," he insisted quietly and opened his hand so that Bertie would see the bottle of lube he was still holding.

Bertie didn't speak. He slid a hand down and tested Arthur's words by sliding one dark-tipped finger inside him. Arthur moved despite knowing better. The slick glide made him kick out, his feet trying to get him back up for more and sliding on the sheets. He made a weak noise and shivered when Bertie didn't answer.

"I want more. You said everything. I'm ready." He was all words in the face of Bertie's silence and the weight that wouldn't let him move. Bertie's sound was animal, but his touch inside Arthur was knowing. Arthur couldn't even squirm, and the thought was almost as hot as knowing what it was doing to Bertie, how Bertie was fighting just to speak like a man.

"Mine." He managed a word as he used two fingers to stretch Arthur and stroke deep inside, and Arthur shut his eyes and whined when he couldn't bend his knees more, couldn't get his legs wider. Bertie spoke again harshly into Arthur's skin. "Treasure."

Arthur shut his eyes and thought he nodded, but it didn't matter, not with the sounds he was making, higher and higher pitched as Bertie took him with just his fingers and watched and inhaled the scent of Arthur's need.

If Bertie had shifted and wrapped his tail around him, Arthur could not have been more helpless, but it wasn't fear making his blood pound and his throat dry. "Bertie," he groaned with his head to the side and stilled, uncomfortable and shocked, when Bertie pulled his fingers out.

He swallowed before he turned his head back. Bertie's eyes were black and hot as he continued to hold Arthur's hands above his head, one-handed, no effort in the gesture at all. It made Arthur think of virgin sacrifices, of girl dragons, of how Bertie might have been with him if Arthur hadn't demanded this.

Bertie would have taken his time, would have driven Arthur insane with how slow and careful he would have been. He would have whispered words into Arthur's skin and pressed into him gently, as if Arthur was precious, and though Arthur was trembling uncontrollably, he shook his head. He couldn't take that now. He'd break.

"Arthur?" Hot breath was pleasantly rough on his skin. Bertie's cock was pressing against him. Arthur shifted and nearly came at how Bertie pushed him down, at the hungry roar when Arthur immediately shifted up, demanding to be taken.

It wasn't the kind of thing a virgin sacrifice should probably do, but he needed it to live, and maybe so did Bertie. Bertie looked at him and pulled his hands from Arthur's wrists to grip his thighs and angle him up.

Arthur went tense.

He didn't mean to, he didn't want to, but he did, right as Bertie's cock pushed in, big and iron-hot.

Arthur arched up and froze with his body straining, his thighs tight with Bertie between them. Bertie went still. He stared down at Arthur and frowned when Arthur shook his head. Bertie wasn't all the way inside yet and it was already uncomfortable. It was already incredible.

Arthur was his boy, he could feel it shimmering under his skin. He could belong to this dragon if he could do this. He lifted his arms so his hands could run over Bertie's skin and feel the power in his shoulders, greater than magic. He pulled it down to him, panting and letting out a whine when the move made Bertie's cock slide in deep.

"Arthur," Bertie rasped in a man's voice, as if Arthur could be reasoned with, and bit against Arthur's shoulder. Arthur drew in air and waited, counted the seconds until he could move again, and then he tossed his head. He could be a better pet than this. He could be the best.

"More," he ordered, moving up with a slight hiss. Bertie was everywhere, his weight over him, his pulse pounding inside Arthur for another moment before Bertie inched his hips back to thrust back into him. His stubble scratched and rubbed against skin already raw, but the pain was light, a distraction as Arthur stretched and exhaled and burned.

"Just... yes," Arthur breathed as it eased, as he just felt full, finally, with Bertie deep inside him, then deeper when Arthur arched up to meet Bertie's new thrust. He moaned and bent one knee in to his chest, grunting at the discomfort and then ignoring it completely until Bertie lifted Arthur's leg over his shoulder and pressed in. Arthur made another hungry sound, one after the other.

He wound his fingers into Bertie's hair and then ran them down his spine so he could feel the power in every movement. *Power*, and Arthur got to touch it. Bertie was heavy and solid and Arthur felt like he was splitting in two.

He grabbed handfuls of Bertie's back, his ass, anything to bring Bertie in closer, deeper.

He wasn't slow anymore. Arthur heard himself whining but only pushed himself back up against Bertie's weight, needing it on his cock and over him. Everything was slick, even the skin over Bertie's flexing muscles. Arthur imagined that coiled strength and threw his head back to feel Bertie's teeth at his throat. He shifted up just to hear Bertie's roar.

This was magic, Arthur thought distantly as Bertie surged into him, and spread out his hands to feel it. Sparks filled him. Fire. Life. He looked in the mirror when the direct sight of Bertie made his vision go white. He saw himself, small, and he saw Bertie, glowing like fire, pumping into him. His teeth were at Arthur's throat. Arthur turned into it so he could stare directly at him, Bertie the dragon king. *His* dragon king. There was no shame in serving something so beautiful.

"Arthur," Bertie called him back and arched over him to grab his hands and pin them back above his head. No effort in the act, only in the words that scraped out of him. "My boy."

Arthur couldn't think, couldn't respond, could barely breath at the slide inside of him and the brush of his cock against Bertie's stomach, but it was the grunt, the parted lips and pointed teeth, the hands fierce on his skin that made him try to push up so Bertie could push him back down. Bertie responded by taking him, faster, harder.

"*Bertie.*" Arthur wasn't aware that he was begging until Bertie answered him.

"Mine. I want to see you as mine." Bertie twisted his head to run his tongue along Arthur's neck as he drove in deep. When Arthur moaned weakly underneath him, he rose up. Arthur grunted as he felt Bertie pull out of him, and then again as jets of hot come splashed across his thighs and stomach in almost the same moment, shocking him motionless for the second until he saw himself, in the mirror, out of it, dripping with Bertie's come and shivering all over at the *heat* of it.

He hadn't expected that and couldn't move for a few seconds except to breathe hard and stare up at Bertie, who was staring hungrily down at him as he caught his breath. He still had Arthur pinned, his face was close, and the pleasure in his expression made Arthur hold still. He wanted Bertie to have his fill.

But he was hard and when he shivered, his stomach tight with the desire to move and his muscles shaking with the pain of staying crushed under Bertie, Bertie let out a long breath.

He licked his lips and made a rough, pleased sound when Arthur didn't move. Arthur's shoulders and hips ached and he felt empty with Bertie no longer inside him, but he held still and watched and shivered as Bertie leaned in to nuzzle at his cheek. He seemed softer, human, again.

Bertie closed one hand around Arthur's cock, which was sticky and wet, and he stroked through his own slippery mess with his breath warm on Arthur's face. "I should have liked to have prepared you, Arthur," he murmured seriously as if Arthur wasn't gasping and thrusting up into his hand.

"I'm sorry," Arthur whispered back, his throat dry. That wasn't how it was supposed to be. He was to be protected and admired, cared for. He shouldn't have taken that away from Bertie, even if Bertie wasn't angry with him. But his voice broke and he couldn't rise up. Need spiked in his blood, behind his eyes, but for all his soft words Bertie was relentless, and he wouldn't look away as he kept his grip firm. Arthur couldn't think, not to do more than let another moan stutter out and rock up into Bertie's deliberate strokes.

"Don't be. You were breathtaking, pet. To think one such as you…. I would have waited much longer for much less. For you, Arthur, I would wait until Doomsday, don't you see? For you I'd serve." His lips teased the spot where his teeth had been. Arthur moved his head, following that hand, that voice, without thought.

"Please." The one word cracked, but Arthur said it again, "Please, Bertie," and shuddered when Bertie nudged his head aside and whispered, "Then say it, Arthur, say what you are," beneath his ear.

"I'm…." Arthur couldn't finish. Bertie had marked him and it wasn't enough. He arched up into Bertie's hand. "I'm…." Bertie's heat covered him but it was the coaxing at his ear that made him shudder and shoot his come into Bertie's hand.

Arthur couldn't see for a few minutes. Maybe he was unconscious, maybe his eyes were just closed, but when he finally blinked, it was at the awareness of Bertie releasing his hands and moving over him, shifting just a second before what had to be his tongue swiped along Arthur's stomach.

Arthur shivered, the sensations rocketing through him way too strong for anything else, and looked down at the top of Bertie's head and the pink tip of his tongue. Fairy semen tasted like sugar, and yet

Arthur had never seen Clematis do anything like lick up their mingled come.

Bertie had a small, warm, wet towel in his hand too, and Arthur frowned a little because he didn't remember Bertie getting up to get that at all. After a few more licks, Bertie started cleaning Arthur up with the towel with soft, slow thoroughness that would have done Arthur proud if he'd been restoring a piece of a priceless collection to its former glory. He looked up when Arthur couldn't stop a small, discomfited murmur at some of the more intimate places the towel went. Bertie seemed quite pleased, and Arthur felt the embarrassed heat spread down from his cheeks to his neck. He opened his mouth.

"Not a word. I'm enjoying this." Bertie spoke before Arthur could think of anything to say but turned away from him to throw the towel away. Arthur took the moment to scoot up and get his body fully on the bed and ease his tired muscles into a new position, but he stopped when Bertie focused attention back on him. A half second later and Bertie was climbing over him, taking deep breaths under Arthur's chin and then coming up to place a small kiss just to the side of Arthur's mouth.

Arthur's thinking was still annoyingly cloudy, but he frowned a little anyway and tried his best to be serious. "You aren't kissing me again until you brush your teeth," he warned softly, though it wasn't what he'd meant to say at all. Bertie only gasped in mock outrage.

"Such an unromantic soul! Your breath isn't exactly peachy either, Arthur." He flopped over onto his back, rocking the bed. Arthur had a second to adjust to the sensation of being abandoned before Bertie slid an arm underneath him to pull Arthur over on top of him.

He might claim to be a small dragon, but he moved Arthur's weight easily and didn't even grunt when Arthur landed, spread out, over his chest. It made Arthur feel as light as a fairy, as if he should spread kisses as sparkling as glitter along Bertie's skin. He would, if he wasn't so bone-tired.

"What?" Arthur started to ask. Bertie's hands smoothed down his back and Arthur couldn't help but think he was being petted, and then about how much he liked it. He didn't stretch into it like Bertie would have done, but he didn't pull away.

"So I won't crush you this time," Bertie explained after a few minutes of stroking Arthur's back. He made it sound as if it was only natural that Arthur would sleep with him in his room full of treasure and his only concern was that Arthur be comfortable. Arthur wanted to tell him that he wouldn't mind Bertie's weight if it meant he knew Bertie was there, that he could wake up to it happily as long as Bertie was with him, but the words felt like too much. He settled for moving his head so his mouth was against Bertie's skin.

"You'll turn dragon again?" Arthur's voice was husky and his words were slow, but at least he got them out. The earth... *Bertie*... moved underneath him, carefully breathing in and out. "Does it...." Arthur thought of the version of Bertie he had brought out by demanding to be taken, but then couldn't think of exactly what he wanted to say and tried to sum it all up. "Did *that* feel okay to you, as a human, I mean?"

"Okay?" Bertie's laugh made Arthur shift and slide their legs together to stay where he was. "I love my scales, pet, but there are several advantages to having skin, and feeling it against yours is one of them."

"Oh" was about all Arthur could manage in response to that. He shifted again, enjoying being skin to skin too. If he moved his legs to either side of Bertie's body, he'd be straddling him, almost like he had downstairs. He licked his lips at the idea and thought of something else he'd never had a chance to try. "Can we do that again?" he asked against Bertie's throat, his face still burning up. "But like this?"

He couldn't believe he ever asked that Bertie take him. He didn't feel that certain now. He couldn't forget Bertie pleading for the chance to prepare him next time, or Bertie whispering to him as he made him come. He trembled at the idea of demanding anything from Bertie again, even if he knew Bertie would probably give it to him.

Bertie patted his back so slowly that Arthur *knew* he was thinking about Arthur's past experience. "Of course, Arthur," he agreed. "I'd be delighted. However I think I will eat your fairy friend after all." Bertie was too quick, especially now when Arthur could barely think. He took Arthur's request as a criticism of the way Clematis had treated him. Arthur tried to speak, to explain, but got shushed again. After a few minutes of quiet, Arthur's muscles stopped shaking. He shifted to get more comfortable and Bertie's hand curved over his back. "I would give you anything, pet. Haven't I made that clear?"

Arthur tried hard to think about that, but it only made him tremble and sigh into Bertie's heat and give up. He could think about it tomorrow.

"But dragons don't share," he agreed halfheartedly and frowned when Bertie let out a pained laugh that shook the bed.

"So you understand my predicament," Bertie answered at last, then smoothed his palm along Arthur's back to lull him back to sleep. "Now rest. You've certainly earned it."

"Yes, my lord," Arthur answered obediently and rubbed his cheek against Bertie's shoulder as his eyes closed.

CHAPTER 11

IT WAS not a surprise this time to wake up hot and naked and not entirely clean, though turning to find a sleeping dragon taking over his pillow was still jarring. Arthur must have rolled off Bertie while asleep, because Bertie was curled up on one side of the bed with his head flat on the pillow Arthur had been using.

Arthur stared for a moment longer, trying to reconcile something that looked almost like a sleeping puppy, a *giant* sleeping puppy, with the lover who called him "darling" and who had fucked him senseless only a few hours before, and who would probably offer to make breakfast when he woke up.

If he still wanted Arthur around, that was. Bertie had said he would, that he wasn't like any fairy, but people said a lot of crazy things during sex while they felt good. Arthur shouldn't take those particular words seriously, no matter how much he wanted to. He shouldn't even be lingering in bed. This was a workday despite last night, and he had things to do. Like clean up and see to Bertie's tea and call his sister and then finish editing the sections he hadn't been able to focus on yesterday after reading that story.

Not that he thought he'd have much luck focusing on them today either. Not with his skin tingling, his body stretched and sore, and a weak, raw feeling hiding just beneath the surface of his thoughts. He did what he always did when the feelings were too much: he thought about work and what had to be done, and then he made himself move.

The mattress was so soft that the whole bed rocked as he slid to his feet, but Bertie's breathing stayed even. There was no sign Arthur had disturbed him, so after a short pause, Arthur padded over to the bathroom, minding the coins that they must have strewn farther over the floor last night, and closed the door behind him.

He didn't take a shower despite the temptation. He didn't think Bertie would mind, but the noise it might make left him anxious. He should wake Bertie. He knew that. He should wake him the way he wanted to, with a careful touch to the top of his head or by whispering his name, and then he'd know the second Bertie opened his eyes if Bertie still wanted him around as more than just his assistant.

Instead, he washed up in the sink and looked around until he found toothpaste to finger-brush his teeth. Then he stepped back into the bedroom to see if Bertie's eyes were open.

They weren't. Bertie had moved over a little into the space Arthur had occupied and wrapped one gleaming arm around another pillow that he must have dragged up from the floor, but he wasn't awake.

Tea, Arthur thought quickly as he considered the pillow taking his place, he had to get Bertie's tea. To do that he had to get dressed. Bertie might wander around the house naked, but Arthur wasn't that guy. It was unfortunate that he'd left his clothes downstairs.

He hurried out and down the hall to the landing, though he knew no one else was in the house. It was colder downstairs, probably because Bertie was upstairs, but it wasn't freezing. Arthur shivered to walk barefoot on the kitchen floor, but he set up the pot for the tea before beginning the search for his clothes.

He found his underwear and jeans crumpled on the floor by the couch and wrinkled his nose as he slipped them on. Then he grabbed his T-shirt from the table and his sweatshirt from where he left it, with his bike and helmet by the door. There was no sound coming from upstairs, so he got down onto the rug to find his socks. His shoes were easy to find, sitting side by side with his laptop, but not his socks.

"Seriously?" Arthur complained softly because his toes were chilled from the contact with the kitchen floor, and he ducked down to look underneath everything. His socks were there, balled up together as if they'd been kicked or shoved under the couch in a moment of passion, which he supposed they had been.

They were also wrapped around something flinty and black and edged. It almost cut him when he touched it, and he had a shocked moment of recognition even before he held it up to the light.

It was a scale. One of Bertie's larger scales, the kind that came from his back. It was roughly symmetrical and see-through from certain angles, then a solid, opaque black from others. There was no blood, no trace of skin anywhere on it, though it must have come off some time last night.

Arthur remembered an uneven, dull patch of skin on Bertie's back and immediately shoved the scale away when he realized that he must be the reason it had come off at all, the way he'd been running his hands up Bertie's back. He left the scale on the cushion of the couch as he got up and put on his socks and then his shoes, just in case Bertie didn't want him around this morning.

Just in case, he told himself again, and kept his eyes on the scale as he finished dressing. He had so many questions about it, like what it was made of, if it was like a rhino's horn, and why dragons lost them at all and how long it took to grow a new one— questions he couldn't ask if it looked like he'd been trying to pull the scale out.

He hadn't, but that didn't matter, not when all Bertie would have to do was open his mouth to smell Arthur's guilt. Arthur had come here with that scale in mind and now he had it. He didn't want it. Just looking at it made him shiver with cold, as if he'd never gotten dressed at all. That it was beautiful meant nothing, because the kind of people who sold things like that, who put a monetary value on them, wouldn't see anything but how much it was worth.

But it was so incredibly beautiful. Arthur shook as he picked it up, feeling that same faint buzz that he had when holding a piece of stone carved by artists in Ancient Rome. Obsidian couldn't come close to how smooth it felt, how fragile it seemed when he turned it to let the early morning light play on the surface.

"Priceless," he said out loud, because it truly was without price, and jerked at the knock on the door. It was early, just after dawn. No one should be at the door. He turned without thinking and walked over. He could make out the shape of a man and frowned as he swung open the door.

Drew was standing opposite him, improbably wearing shorts at that time of the morning. He had his hair slicked back, but he hadn't shaved. His stubble wasn't nearly as attractive as Bertie's ever-present shadow, but it made him seem rougher, slightly dangerous, and Arthur assumed it was deliberate. He was smiling too, a crooked, inviting smile, but it slipped when he saw Arthur. Then he didn't look happy, or nearly so inviting.

Arthur returned his glare. It was too early for a delivery, even if Drew had his bicep-revealing uniform shirt on. More importantly, they hadn't ordered any groceries for today. By which Arthur meant that *he* hadn't ordered any groceries for today, because it was something else he did for Bertie now, unless Bertie decided on a last minute menu change.

He wasn't in the mood to deal with any uninvited guest, but especially Drew, Drew with his smirks and his eyes always drifting over Arthur to look at the space behind him. He seemed surprised to find Arthur answering the door again. Maybe Ravi hadn't mentioned Arthur was still working for Bertie. Of course, if Arthur hadn't slept with Bertie last night, he wouldn't have been here now for Drew to find, and that had probably been Drew's intention.

Drew was there this early because he hadn't expected Arthur to be there. Arthur was tired and confused, but he didn't think Bertie had asked Drew to be here. Bertie didn't like the way Drew smelled, he'd said so, right before telling Arthur he was free to drive away all his pests.

"What are you doing here?" Arthur barked out, not remembering until it was too late to keep his voice down. Drew recovered from his surprise quickly and took a few moments to look over Arthur again. It was a long, slow look that probably didn't miss a thing and which made Arthur blush again despite himself.

Drew had already made it clear what he thought Arthur was doing here in Bertie's house the first time they met, but Arthur's appearance now only confirmed it. He'd dressed quickly, sloppily, leaving his hair the mess Bertie's fingers had left it. His lips were dark, his eyes shadowed with a lack of sleep, and unlike Bertie, Arthur had marks at his throat that would last for days.

Drew's smile was suddenly a lot warmer. He looked almost friendly except for the cool look in his eyes. Arthur was reminded once again that Drew looked a lot more like the paintings of knights than Arthur did. But Arthur lifted his chin and just frowned harder.

"*What* are you doing here?" he demanded again, clenching his hands so tightly that it hurt. Drew's gaze skipped over him again, lingering at his side before coming back up to Arthur's face.

"The same thing you are, I bet, only you beat me to it." He nodded down at Arthur's hand and Arthur followed the gesture and ended up staring at the black scale wrapped in his fist. He'd forgotten about it, but the early morning light made it seem wet.

"What?" Arthur asked blankly, with the edge in his palm like a shard of glass. It made him think of a blade and the display of short swords on the wall next to him. They were probably dull, but Arthur might like the weight in his hand. If it felt anything at all like holding Bertie's scale, Arthur might enjoy holding a sword after all.

"The dragon," Drew explained with a roll of his eyes. "I bet he doesn't even know. But I got it the second after I saw you, when I saw him and how he looked at you. I guess short and skinny is his type. And now you've got that...." He pointed at the scale. Arthur raised it without thinking. "That's a scale from his back, right? Did he give it to you? It's worth more if the old lizard gave it to you freely, not that it's worth nearly as much as his treasure. But you could probably get that too, if you're good enough."

Arthur shuddered as something snapped. He wasn't sure if the sound came from inside of him or from somewhere in the air around him, but it was the noise the ground made when it broke apart, the half-second warning most people flinched and hid from. The scale in his hand was like the jagged edge of a rock or an arrowhead, like a vorpal sword, though Arthur wasn't out to slay any dragons.

"Shut up." It was someone else's voice, because it was way too calm to be Arthur's. But the sound of it was familiar, as familiar as the heat around him and the haze over his eyes. He lowered the hand with the scale in it and let Drew look at the sharp, glistening edge of it.

"I could tell." Drew ignored the warning because he was stupid. He was a stupid jerk, just like his sister's ex-boyfriend, just like anybody who looked at the world and thought of what they could take from it and not what they could give it. "Nobody would be with a dragon for any other reason," Drew started and then suddenly, abruptly, went quiet, as if he finally noticed that Arthur wasn't agreeing with him.

Arthur narrowed his eyes.

"Treasure?" He moved forward, startling Drew into stepping back. "If you think it's just about treasure then you really are stupid. It's so much more than that. Gold?" He snorted and gestured with the hand holding the scale, watching the sharp edge of it and how it gleamed in the light. Drew took another step back. "*Gold?*" Arthur asked again, almost spitting the word. "You saw *him* and you thought about gold?

"He is—" Arthur briefly couldn't find the words. "—power and beauty and knowledge and compassion and you wanted to see some jewels?" Arthur nearly tossed the scale at him out of pity. But then he remembered what someone like Drew might do with a piece of Bertie and narrowed his eyes until Drew was off the front steps.

"Leave. Leave now and don't come back." He took another step forward to follow, putting one foot across the threshold and for a second felt a swirling rush of warm air around him, pulling him back and pushing him forward. It made him think of Bertie and he got a sick, cold feeling in his stomach.

Drew looked at him and then up over his head, just for a second. Arthur straightened, trying to block the entire house from Drew's sight. He was shaking, but he didn't think Drew saw it. Then he gestured out at the street.

"Stay away from Bertie or I'll have you fired." He meant it. He'd never threatened to fire anyone before but he could do it, and would, if Drew said another word. "He's not for you."

"Just you, Arthur dear?" Drew was stupid *and* defiant even though he was quaking with fear. Arthur grabbed the door and slammed it closed. He breathed hard behind it for a second and then locked it. The air moved around him. It felt hot on the back of his neck and he turned.

He knew before he looked that Bertie was there, but he looked anyway, all the way up the stairs to the landing. Bertie was watching him, his eyes dark and fierce beneath low eyebrows. He did not wink and there was no sign of a grin.

"I wasn't taking it," he insisted instantly, staring back at Bertie because where else could he look? Bertie was unmoving, almost a statue, until he opened his mouth, exposing rows of pointed teeth and that tongue that even now was tasting everything Arthur was trying to deny. "He was wrong, Drew was...." But Drew hadn't been wrong, so Arthur stopped. Arthur *had* come here partly for that scale.

Arthur dropped the scale and knew as he did it that it only made him look worse. He was standing there fully dressed, like he'd been ready to run, and he was holding that scale while Drew said every horrible word.

The room was getting hotter, and Arthur didn't think it was just due to Bertie's presence. He stepped back from the door as if that was going to do any good and felt something brush against him, a force almost like hands or that dizzying feeling when strong magic was close.

Arthur had never felt anything stronger than the kinds of spells kids tried out on each other for fun. He took another step back and shuddered at the rush of air on his skin when the room itself was so hot and still.

It wasn't coming from Bertie, he realized in one tense moment. It was coming from the house. Whatever magical wards Bertie had put on the house were reacting to something, probably Arthur and the guilt that wouldn't even let him look at the scale anymore. He raised his head and flinched again at the way Bertie was looking at him, as if he didn't know Arthur at all. If he hadn't known Bertie so well, he would have said that Bertie was waiting for him to make one wrong move so he could roast him on the spot.

"It's beautiful, but I don't want it." Arthur spoke up again, then frowned and shook his head at the answering silence. "It's yours and I wouldn't... I wouldn't do that to you. Not just because I...." It was all out there anyway, it had to be, but maybe the scent was drowned out by the dry, singed smoke drifting downstairs. Arthur put a hand out and then dropped it because why should Bertie believe him? He *had* lied. He'd lied from the second he walked in this house.

"Not just because I know you," he finished, though the truth raced through his blood like panic, making him flushed and sick and more scared than he'd been when he met Bertie and thought he might end up charred and eaten.

"I... I thought about it, though. Before I knew you. Before I worked here. A scale like that is worth money and I thought it would be harmless. If one fell off, you probably wouldn't even miss it and then I could take the money and pay off enough bills to give myself some breathing room, maybe go back to school."

He looked down because no way could he look into Bertie's face while he admitted to thinking about selling off a part of him through someone like Dante. He didn't want someone like Dante to come near Bertie any more than he wanted Drew to. Drew didn't see what made Bertie special; he just saw a dragon, a monster from a story that repulsed him, but one that he still wanted to use.

"You aren't... what he said. You aren't that, you're so much more. You're incredible. I didn't realize that when I first had the thought, because I hadn't met you." Arthur didn't even deserve to be this close to Bertie. He took another step back and for the first time, Bertie moved. The scrape of his claw against the balustrade made Arthur glance up.

Bertie had one hand wrapped around the railing, his grip hard enough that a claw was digging into the wood. The repairs would be costly, though that would mean nothing to Bertie. Of course it wouldn't.

Arthur scowled again and felt his chin go up. "Not that I expect you to understand not having money or working all the time. Why would you? But let me tell you, it's exhausting. It's so exhausting you can't think about anything else but work and money and how you don't have any, and if you do it too long, you just know your dreams are going to be just that... dreams. Dreams don't come true without money, and I wouldn't change having Kate with me, but you get desperate sometimes, tired and hungry, and I thought... I thought it wouldn't hurt."

"Stupid," he added a moment later, his brief moment of anger fading away when Bertie didn't say anything. "But I really thought... if you didn't want it. They said scales just fall off." He exhaled. "I guess I just wanted to think that. But it didn't matter. The second I got here I saw you and I knew there was no way." He took a step back.

"Arthur." Bertie spoke for the first time, his voice so rough that Arthur knew it was a sharply growled warning that Arthur was treading on dangerous ground. Arthur shook his head again at the blast of heat that followed the word, the sensation of too much magic or the ground itself rising to trip him up or shove him forward.

"I'm sorry." Arthur stood where he was for a moment longer anyway and stared through the growing haze. "I'm sorry for thinking it at all, though I never ever would have done it. You should believe that."

He couldn't tell if Bertie did or not, or if the magic in the house did. He was so hot he was shivering and Bertie was looking at him as if Arthur had failed him, as if Arthur wasn't the honest, fearless warrior that Bertie had thought he was. Arthur supposed he wasn't. But he wanted to be. That made it so much worse.

He looked up and did his best anyway. "I want you to know… I couldn't breathe the first time I saw you, and it hasn't gotten any easier since then. In fact, the more I'm around you, the stronger it is, this feeling in my chest. It's not fear. I'm not even a little bit afraid of you. Not like that. You aren't going to devour me. You wouldn't have to because I'm…." No, he wasn't that and stopped himself. He changed his words. "I want…." He was revealing too much, but it wasn't anything that Bertie didn't know already. He had to know, and if he didn't, it was out now, belly up and waiting to be gutted. Arthur couldn't take the words back, but then, why should he bother if he wasn't coming back? Arthur wasn't just a nobody, he was a potential thief. Someone who had thought about money, no matter his reasons. Bertie wouldn't want him.

He straightened and turned away before the house could make him. He couldn't look around; he just kept his eyes on the door. He grabbed his bag and his laptop and kept on going, throwing open the door before he dared to glance back.

The room seemed to shimmer, as if his vision was swimming, and he thought Bertie was changing form but couldn't tell.

"I'm sorry I'm not your boy, because I wish I was," he admitted the truth, the whole truth, quietly and then turned to push his bike out the door so he wouldn't have to hear how Bertie wouldn't call him back.

HIS chest was tight, though it wasn't just the fast race across town back to the apartment that made breathing painful. The morning air was cold, colder now that he was outside of Bertie's house, but he didn't let himself think about it. He just carried his bike up the stairs and fumbled for his key and got inside with enough noise to bring Kate's head up from the couch.

She looked sleepy and startled for one second, and then just concerned. Arthur turned away before she could say anything because he knew what it looked like, having spent the night there only to come crashing back home way too early in the morning. He also knew he was probably flushed and that his eyes were probably just as red. The sting made him blink as he shoved his backpack into a corner and hurried past her into the bathroom.

A shower made him feel clean and kept Kate from asking him questions, but that was all it did. He could still feel the ache when he moved, sore muscles getting sorer by the second and reminding him, every time he moved, of what he'd just lost. He tried to distract himself by thinking of what he had to do next: dry off, get dressed, eat, look for new jobs. Practical items on a simple list, things to be checked off in order that wouldn't give him time to think. It might have worked if he hadn't run the soapy washcloth over his thighs and thought of Bertie, and then thought *give Bertie his key back*.

He discarded that mental note, then the entire list, and tried to start over. He'd left the tea things in disarray in Bertie's kitchen. He... Bertie would... have to take care of that, if he didn't forget. Maybe Arthur *should* write out a list, a list for Bertie, that he could drop off with the key.

He wasn't sure the house would let him in, but he could leave the key in the mailbox with the notes Arthur hadn't had a chance to share and the names of people who would take care of Bertie's books if Arthur couldn't. He could do that. Not today, but he could. He had to make sure of things.

Tomorrow, he decided, though he wasn't sure he could tomorrow either. But he made himself think about it, adding household items Bertie was running out of instead of looking at the bruises and hickeys on his chest and the marks of fingernails at his wrists, and mentally writing out the order to the stacks of books around Bertie's living room so Bertie would understand them, instead of thinking about how hollow he felt inside and how that dragon had looked, clinging to the balustrade and staring sadly down at him.

When he finally came out of the bathroom in just the same pair of jeans, Kate was standing in his bedroom doorway with her eyes averted and a cup of coffee in her hand. The fact that she'd actually made coffee from their carefully saved supply made him stop to swallow back everything but "Thanks." He took the cup after throwing on a new shirt with long sleeves and Kate finally looked at him.

"Want breakfast?" she asked nicely, without any indication that she could see how upset he was. He shook his head, but it didn't stop her from turning and heading back toward the kitchen.

"I'll make eggs. They were on sale yesterday at the mercado down the street. I walked down to get some," she explained over her shoulder, leaving Arthur to follow her. He took a sip of burning hot coffee and then put the mug down as soon as he could.

Kate reached up into the cabinet for one of their two pans.

"You went out?" Arthur cleared his throat. "That's good."

"Yeah, well. I felt like celebrating." She rolled one shoulder, making the old T-shirt of his that she was wearing as pajamas fall a little bit. "They called me back to interview again. At the shop. I guess whoever they picked the first time didn't work out."

She was trying to keep the excitement from her voice, but Arthur turned toward her after the first part and he could see the smile she was trying to fight.

"You're serious? That's great!" He didn't care what she thought. He came forward to wrap his arms around her shoulders only to freeze when Kate reached up to put a hand on his arm.

"I don't have the job yet," she added after a few seconds and then pulled her hand away. Arthur took longer to step back, and by then she was watching him, so he spun around to go back to his coffee.

Kate didn't let him take a sip before she spoke again. "What happened, Arthur?"

She sounded older than she was, a lot like their mother, and Arthur spent a minute thinking about what their mom would have thought of how they lived, what Arthur had done. It wasn't any less painful than what Kate was asking.

"I'm in love with my boss," he admitted to the cup after a while, and Kate made a sad but not exactly surprised sound. "Or ex-boss," Arthur corrected himself and hated having to, "since I guess I can't go back there." He couldn't go back to that house or to those books or to Bertie. They weren't his. Maybe he'd been right all along; he wasn't worthy of them. "He...."

"What? What did he do? Fucking *Beings*, just because they have some magic...," Kate started but shut up when Arthur raised his head to glare at her.

"He didn't do anything. I did it. It's got nothing to do with his magic. Or...."

Arthur paused, frustrated and sick at how stupid he was. "I suppose it does." He turned away when Kate looked startled so he could direct his anger back at himself where it belonged. "If there's anything you should know about dragons, it's that they love treasure." He wanted to put a hand to his mouth but knew Kate was watching him. "They love it, but their treasure isn't what everyone thinks it is."

"Then what is it?" She was listening attentively now, not really as prejudiced against Beings as she'd pretended to be. She wanted to know about them as much as Arthur had.

"It's... beautiful things, but it's not gold or silver. It's not jewels either. It's not about money at all, just things bold and pure and brave." He closed his eyes and ignored the crack in his voice. "He wanted that to be me. He wanted *me* and I'm not... I failed him."

"You've never failed anything in your life." Any other time Arthur would have thought about teasing Kate for how fast she answered, but Arthur only opened his eyes to stare at the carpet because she was right. He'd never failed anything before. Naturally, he picked the worst time to come face to face with his limits. The moment he had an entire dragon naked and his for the taking, he'd focused on a single scale.

Bertie *should* be disappointed in him. Arthur shivered and leaned into the counter at the memory of Bertie's eyes. He couldn't think of them without seeing the shining disappointment, the heavy expectation that hadn't lessened when Arthur started his rambling explanations. Only in those last few moments when Arthur had been so incredibly stupid to say what he did had he glimpsed anything else in those liquid depths. The world had been wet and shimmering, the air thick with heat. Arthur hadn't seen anything clearly, but he knew that Bertie was kind, not fierce, and softhearted when he should be angry. It had probably been pity that stopped him. Pity for Arthur admitting that he loved him, for Arthur not being good enough.

"What?" Kate stepped closer as if Arthur had said some of that out loud. He glanced over and resisted the urge to wipe at his stinging, hot cheeks. His eyes burned. "Not good enough?" she repeated furiously and came at him with her fists clenched at her sides. Arthur had the fleeting thought that he must have looked similar in the second before he punched her boyfriend in the face, but forgot about it when she raised her voice. He hadn't seen her so emotional in a long time.

"Kate, you don't understand what I did," he tried.

Kate shut him down with a brutality that shocked him quiet. "I don't need to, because I get that you messed up and that you've never done that before, Arthur. You don't disappoint people; you'd wear yourself down to nothing first. But trust me, messing up? The rest of us do it all the time. You only failed when you ran away." She crossed her arms. "If your writer dragon boss is as smart as you insist that he is, if he is as smart as I know *you* are, he should know that."

"I—" Arthur swallowed, not sure what he wanted to say at all. He frowned, but Kate's glare didn't let up. "I could have stolen from him." Not that he had. He wouldn't, and he'd realized that his first day, in that first minute. He had realized that before he knew the truth about dragons and their scales. It wasn't in him, and he would never have risked hurting Bertie, not for anything.

"Did you?" Kate's eyes went wide but she relaxed slightly when Arthur shook his head to deny taking anything from the house. "Then why did he tell you to leave?"

Arthur felt his throat lock up. The house had been an inferno, raging with everything unspoken, feelings strong enough to knock him from his feet. But Bertie himself, a midnight black dragon with wounded eyes, hadn't done anything but say his name. "Arthur," he said in that rough bark after his gaze swept over Arthur's shirt and jeans and shoes and after Arthur flinched away from him. He hadn't told Arthur to leave at all.

"He didn't," Arthur realized out loud, then turned to blink at his sister for one panicked second before spinning around to find his shoes. "Shit." He had to go back.

"Arthur?" Kate followed him with a question in her voice but she handed him his jacket without a word and pushed his bike back toward the door while Arthur was struggling to hold onto the helmet. So much for him being smart. Whatever Kate thought, Arthur was clearly an idiot. He flung the door open wide and stopped dead to see Bertie across the threshold.

"Arthur." Bertie froze too. He had one hand up as if he'd been debating knocking on the door when Arthur had opened it, but he lowered it after a few seconds and ran a nervous touch along his coat.

It was a chilly morning and Bertie was his own furnace, but of course he was wearing a long coat and a scarf. They were both probably impossibly soft to the touch and cost more than Arthur's rent for two months and would have made Bertie stand out in their dirty old apartment complex even if he hadn't been glittering and beautiful.

Arthur thought Bertie had showered too, or at least cleaned up. His face was dark and shadowed, but he had on one of his dress shirts and black dress pants that looked crisp and pressed. Arthur was conscious that he was in a T-shirt and jeans and his skin and hair were still damp. He wasn't blushing; he was too terrified for that.

"You're here," he said faintly, and remembered his sister only when she shifted behind him.

"You said you wanted to be my boy." Bertie exhaled it as if it was the only thing he could think to say and then left the words to drift through the air without qualifying them. Maybe to him that was reason enough to get dressed and drive across town after someone who had run away from him. But even with the heat in his voice, Bertie was shivering.

"Would you like to come in?" Kate offered without warning, making Arthur jump. She pushed his bike back against the wall before he could respond.

"Ah. Yes, if you don't mind. It's rather brisk out here." Bertie glanced at Arthur before he stepped inside and then stopped past the threshold to look at Arthur again. His eyes had Arthur hypnotized. Bertie was waiting again, waiting for Arthur to do something. Arthur absently closed the door and then stood there, watching Bertie look around the little apartment.

Arthur knew what he'd see: the couch that was clearly also Kate's bed, the tiny kitchen, the lack of any other real furnishings except for the bed in the tiny bedroom, which was just visible since they'd left the door open.

It wasn't much warmer inside the apartment than outside. Bertie shivered again and finally looked over at Kate, but it was only for a second and then his eyes were back on Arthur.

"Arthur," he said again in a low enough rumble that Kate might not have heard it. Arthur looked back at him and then cleared his throat. He let his bike helmet fall to the floor.

"Bertie." He squared his shoulders and moved back and out of the way so Bertie could come forward. Then he turned to look at Kate, who looked at him like she'd never seen him before. It made him feel warm, as if there was something different about him now that Kate could see and that she liked.

There wasn't anything Arthur wouldn't do to keep her happy, no matter how much it might terrify him. He swung his gaze back to Bertie.

"Bertie." The name was soft in his mouth, but Arthur could hear the weight in his words that said he was offering up his treasure. Kate might not understand it, but he knew Bertie would. "Bertie, this is my sister, Kate." Bertie must have heard and understood, because his expression brightened with interest as Arthur went on and said the rest. His hands, his pockets, his mouth, all felt empty without Bertie there. He shivered. "Kate, this is Dr. Philbert Jones."

"Please, call me Bertie," Bertie told Kate and took his eyes off Arthur again to study her. Arthur kept his gaze right where it was, watching the wicked grin grow wider when Kate hesitated but then extended her hand for a handshake. Bertie looked over her messy, pillow-styled blonde hair, stared for a moment longer into her blue eyes, and then dropped the grin for a real smile. He didn't lick his lips, but he did inhale. "I can't tell you how pleased I am to meet you."

Kate didn't say anything to that, not even to agree to call him Bertie, but when the handshake was over she stood there for another second to frown at him. If anything, that only made Bertie seem more pleased.

"Arthur wouldn't steal anything." If Kate was afraid of the fire-breathing creature in front of her, Arthur couldn't see it. He didn't know if Bertie could, because Bertie wasn't looking at him. He inclined his head at Kate, the way he had when Arthur first met him and promised to work hard for him.

"Have you tried telling Arthur that?" Bertie asked Kate seriously, though his attention was on Arthur. Arthur flinched and scowled at him.

"I wouldn't," Arthur insisted again, finding his voice at least. Bertie's smile drifted away.

"I know, pet." He didn't seem to see Kate's lips part at the nickname. "You wouldn't, and you wouldn't need to in any case."

"What do you mean?" Arthur's heart was racing. He had yelled at Bertie that he hadn't intended to steal the scale and Bertie had implied that he'd known that all along. Now Bertie was telling him something that would probably make perfect sense to a dragon and no one else.

For the first time in a few minutes, Bertie licked his lips and looked hesitant. He held out his hand and offered it, palm up, to Arthur. "Why would you steal what I would give you?" He spoke formally but rolled his shoulders in an uncertain gesture and Arthur's eyes wandered over his shoulders, thinking of his back, of the dozens of large scales and the one that was missing, and if that was true.

Arthur shook his head. "I don't want one of your scales. Not that one, not any of them." Another thought occurred to him and he put a hand to his stomach. "Don't," he ordered fiercely. "Don't pull one out for me either." Just the idea of Bertie ripping out a scale for any reason made him sick. He shook his head again. "Even if it doesn't hurt"—though somehow he was sure it did—"don't. I would never ask you to."

"It's little more than a fingernail clipping, Arthur," Bertie remarked, his voice low and rich with something he wasn't saying. Arthur snorted, because he doubted that losing a scale was anything at all like clipping a fingernail, but then Bertie blinked and didn't say anything else and Arthur realized he was still waiting. Waiting for something, some reaction from Arthur that Arthur couldn't say now.

He looked over at Kate, who had a strange expression on her face, as if she didn't know what to make of any of that. But she finally shut her mouth and stared back at him. Her cheeks were slightly pink, her expression a little flustered.

"I'm going to make breakfast, but I am going to shower and get dressed first," she announced, loud enough to bring Bertie's eyes back to her. Then she crossed her arms over her chest in a vaguely self-conscious move before she stepped back and hurried out of the room.

"I really shouldn't be so surprised, but you continually surprise me, Arthur," Bertie whispered once she was gone. "She's another pearl, isn't she?"

"Yes," Arthur answered without thinking, then realized Bertie was referring to him. After this morning, Arthur was still his pearl. He stopped and looked up. This close and without Bertie's interest aroused by everything he was smelling, Arthur could see the brown in Bertie's eyes and it made him look more human. But he wasn't, and Arthur needed to make sure they understood each other. All the things Bertie kept saying, if Bertie meant them, then Arthur should speak to him the same way.

He shifted and watched Bertie watch him. "But she's mine."

It got him a nod, as though that was only natural. "Then we should take good care of her, shouldn't we?" Bertie agreed easily. Arthur nodded back at him, though his thinking was getting slow and his legs were getting wobbly. They would take good care of her, because Kate was Arthur's treasure, and that was what one did with treasure. Treasure was held and cared for and protected.

Arthur swallowed. He was grateful Kate had left the room so she wouldn't see him like this. He always felt different around Bertie, but this weak feeling was new. He hadn't felt this naked when he actually was naked. He bumped into the wall and realized he'd taken a small step backward.

"I thought you wanted me to leave," he said, because he had to say something. "The house… I felt it move."

"Arthur. Darling. My house and any magic in it do what I want, and when have I *ever* wanted you to leave?" Bertie took a second to obviously compose himself and answer patiently. It made Arthur feel pretty brainless, but then, he deserved it. He'd had his clothes and shoes on and Bertie had come downstairs and must have thought Arthur had been sneaking away. Then Drew showed up, angling for treasure, and Arthur kicked him out and afterward Arthur started babbling about stealing from him and then….

And then Arthur had practically told Bertie that he loved him and run out the door. Perfect. When he failed a test, he failed *spectacularly*. He shut his eyes for a moment and then took a breath and opened them again.

"Never?" he guessed carefully, though he knew the answer. He had a feeling the house had been trying to keep him, that Bertie had been so upset the shaking had just happened, an uncontrollable reaction to Bertie thinking Arthur was leaving. He shook his head just in case Bertie thought he might still leave. He wouldn't, not ever.

"Never." Bertie agreed with another nod, then paused. "Well, perhaps in the beginning, when I thought you were delicious, but let's just say I had no greater designs on you than perhaps someday getting you naked on my couch. Then, perhaps, I wouldn't have begged you to stay *quite* as much as I would now, but in my defense, it didn't take me very long to see how special you are, Arthur."

"Special?" Arthur couldn't breathe, couldn't focus. "Begged?" he repeated blankly. Bertie had asked, but Arthur hadn't thought of it as begging. Then again, this was a dragon, an aristocratic dragon, as Bertie had often pointed out. Maybe asking that much *was* begging to him. If Arthur hadn't been so scared, Bertie would never have had to ask at all.

Bertie made a sound of frustration, a small growl, not quite a roar. Arthur's knees went weak. He leaned into the wall, but it didn't do much good, so he put his head back. Bertie took a step closer and Arthur abruptly hated the jacket he'd thrown on earlier because he was so hot. He shrugged it off without caring where it landed. Bertie's eyebrows went up.

"I'm sorry," Arthur apologized in a dazed whisper, though there was a small smile at the corner of Bertie's mouth now, and he was in Arthur's space and studying him intently. The raised eyebrows made him look imperious, and he must have had a cigarette in the car because he smelled like sharp, potent herbs.

"Arthur," Bertie began, probably wanting to know what Arthur was apologizing for, but his voice was a heavenly rumble just above Arthur's ear. Arthur, as he had since the beginning, nearly fell to his knees and only didn't because Bertie was too close now and he couldn't.

He wanted to beg Bertie to let him stay, not that he had to. He was free to stay. Bertie had begged him, and though that made no sense, Arthur wasn't going to argue it. But the fact that Bertie had begged, had done it for Arthur's sake, made him apologize again.

"I'm sorry," he whispered. *Grovelly* was the word Bertie had used once, and Arthur made a vague note to himself to let Bertie use it whenever he wanted; the publisher could deal with it if it wasn't a real word. It felt real enough to him. He'd do anything to make it up to Bertie, anything at all to make him happy. "I didn't mean to hurt you. I shouldn't have left. I'm sorry."

"Forgiven." Bertie growled it as if he needed Arthur to know he meant it. Then he smiled and moved; his hands hovered over Arthur's ribs. "But the rest of what you said, Arthur. The rest of it. That's what I need to hear. Please. I have been waiting for so long, wanting for so long, since you looked at my possessions and saw the worth and not the cost. You don't know, Arthur, the things I want to do to you, how I would keep and protect you, how it burns to watch you leave. But if you wanted to leave, I would not stop you."

Arthur tried to think of those words as a dragon would hear them and not a small, skinny human. He wanted to ask what things Bertie would do to him, but there were already marks at his wrists— enough of a hint—and anyway his sister was around and he knew that if Bertie started to tell him, Arthur might want to do them. So he gave a small shake of his head and stayed where he was.

They touched, through Arthur's T-shirt at first, and then Arthur shifted to make it ride up and to feel Bertie's hands on his bare skin. But they stayed still and Arthur lifted his chin just as Bertie pulled back to look at him.

"Would you really like to be mine, Arthur?"

Arthur couldn't tell which of them was shaking. He thought maybe they both were, though Bertie might be hiding it better. Arthur's chest was so tight he sucked in a deep breath. There was a safer answer than the one he could give.

"If you want me." That was what he *could* say. But Bertie wasn't looking away and there was something unsteady and weak in his voice and his hands were holding onto Arthur as if he was scared Arthur would run away again, the way Arthur already had more than once.

Arthur curled his hands and leveled his gaze to Bertie's. "Yes."

For one long moment Arthur's pulse was loud in his ears, almost as loud as the noise of the shower and the barely suppressed roar from Bertie who pushed forward to crush Arthur against the wall. Arthur shivered at the change in temperature but couldn't make himself mind anything else, not with hot lips at his ear.

"My boy." Satisfaction deepened Bertie's voice, made it rough, and it hit Arthur somewhere primal. He shut his eyes and didn't protest when Bertie, not quite human Bertie, pressed him to the wall. His voice was bestial. "Then I would hear you say it, Arthur."

"Say it?" Arthur swallowed and opened his eyes, confused only for the second until he saw the depths of darkness in Bertie's eyes. He tilted his head up so their mouths were close. "I'm…." It was unexpectedly difficult. "I'm your treasure."

Bertie's lips brushed his. The growl was slow and aroused and Arthur tried to remember his sister was nearby so he could control himself. Bertie had other ideas, sliding one hand down his chest. "Again, pet," he ordered without looking away.

Arthur shivered. "I'm your treasure." It was easier this time, easy to imagine saying it with Bertie inside of him again, easy to want to say it. "I'm your treasure."

Bertie's kiss was hard and wet and starving. Arthur took handfuls of his hair to make it last longer.

"Are you sure?" Arthur asked him a few minutes later, his lips fat and buzzing and wet from Bertie's kisses. Bertie's hands were achingly slow under Arthur's shirt, tracing over his ribs to leave the skin flushed and warm before wandering away to leave Arthur panting.

"Very sure," Bertie affirmed, scraping his teeth along Arthur's jaw, petting down Arthur's stomach to the light trail of hair. When

Arthur shifted forward, Bertie took his hands away, and Arthur couldn't even frown.

Arthur felt like he was coming apart. Breaking apart, he realized, over his loud, pounding heartbeat, but Bertie kissed him again slowly, and he didn't go anywhere.

Kate couldn't take that long of a shower, Arthur thought, but distantly, and then couldn't hold back a moan. It was just Bertie's mouth and that voice, slow and intense and constant, as though he had all the time in the world when he didn't, he couldn't.

Or maybe he did, because Arthur had said he wanted to be his. His boy, or his pet, his everything. That's what dragons did, what *Bertie* did: they devoured everything.

"Your pearl?" he asked, breathing raggedly at the build of heat.

"Pearl," Bertie exhaled over Arthur's cheek before kissing him again. He murmured against Arthur's lips and groaned quietly when Arthur parted them and pushed up for more.

Arthur hadn't expected Bertie to be trembling too, or to be breathing just as hard as he was when he finally, really pulled back.

Bertie's eyes went all black, the pupils swallowing up the brown as he watched Arthur dart out his tongue for more.

Arthur could still hear the shower, but he doubted Kate was in it. She probably just wanted the noise. Later, when he could think again, he was going to be embarrassed about that. He was also going to blame Bertie.

"Kate is going to make breakfast," Arthur remarked as he extracted a hand from Bertie's hair and slid it down to Bertie's chest. Bertie made a soft, grateful sound and nodded to encourage him. "You could stay, if you want…." Arthur glanced down and then back up. "For a little longer?" he finished quietly, joking and pleading at the same time. Bertie's grin was sharp and his stare pinned Arthur to the spot. Arthur couldn't move, but then, he didn't want to, not for a long, long time.

Bertie must have had the same idea, or read his mind and his scent, because he wet his bottom lip and then leaned in to whisper his answer into Arthur's ear.

"As long as you like, darling," he promised, and he was so hot he might as well have been breathing fire. Arthur slid his hands to Bertie's back and held him close.

"Yes, love," Arthur whispered back so Bertie wouldn't hear and pressed in closer to let the fire take him.

FACTS ABOUT DRAGONS:

1. They have existed since before the first written human records in almost every human culture.

2. They "came out" around the turn of the last century when the other magical Beings started to emerge from hiding both during and after the First World War, though many did not come into public view until the mass exodus of Beings from the countries torn by war and strife during the Second World War. This includes Russia, China, Northern Africa, the islands of the Pacific, and most of Europe.

3. Like fairies, they are said to possess powerful magic.

4. Because of their rumored hoarding of treasure, many who don't know dragons value them only for the perceived financial gain to be found in taking advantage of, or even killing, a dragon.

5. They often but not always give their children powerful names.

6. They can and will intermingle with humans or other Beings, up to and including sex, marriage, and children.

7. They often have a "type" when it comes to human lovers ("Bold of purpose, fair of face, pure of heart." "Pure of body" entirely optional, though often preferred.)

8. Like werewolves and other weres, dragons can shift form at will.

9. They can definitely breathe fire.

10. They like stories of all kinds.

11. They are protective and possessive about their treasure.

12. They define treasure as anything that they love, and love deeply.

13. They long for someone that feels the same way.

14. They are pretty fond of back rubs.

R. COOPER has been making up stories since she was a wee R. Cooper. She has a weakness for strong-minded characters doing unspeakably hot things to each other and thinks dirty martinis are for the weak (or perhaps just thinks olive juice is gross). If she listed all of her turn-ons, it would take up this whole bio, but they include smart people, tailored suits with serious ties, shoulder holsters, funny people, sacrifices made for love, power struggles, the walking wounded, bravery, and good old-fashioned shameless sluts.

She also likes ice cream. Strawberry.

Visit R. at http://r-cooper.livejournal.com/. You can contact her at RisCoops@gmail.com.

Also from R. COOPER

Some Kind of
MAGIC

R. Cooper

http://www.dreamspinnerpress.com

Play It Again, Charlie

R. COOPER